THE STONES

Complimentary Copy
NOT FOR SALE
eLectio Publishing
eLectioPublishing.com

BETH HAMMOND

eLectio Publishing
Little Elm, TX
www.eLectioPublishing.com

The Sound of the Stones
Copyright © 2015 by Beth Hammond
Cover Design © 2015 by Beth Hammond

ISBN-13: 978-1-63213-132-4
Published by eLectio Publishing, LLC
Little Elm, Texas
http://www.eLectioPublishing.com

Printed in the United States of America

5 4 3 2 1   eLP   20 19 18 17 16 15

The eLectio Publishing editing team is comprised of: Christine LePorte, Lori Draft, Sheldon James, Court Dudek, and Jim Eccles.

Without limiting the rights under copyright reserved above, no part of this publication may be reproduced, stored in or introduced into a retrieval system, or transmitted, in any form, or by any means (electronic, mechanical, photocopying, recording, or otherwise), without the prior written permission of both the copyright owner and the above publisher of this book.

If you purchased this book without a cover, you should be aware that this book is stolen property. It was reported as "unsold and destroyed" to the publisher and neither the author nor the publisher has received any payment for the "stripped book."

The scanning, uploading, and distribution of this book via the Internet or via any other means without the permission of the publisher is illegal and punishable by law. Please purchase only authorized electronic editions, and do not participate in or encourage electronic piracy of copyrighted materials. Your support of the author's rights is appreciated.

Publisher's Note
The publisher does not have any control over and does not assume any responsibility for author or third-party websites or their content.

This is a work of fiction. Names, characters, places, and incidents either are the product of the author's imagination or are used fictitiously, and any resemblance to actual persons, living or dead, business establishments, events, or locales is entirely coincidental.

For my parents, who support me beyond measure.
For my husband, who never batted an eye when I told him I would write a book.
For my children, who peeked over my shoulder every time I drew.

Above all, for my Savior.

John 3:16

The Winds of Change

The wind felt different today. Something nagged at her, not unlike every day before. But today felt more intense; anticipation hung like a blanket. The blanket didn't quite touch her skin but wrapped around her like a cocoon, encasing her with a sense of urgency. She quickened her stride. The smell of fall was heavy in the air as a crisp wind whipped past. Frankie tugged her jacket closed. Her steps were swift as she made her way down the small-town sidewalk.

She gave a passing glance to the old used bookstore to her right. Her heart stuttered. A going-out-of-business sign hung crooked in the window. Its message sent a sharp pang of regret through her chest. She didn't remember stopping. Her face pressed against the glass, fogging the window with each shallow breath. Boxes littered the floor and countertop, empty, yawning, and eager to be filled. She watched her hand numbly as it reached for the door. A gust of wind nudged her forward as the door swung wide. A tiny bell sounded its charming ding, and papers skipped around the room in welcome.

The air felt warm and inviting after her long walk in the chilled afternoon. The smell of old books and stale coffee brought images to mind of another time in her life, a simpler time when books could carry her away to worlds where she felt a sense of belonging. Life seemed more complicated now. She didn't get the same escape from literature that she used to. In her seventeen years she felt more yearning with each passing day. A yearning for what she did not know. Perhaps it was for freedom from the foster system, or the structure of school. Maybe it was normal teenage frustration. But in listening to her friends she didn't think it was any of those things exactly. Something pulled on her, tugging like a hidden magnet but never revealing its purpose.

The door clicked shut behind her, cutting off the wind. The crumpled papers that had greeted her in welcome now lay still at her feet. Her senses prickled as the cocoon of anticipation enveloping her turned to purpose. The purpose was not clear, but the desire to fulfill it nagged like an itch begging to be scratched.

An old man strode from the back room carrying an empty box. He hummed cheerfully, and his white hair stood in all directions as if dancing to his music. His wiry brows shot to the top of his forehead, mingling with his untamed hair.

The Sound of the Stones

"Well, hello there, young lady." His voice was like a warm sunny day. A smile spread across his face, lending to his friendly disposition as he placed the empty box on the counter.

"Hey." Frankie gave a small wave and shoved her hands in her jeans. She looked around at the disheveled state of the store. The old man's eyes lingered for a moment. Frankie felt a flicker of something like a memory when she turned back to him. Her mind almost grasped it, but when he turned his eyes toward the box on the counter it was gone.

"Um, what happened to the Davenports?" she asked, and tucked a piece of hair behind her ear.

The old man looked up, his face pulled in concentration. "Oh, well, I'm afraid they are getting on in age. They decided to sell." He gave an apologetic shrug.

"Oh," Frankie replied. A pang of regret coursed through her at the realization that she would not see the old couple again. She swallowed the emotion and went straight to the shelves that held fantasy books. She had bought and resold most of the books there. She wasn't looking for anything in particular. She just wanted to walk the shelves again. She ran her fingers over the worn bindings on the books and hummed. It wasn't a distinct tune, just something that stuck in her head from time to time.

"What's that you're humming, young lady?" The old man held a book absently in his hand as he padded down the aisle toward her. His eyes were sharp, with a hint of curiosity. Frankie shook her head and cleared her throat.

"I really don't know." She shrugged one shoulder and her sleek black hair spilled over her flannel shirt. "Just something I get stuck in my head from time to time." Her cheeks flushed pink and she turned back to the books. She bit her lip, willing herself not to hum. She could feel the old man lingering.

He made a noise in the back of his throat, but after a moment went back to shuffling boxes. Frankie made a few selections and went to the counter where the old man tucked books into a box. She placed the books on the glass counter and pulled a wad of money from her pocket. She didn't want to leave, but couldn't think of a reason to stay.

The old man rose from the depth of the box. "Ready?" he asked, but the tone in his voice held an odd resonance that made Frankie blink. That flash of something familiar flickered in her mind again. She stood staring for a moment and the old man tipped his head to one side.

"Yes. Thank you," she said, and smoothed the money on the counter. Her dark eyes narrowed and studied the old man's features as he handled her book selection. He hummed appreciatively at her choices. Something like a slow frost tickled her mind. He looked up and gave a conspiratorial smile.

"You have good taste."

Frankie's face flushed. "Thanks."

The old man slapped a hand on the counter and Frankie jumped.

"How would you like to help me pack up here? I would need you for the next few days, and pay you twenty dollars an hour at the end of the week." He raised a finger. "And you can keep all the books you want." The expectation on his face was clear.

Frankie realized her mouth was hanging open in response to his slapping the counter. She closed it. She didn't need the money but spending more time here was exactly what she wanted.

"Hmm? What do you say, young lady?" He smiled a full-toothed grin surprisingly white for his age. They weren't dentures in that they were not perfectly straight, but lent character to his warm, weathered face. Frankie narrowed her eyes, studying his face for an answer to the strange sensation flitting through her mind. There...there it was. She almost had the thought situated.

"Oh, come on. I really could use the help." He waved a book enticingly. It was gone again, the fleeting sensation chased away by reality. She watched him wave the book and snorted.

"All right." She couldn't help the grin tugging at her lips.

"Ah, good, good," he said. "I am Mr. Malack." He held out his hand.

"Frankie...Frankie Sheba." She accepted his hand.

He nodded politely. "See you tomorrow, say three thirty p.m.?" he asked.

"Sure." Frankie scooped up the books and left, feeling something she couldn't quite put her finger on...hope?

A Different Kind of Oppression

Frankie gritted her teeth as she stepped into the lavish home in which she was fostered. She had bounced around foster homes for much of her early teens. She had been with the Abensteins for three years now. She would be eighteen soon and couldn't wait to get out of the foster system. The Abensteins' home was nicer than most she had spent time in for sure. But Mrs. Abenstein was an uptight older woman who didn't much care for Frankie's choice of style, worn jeans and a baggy shirt, nor did she care for her name.

"Frances!" Mrs. Abenstein's high-pitched voice called from the kitchen. Frankie's eye twitched at the use of her proper name. "Set the table, dear."

Frankie put down her armload of books, reverently, on the foyer table. She took a deep breath, trudged to the kitchen, and gathered the plates. She performed the task with a practiced, pleasant expression. Mr. Abenstein sat stiffly at the dinner table, his glasses perched on the end of his nose, reading the paper. He looked up and his mouth curved with genuine warmth as Frankie set down the plates and flatware.

The Abensteins were an older couple but not ancient. Mrs. Abenstein had taken empty nest syndrome hard when her two children moved away to start their own lives. Mr. Abenstein had agreed to foster children, as long as he didn't have to trip over toys and change diapers. They decided that a teen would be the best choice. They had the best intentions but Mrs. Abenstein could be a bit much to stomach.

She insisted Frankie call them Mr. and Mrs. Abenstein. "The better to instill respect, Frances," Mrs. Abenstein had said upon Frankie's first meeting with them. Mrs. Abenstein's brows had been raised loftily, her lips pursed as if sucking lemons was part of her daily routine. Mr. Abenstein had smiled and readjusted his glasses, only to have them slip down the bridge of his nose moments later. They reminded Frankie of birds. If Mrs. Abenstein was a hen, Mr. Abenstein was an ostrich.

Frankie took small bites of roasted potato and pushed food around her plate. She smirked secretly as images of a hen and ostrich strutted through her mind.

"I see you brought some books home." Mrs. Abenstein pursed her lips. *There's that lemon.* Frankie's smirk dropped, the amusing bird images flitting away to be replaced with a sense of dread.

"The old bookstore is closing. I'm helping pack up. Mr. Malack, the man handling the store closing, said I could take books that I like." Frankie realized she was talking through a mouthful of potatoes and swallowed hard. Mrs. Abenstein dabbed at the corners of her mouth with a cloth napkin pointedly. Frankie cleared her throat and stared at her plate.

"You know, Frances, reading is a good thing but"—she gestured to the stack of books across the room with a fork full of chicken—"you should read the classics. That is the way to sharpen your mind." She raised an elegant brow. "That fantastical stuff you read is full of nonsense." She punctuated her feelings with a curt nod of her head and her short, curly hair nodded with her. She glanced toward her husband for support. He stopped chewing and cleared his throat.

"Well, my dear, I see no harm in reading such fiction." He met Frankie's eyes and his lips curved up at the sides. "She does what she's told and gets good grades." He shrugged a shoulder, turning his eyes back to his plate. "Certainly it's no worse than watching soap operas," he mumbled, then took a mouth full of food much the same as an ostrich would thrust its head in the sand to avoid confrontation.

Mrs. Abenstein choked on a buttered roll. She coughed and sipped her wine with rose-tinged cheeks. Frankie glanced over in time to catch Mr. Abenstein's fleeting wink.

Conversation faltered after that. "Thank you for dinner. It was delicious," Frankie said, when it became clear they were finished eating. Mrs. Abenstein nodded and dabbed the corners of her mouth with a napkin for the hundredth time.

Frankie helped clear the table in silence, much like every night before. They exchanged a few pleasantries, but it was formal and Frankie felt out of place. She always felt out of place. In fact, the only place she ever felt at home was in the fantasy world of a book. She had lived with the Abensteins for three years yet felt as much a stranger in their home now as the day she moved in. They weren't cruel. In fact, they were very good to her. Mr. Abenstein even got her on some level. But she didn't feel a bond with them.

"I have homework," she blurted, after the kitchen was spotless. Mrs. Abenstein nodded distractedly. Frankie climbed the stairs to the safety of her room, toting her stack of books. She flopped down on the bed and opened a book to page one, drifting into another world for a time.

It Is Time

Frankie took lighthearted steps. The fall air smelled sweeter and the wind was swift and playful, flushing her cheeks a happy pink. She reached the bookstore and opened the door. The bell chimed in welcome.

"Mr. Malack? It's me…Frankie," she singsonged. She heard shuffling in the back, followed by muffled grunts of irritation. Scattered about the room were empty boxes marked with various titles, romance, historical, self-help, and the like. She gathered an empty box and started to load them with the appropriate genre. She finished packing one box and dragged it to the center of the floor with other filled boxes. She wiped her hands on her jeans and looked at the box with self-satisfaction. Mr. Malack popped out from the back room. His brows were drawn, but when he saw her they shot up high, as if pointing to the disheveled state of his dust-covered hair. He looked at the packed box she was admiring and his mouth lifted at the corners.

"I knew I was right about you." He pointed a finger in the air in illustration. "I know about people, you see." He winked at her. The dichotomy of his self-assured demeanor against his wild hair and dusty garb sent Frankie into a fit of giggles. She punctuated the giggle with a snort, and then looked surprised by the noise she made. Mr. Malack threw back his head and laughed. The sound of it was so comforting and familiar; a small place in the back of her mind scrambled to locate the memory that would explain why. As quick as the prick of a needle, the flash of familiarity was gone, leaving Frankie with a sense of abandonment.

"You were busy when I came in, so I just took an empty box and loaded it with the proper genre." She gestured toward the box, then let her arm fall to her side when she realized he already knew that. She shoved her hands in her pockets and kicked at a piece of lint on the floor.

"Fine, fine," he said, glossing over her embarrassment. He patted her on the arm and glanced over his shoulder toward the back room with a scowl. "Yes, I'm just cleaning things up back there." He shook his head and made a clucking noise with his tongue. "So many books," he said, and fixed her with a stare. He studied her with piercing eyes for a moment and nodded. The gravity in the room seemed to cement her to

The Sound of the Stones

the floor. There it was again, that sense of something she should know. Mr. Malack smiled and things were normal again.

"Shall we keep going, my dear?" he asked, as he grabbed for another box.

"Sure," she said, trying to swallow the sense that she was missing something.

They worked late into the evening. Frankie found that she very much enjoyed the company of the old man. He was warm and intelligent. Not the sort of stuffy old coot you felt judged by. The sun began to set, and the fluorescent lighting in the store grew harsher by the minute. Frankie finished packing another box and glanced out the store window. She dusted off her hands and sighed contentedly.

"Mr. Malack, I think it's time I get home." She looked around at the progress they had made. The shelves were halfway cleared and the boxes neatly stacked. Mr. Malack looked at her over his own box and nodded.

"Of course, my dear. Tomorrow then?" he asked.

Frankie nodded. "Tomorrow," she said, and headed for the door. She hesitated, her hand poised for the handle. She felt a slow frost prickle up her neck and settle in her mind. She looked back over her shoulder. Mr. Malack waved. The prickle was gone. She tugged her jacket close, waved back, and ducked out the door. A brisk wind whipped inside the store and the bell rang in farewell. When the door clicked shut, silence fell.

Mr. Malack watched her disappear into the dusk and sat on a stool, his back resting against the counter. He looked toward the ceiling, his head bent to one side, as if listening to a faint whisper. After a good long while he nodded.

"Yes," he said, "it is time...at long last. It is time." He clapped his hands once and rubbed them together brusquely, then picked up another box and continued to pack.

A Story Begins

Frankie was running late. It was pouring outside and by the time she reached the store she was soaked. She tried the handle of the door but it was locked. She pressed her face to the glass. It was dark and empty. Her heart sank. She didn't know whether from the closing of the store, all the books being gone, or from the thought she would not see the old man Malack again. She trudged home like a limp dishrag.

Dinner was much the same as the night before. She didn't bring any new books in, so that topic was thankfully avoided. The Abensteins chatted, but she didn't really hear them. Her mind was still back at the dark, empty bookstore. She helped clean up after dinner and headed for the stairs. She was halfway up when Mr. Abenstein spoke.

"Frances?"

Frankie paused, and turned to find him looking over his shoulder. Mrs. Abenstein was on the phone in the kitchen, her high-pitched chatter leaking into the foyer. Mr. Abenstein sighed and nodded, then pulled a bag from behind his back. He held the parcel out to Frankie with a hesitant smile. Frankie moved back down the steps, reservation bubbling in her stomach. She took the heavy bag from his hand. Mr. Abenstein cleared his throat and gestured toward the front door.

"A nice old man stopped by today. He gave this to me and asked that I give it to you. He said he was in a hurry so...." He waved a hand at the bag in illustration. He leaned in closer, glancing over his shoulder again. "I hope it's a great fantasy book," he whispered, his eyes filled with boyish wonder.

Frankie grinned. "Thank you," she whispered, and headed to her room with lighter feet. She closed her bedroom door and pressed her back against it. She clutched the package to her chest, and after a few breaths, moved to the bed. She slipped something heavy from the bag. It was wrapped in thick brown butcher paper and bound in twine. A note was tucked into the string, folded neatly in thirds. She opened the note and money tumbled out. She tucked it into her pocket without counting it and read the note.

My dearest Frankie, I am sorry that I left so quickly. An urgent matter came up, and I had to finish my business here without further ado. I leave you this fine book, in hopes that you will enjoy the greatest story ever told. May it take you places no one has ever been.

Sincerely, Mr. Malack

Frankie folded the note tenderly and put it her pocket. She slid the twine from the package and opened the paper. The book was heavy in her hands, the white, pebbled leather cover unmarred. A crystal plate, in the center of the book, was inlaid and glistening, in the shape of a double door. The doors had intricate scrollwork on its surface. She opened the book to the first page and the binding made crackling noises, indicating it had never been opened. She ran a finger over the fine vellum paper edged with gold. On the first page was an intricate drawing of a charm. It was a circle with seven lines in the center, running from top to bottom, and evenly spaced. On each line was a dot or circle. They were spread out over the lines to make a pattern. Frankie gasped and slammed the book shut. She lifted the sleeve of her shirt and looked at the wine-colored mark on her forearm that was a source of self-consciousness. She covered it up at all times. It was eerily similar to the drawing in the book.

Frankie stared at the book for a moment, then turned to the next page and started to read…

You Don't Know Me

It was a clear day and the sky was a vibrant blue. Ashra turned her face toward the sun, allowing it to warm her skin. She inhaled a deep breath and closed her eyes, savoring a few brief moments alone. She didn't particularly want to be in the mines today. She sighed, sending stray hairs from her face. *Let today be a safe day. Let today be filled with better things.*

"Destiny often calls in the darkest of times."

An airy voice pierced her silent prayer. Ashra jumped, then turned to find a strange old man watching her. His garb was an unusually clean white robe, unsoiled from the ruggedness of Krad City. His hair was glacial and wispy and his eyes were alight with amusement. He wore a warm wrinkled smile. She stared at him, unashamed. Perhaps he was a man overcome with life in Krad City. Sometimes a person lived long enough in the harsh environment to reach a very old age. Those "lucky" enough to live so long eventually ended up mad, overtaken by thoughts of grandeur, unafraid of death. When that happened, they became dissenters, spewing ideas of release from Krad oppression. *It won't be long before they kill you, old man.*

"I'm sorry, do I know you?" Ashra cocked a brow and pursed her lips primly.

His eyes flashed knowingly. In that instant, his wrinkles smoothed, and he looked perfectly sane. Ashra felt exposed. He looked at her for a few moments and searched her eyes. Her brow dropped from its annoyed position and she swallowed loudly. She couldn't look away.

"I know what you can do." He raised his chin in challenge. His grin widened, showing even more of his teeth. They were surprisingly white for a man of his age.

Ashra's eyes flashed fierce. Heat climbed up her neck and her cheeks flushed pink. "Look, old boy, I don't know who you are, or what kind of game you're playing, but I can assure you that you do NOT know me! I've never seen you in my…" She was cut off by an irritating chuckle.

She would have continued to berate him but the air began to shift, then it stilled. There was no longer a gentle morning breeze. The sounds of the mines ceased. She could hear nothing but eerie silence and the beating of her own heart, loud in comparison. It was as if she stood in a vacuum, devoid of time and sound. The old man narrowed his eyes and took a deep breath through his nose.

"The time is drawing close for you to reveal who you are." His voice held an odd resonance. He moved his lips, but his voice bled directly into Ashra's mind. He wasn't smiling anymore. His face was serious, almost threatening. As Ashra's face changed from anger to confusion, his own expression turned from urgent to empathetic. She recognized that look. It was one her mother often held when she looked at her. She wanted to refute him, but the words wouldn't come. She looked on mutely.

He nodded his head and turned away, his white hair dancing in the wind. The breeze was back, as were the sounds of people working in the mines. No one noticed the old man. He rounded the corner without a backward glance. She stared after him for a long few moments, wondering at the strange encounter. Then she shook it off and told herself it was just a crazy old man. *Wasn't it?*

Desperate Times

Dust and rock fragments rained down from the mine wall, finding homes on Ashra's clothing, skin, and hair. The fine powder stood out in stark contrast to her olive complexion, giving a silver sheen to her long dark mane, pulled into a knot at the base of her neck. Wisps of hair flared around her small angular face, lending to the effect of fierceness flashing in her dark almond-shaped eyes.

"There's a nice pocket in here," Ashra informed Blithe. She held her breath and braced herself for his snarky remark.

"I know," Blithe snapped. His lip curled ridiculously, and the words rolled off his tongue like bitterroot. He narrowed his gray eyes at her and lifted his too long nose, the better to look down on her. He knew the crystals were in there. He was a Krad, Crystal Sensitive, and she was just human. She worked in the crystal mines digging out the Krad Glasne's means of control. They were the mighty Krad. She was just a lackey, a cog in the mechanism. Such was the air he held himself with. Ashra lifted her chin and sniffed, a small spray of freckles accentuated by the scrunching of her nose. A smirk pulled at the corner of Blithe's thin lips. He wordlessly dared her to lose control. She cleared her throat and turned her attention back to the wall, resisting his provocation.

She was not supposed to know where to find the crystals. Furthermore, she was not supposed to know how they worked, but she did. The crystals sang to her in an ancient language. They had special powers encased in them, remnants from the early dawn of time. They held vibrations, like echoes from the Creator. Each had a unique purpose. Some crystals produced heat, some were used for ailments, and some recorded energy waves that could be played back for those who could hear them. They each hummed their purpose. Ashra could hear the crystals. Rolling vibrations formed songs. Her mind sought them and gave off their own, provoking song, its own answering call. It was a back-and-forth, a give-and-take. There was an art to it, and she was an artist.

The crystals that held energy waves like etchings were the ones Blithe was looking for. The difference between Blithe and Ashra was that Ashra could communicate with the crystals, while Blithe and other Sensitives could only hear them. The Krad needed the right kind of crystal to fabricate crystal modicums. More humans were born every day, and every day those modicums were placed into the hippocampus of fresh, tiny human minds. Brain waves were recorded, and Krad Sensitives interpreted the waves embedded in the crystal. The Krad monitored thoughts, fears, and desires. This was how the human race was suppressed, controlled, and held captive. It all started long ago, much longer ago than human memory could reach.

Ashra set her jaw tight and bit back words that fought to escape. She would love to show Blithe and all of the Krad mongrels just how incompetent they really were. She knew the mines like a favorite book. The walls were full of verse and chapter, and she could read every one just by listening to what they said, and how they said it. Ashra continued to hide her gift with carefully guarded expressions. No one else could know what she was capable of. She wasn't sure what they would do to her, but death was probably the least of the punishments she would receive.

Blithe turned to the wall, straining to hear the crystal vibrations held within. His face was pinched, his body contorted as he followed along the narrow rock passageway. He stopped from time to time to listen, nodding to himself. Ashra resisted the urge to roll her eyes.

"It runs from south to north at a fifty-one-degree angle from here, to here." He gestured at the wall, not bothering to look at Ashra as he spoke. "Have it finished in three days."

Ashra blinked, then nodded. Blithe skulked from the mine, nose turned up and hands gathered behind his back in a hard knot. A smug sneer pulled at his lips. Ashra visualized hurling a rock at his head, and felt better for the daydream. She blew hair from her face and shoved tight fists in her pockets.

Blithe was an arrogant nit. He was also wrong. The crystal vein did run from south to north at a fifty-one-degree angle for a small portion of the wall, but then it took a hard turn up for ten feet, and then over at an almost ninety-degree angle for the rest of the passage. Ashra shook her head and turned to leave. She kicked a stone in place of the face she pictured. It skidded across the ground and came to rest against the far mine wall with a satisfactory crack. *What a ninny.* She shook off the sour mood as best she could and donned a professional face.

Ashra walked to the far end of the walkway where her team was waiting. Haker, Jinka, Scoot, and Pooter stood making small talk. They turned as she emerged. "We have three days to excavate," she informed them in a measured tone, her expression unreadable except for the slight crease in her forehead. She attempted a reassuring smile but it wavered and fell flat before it took hold.

"Ugh…Three days!?" Jinka spat. She was a spirited woman in her mid thirties. She was stout with wiry red hair and had a wide gap in her front teeth that seemed to punctuate her strong personality. It was like her teeth were forced apart by the sheer loudness with which her voice escaped its trap. She was a no-nonsense type of woman with a short fuse and the only other female on Ashra's team. She rubbed the Krad the wrong way and often skirted on the fringe of dissent. In short, Ashra loved her. Ashra did manage a smile at Jinka's protest.

"We'll have to make use of a Giant. It's the only way to meet the deadline." Ashra's voice held no hint of the uncertainty she felt. Grunts of acknowledgment with a twinge of apprehension came from her team.

Giants were another of the Krad race. They were a large mutation of muscle and strength. They had a nasty temper and lacked the ability to control their actions when provoked. Humans often relied on them to help accomplish the scope of work they were forced to achieve. Giants were useful, but risky. Lack of intelligence and short temper were a bad combination. Ashra had avoided using a Giant until now. But these were dire times, and the humans were kept in horrible conditions. They had no choice but to use the dangerous tools they were allotted.

The team looked at Ashra in silent sulk. Her face was smudged with dirt and her clothes were dingy, but they were well mended against their constant use. Ashra stood proud, and appeared tall despite her small feminine frame. Her dark eyes seemed to spark fire with amber flecks glinting against the almost blackness of her irises. She was fierce and soft, loyal and wild in complementary dichotomy. "I'll put in a request and you can get the equipment ready. I'll be back as soon as I can." Ashra looked each of them in the eyes and gave what she hoped was an assuring nod. The three men and Jinka nodded their agreement, heaving sighs of resignation as they moved to ready the equipment.

Haker, the oldest member of the team, approached Ashra, his eyes tense. "You know, even with a Giant, three days is stretching it at best."

His voice was low and gruff. He scratched his scraggly, gray beard. His steely-eyed stare met her sparking, deep brown one with unspoken warning. He was matter-of-fact and never minced words.

Haker could have hated her when she was appointed lead on the team a year ago at the tender age of twenty, but he couldn't. She was good at her job, and too kind to hate. She came into the mines as a child many years ago and breathed life into the dark caves. She withstood the adversity with a steely resolve. While other children buckled and died under the harsh mine environment, she flourished. Each new challenge seemed to spur her strength. He couldn't feel resentful of this young woman. He grew to care for her as he watched how others fed from her strength. Even he, the crass old man that he was, felt drawn to the light within her.

"I know, Haker." She gave him a look that said, *Let's keep this between you and me.* "We'll figure something out. We will make the deadline."

His eyes stayed steel and his face rigid, but she didn't wither under his stare. A glint lit her eyes, and a crooked half grin tugged at the side of her mouth. His stern expression softened a bit, and his hard eyes returned some of her warm expression, even if it was barely detectable. She knew it was there, and that's all she needed. They always pulled through the tough jobs. Ashra was crafty and persistent. Haker kept the team grounded with his matter-of-fact look at life, and together they made the heart of the team. He chuckled to himself as he watched her walk toward Mine Central. The sloping ground beneath her feet seemed to bow to her.

A Fateful Appointment

Ashra made her way up the crumbling rock hill toward Mine Central. The large stone building stood above the rugged quarry hills, overlooking the various mines. The building was clean and sleek, in stark contrast to the landscape of the mines. People stood outside making trades and speaking of small things as they waited for their team leaders to emerge from the building. The Krad issued weekly food and medical rations to all human families, along with quarterly clothing rations. The supplies people didn't need were traded for things they liked better or needed more. For humans, this black market trade felt something like control in the vast lack of freedom enveloping them.

Ashra hated visiting Mine Central. With her particular vocation she only interacted with Krad one-on-one in the mines, but she had to face many Krad when she needed to put in supply requests. She dreaded it, and as such took her time climbing the smooth, stone stairs. She exchanged hellos with people she knew, but her heart wasn't in it. Her feet felt like weights. She put one heavy foot in front of the other with considerable effort until she reached the entrance.

The soaring ceiling made her feel small as she stepped through ornately carved columns. *Humans carved these columns. We accomplished these great things.* All of the greatness the Krad enjoyed was borne on the backs of humans. As far as Ashra knew it had always been this way. She wondered what would become of the Krad if humans somehow broke free. She wondered what the humans could accomplish free from Krad oppression. The thought was scary and exhilarating all at once and she felt a familiar sense of obligation. She didn't fully understand it, but it was ever present and growing stronger with each passing day.

Humans stood in long lines and guards walked about with spears in hand. The guards were Krad Gravity Benders, the third kind of the Krad race. They were agile and dangerous, possessing the ability to repel the earth's magnetic force, giving them an advantage in any fight.

Ashra took her place at the back of the line some twenty people deep and waited with the other humans who were also there to put in requests. The stench of hard work and filth filled the air. Men and women with dirt-smeared faces shuffled back and forth on tired feet. Bender guards wove in and out of the crowd armed with sleek spears.

They were dressed in tailored metal armor encrusted with tiny crystal jewels. The ornate garb made them look ridiculous, like strutting Color Plumes. Those silly birds roamed the streets of Krad City, displaying their colorful feathers, calling to their female counterparts. Krad found them beautiful in their cocky display. Ashra found them pretentious. *Stupid rainbow bird.* Her lips turned up at the thought.

She was startled from her private joke by a shout that sent echoes through the large hall. Two men were arguing about who got in line first. The line was long; requests had to be made for specialty equipment or Giants. Their lives depended on completing assignments on time. It wasn't any wonder that tension filled the vast, stinking hall of Mine Central.

The Gravity Bender nearest the ruckus approached and held the men at spear point. He shouted a gruff command to stop. The larger of the men swatted at the spear in his irritation, and the Bender jumped into the air. He somersaulted above the man and came down, skewering the larger man's head. The skewered man stood stunned. Ashra thought perhaps he was trying to comprehend what had happened. But after a moment it was clear he was already dead, his spine having been separated from his brain stem. *No!*

It happened in an instant. His lifeless body slumped to the ground. His head bounced off the floor once before it settled, and the room fell silent. The Bender pulled his spear from the dead man's head. It made an awful sucking noise as it drew from his flesh. Ashra noted the Bender's boot, placed carelessly on the dead man's back for more leverage. She also noted the complacent look on his face as he completed his task. He could have been digging a hole or taking out the trash for the lack of feeling he showed.

The other man from the altercation stood frozen, his eyes fixed on the bloody spear tip. His expression begged his life to be spared. Another guard latched on to the remaining offender and dragged him from the hall, his pleas for mercy falling on apathetic ears.

"Please, I have children."

Ashra knew she would see him later, in the Death Bowl. Humans deemed unruly were forced to fight to the death. This was not an uncommon occurrence. Humans were killed every day in the name of peace. The body of the dead man was dragged from the building. The

Bender's face held a well-composed, indifferent look as he proceeded with his task. The pool of blood was given a wide birth, but no one else acknowledged the altercation. Humans waited in line for their turn and the hall stayed silent. The pool of blood called a silent warning, "You are ours to control." Ashra could hear something else. From the depths of the sticky, dark pool she heard the voices of thousands of humans cry out. She heard her own soul answering a quaking battle cry. Her body trembled and her eyes threatened to brim over. She could almost feel the floor answering her trembles with its own vibration. She glanced around at the faces of the other humans, searching for any recognition of this shared experience, but no one else seemed to notice. The expressions on the faces around her held practiced aversion. She drew deep breaths, attempting to dim the feeling.

Tightness resonated deep in her chest. She swallowed back her emotions and replaced her horrified expression with a forced blank stare. Her body calmed. The floor lay still once more. She averted her eyes from the dark pool of blood that contrasted against the light gray marble floor, and concentrated on the gentle vibrations from the stone building around her.

When Ashra reached the front of the line she shared her request with the Sensitive on duty. Her actions were commonplace. She pushed her threatening emotions deep, and replaced them with the foremost need, to accomplish her task and keep her team alive. There was no time to dwell. Not now, not while her team had an impossible job to do. Such was her life, and all humans' lives under Krad control.

"If you need a Giant today, you will take Krank," the sour-faced Sensitive said, drawing out his words as if she were too stupid to understand the normal speed of speech. One graceful brow arched over particularly beady gray eyes. The long slender nose perched on his face practically begged to be looked down. Ashra wondered if it was in his job description to hold that nasty expression on his face all day long. *He's a pro.* She was amusing herself with that thought when the name Krank registered. It made her flash cold and hot all at once. Her armpits began to itch from the adrenaline surge. *Krank?!* Krank was the most volatile Giant around. More human deaths occurred with Krank on the job than with any other Giant. He was generally reserved for the mining teams who failed to meet a deadline or infuriated a Krad in Mine

Central. *Well-played, sour Krad.* She thought about scratching her armpits, but the sour Krad was looking her over with obvious disdain. She opted to swish her arms in a vain attempt to relieve the discomfort, only to succeed in eliciting two raised eyebrows from the Sensitive.

"That will be fine, thank you," she answered primly. Her nose was much too short to beg the looking down of, so she settled for a curt bob of the head. She refused to let him know she was troubled by this information. She took the crystal chip from the Sensitive's long, skinny, pale hand. His face settled into boredom as she took the one-inch-by-two-inch slice of clear crystal with various lines etched into its surface. The chip would be used to summon the Giant. She tucked the chip in her pants pocket and watched as the Sensitive narrowed his eyes at her. Sensitives conducted random modicum scans. It was second nature for them. They listened to the vibrations, for signs of dissension embedded in the modicums of humans. Ashra felt the Sensitive scanning hers and inwardly rolled her eyes. She had learned long ago how to control her modicum so the Krad could not read all of her thoughts and memories. The Krad were unaware of Ashra's ability. *Go ahead, big boy, give me all you got.* She blinked innocently at the Sensitive.

"Well, go on then, off with you." The Sensitive motioned with one hand as if shooing away a dog. Ashra lifted her chin in rebellion to the dismissal and gave a curt nod. The prudish Sensitive, with too-long skinny hands, sneered at her as he sat behind the large marble desk. Ashra wanted to spit at him, but refrained from the urge to do so. She would not let them bring out the worst in her. It would only serve their purpose. Life was tenuous. Pride was better left hidden in the secret places of her mind.

Meeting Krank

The lofty pillars of Mine Central cast long shadows over the earth. Ashra stepped from the shade and turned her face toward the sky. She raised a hand against the brightness and took a breath of dusty air. She reflected on the death she had witnessed. She would never get used to that. *Never.* She blinked up into the sapphire vastness. *Help us.*

One foot moved in front of the other. Loose gravel jumped and rolled beneath the treads of her boots as if skittering from her destination. She didn't remember the steps she took to get there. An ominous stone wall rose up before her, Giant encampment. Ashra pulled the crystal chip from her pocket and brought it near her face. She ran her fingers over its smooth surface and listened to its vibrations. With a breath of resignation she held it under a beam of light that streamed from a metal-encased crystal rod. The crystal scanner was affixed to a large stone obelisk. It towered over her, casting a long shadow in the morning sun. The scanner light blinked rapidly over the face of the chip. Tiny metal pieces affixed to the top of the obelisk vibrated against a blue crystal. It created a series of varied tones that burst forth like brass horns. A bone funnel amplified the vibrations from the top of the obelisk. Ashra jumped. She looked around. No one saw her reaction. *Good.* Eerie silence followed.

Ashra worried her bottom lip between her teeth and peered into the camp. Enormous tattered tents flapped like stray tails in the wind. Gnawed bones and bits of garbage lay strewn about the grounds. Giants were not held in high regard. They were shoved off in a camp, much the same as humans, in contrast to the ornate city the other Krad lived. The similarities ended there. Giants were mostly mute and had extremely violent tempers. If they were crossed, they smashed whoever was in their path, even if it was another Krad. It was not uncommon to see two Giants fighting for lack of a better thing to do. Sensitives and Benders gave the Giants a wide berth, leaving the humans to deal with the repercussions. They were like the unwanted stepbrother you couldn't disown, but refused to sit next to at family gatherings.

The stench in the Giant encampment made the smell of human sweat seem preferable. Ashra brought her durable cotton work shirt up to her crinkled nose in an attempt to inhale a more pleasant scent. It didn't help. She scanned the chip again and the same series of short hornlike bursts played. After another few minutes of shuffling feet and smelling stinks, Ashra decided to return to her team, Giantless.

She was formulating another plan in her mind when she heard the sound of a faraway thump. A creeping chill lifted the hair on her arms.. A series of thumps followed, and the lulling pattern gave a false sense of serenity, like a distant drum beat. She stopped to listen and turned her face toward the noise. The thumps grew louder with each passing blow, bringing with them small vibrations through the ground. Ashra felt them through her thick-soled boots and shivered despite the warm air. Dust and tiny rock fragments jumped at her feet like popping corn with each vibration.

She'd never seen Krank up close, but she had seen him from a distance in the Death Bowl. The Death Bowl was another means of oppression, pitting Krad against humans in an unevenly matched slaughter. Humans found dissenting were made to fight. They always lost. Death Bowls were held every few months and were mandatory to attend. They made Ashra sick. Some humans enjoyed the gruesome distraction but Ashra felt them a brutal reminder of what she was, and who controlled her.

She knew, in general, what to expect. She'd seen Krank fight, but she was unprepared for what followed the series of thumps and vibrations. It wasn't the grotesque underbite or the broad forehead that startled her. It wasn't the sick grayish color of his skin or the rippling muscles, bulging beneath shredded clothing, that caused her unease. It wasn't even his height that made her want to run. All Giants looked like him to some degree. It was his eyes. Ashra had never seen a Giant meet a human's eyes the way Krank did.

Ashra stood five-foot-five-inches looking up into the face of the near-fifteen-foot Giant as he approached. *Should I run? Yes, if I'm smart I'll run. No, I can't. I have to stay...I'm not very smart.* Her thoughts were swarming. Her obligation to her team planted her firm. It wasn't pride at stake, it was their lives.

Each step he took sent ripples through the ground. He met her eyes with intensity. His eyes were fierce. They were inquisitive, and they were calculating. Krank, it would seem, was not your typical half-wit Giant. *Uh-oh.* She felt small and insignificant next to his massive frame.

She wanted to run but her legs turned to rubber. She took a breath and it wavered like the ground when Krank walked. She blew it out and managed another breath somewhat less shaky. *Good.* She squared her shoulders in defiance of her quivering body. Krank approached, his eyes never leaving hers. His stare felt heavy, like it somehow changed the density of the air around her. His presence cast a dark shadow over her. She blinked. He stared.

She willed her lips to part and forced air through her clenched voice box. "Krank, you are assigned to me, I need your help on a project, if you would follow me please," she croaked, then cleared her throat as if blaming phlegm for the tremble in her voice. Her right arm pointed awkwardly toward the mines. *Crap!* She was scared but her fiery eyes never left his as she spoke. The gesturing arm hung outstretched as if it had its own hopes of pulling her away from the exchange.

Ashra turned without giving him a chance to respond and followed her arm's advice to walk in the opposite direction from which he stood. She proceeded on wobbling legs, putting safe distance between her and the intimidating Giant. *Maybe he won't follow.* She took quick, bumpuckered steps down the hill, resisting the urge to look back. Her knotted bun bounced behind her with each step. Escaped hairs flapped wildly, mimicking her heartbeat.

Her nervous attempt to seem in control, while at the same time moving with great urgency, made her neck bob back and forth. Heavy boots sent a spray of dirt and gravel in their wake. She looked like a startled long-necked sand bird running from a loud noise. A sand bird was a silly creature. When scared, its small head bobbles back and forth on a skinny neck. Long legs work frantically to carry its body away from the danger, while useless wings flap to the side in a wild display of ridiculousness. At the moment, Ashra was a spitting image. If a Giant could smirk, Krank did. He shook his head and scratched his chin. He studied her for a few moments, then followed behind her with an easy stride.

Breaking Through

The dirt wall behind Ashra didn't make her feel protected at all. In fact, it made her feel trapped as Krank stood before her, foreboding. Her dark determined eyes met Krank's fierce black ones. The stench of fear mingled with sweat, dust, and Giant hung in the air. Ashra stood her ground, posing strong, though her knees felt like they could buckle. She scratched her face, leaving a smudge of dirt behind.

Krank stood easily. His sharp eyes made their way to each team member, as if assessing their fortitude. He was like a quiet before the storm. His eyes settled back to Ashra and he cocked a scar-mangled brow. Her eye twitched. She pursed her lips as she formed her thoughts. She pushed air through her voice box. It came at first like a loud squawk and then evened out into a steady, if not self-assured, tone.

"Krank, I need you to force the pocket of crystal open in the mine wall." She cleared her throat and swallowed, willing confidence. "It starts here." She walked toward the mine wall, gesturing in the direction that the crystal pocket ran. Her voice came out stronger. "If you can break your way in here"—she pointed to the small place uncovered earlier—"I think it will open the pocket this way."

Lost in her train of thought, she continued to describe how the crystals lay in the vein, in much more detail than necessary. Her eyes lit with excitement as her concentration centered on the rock and not the scary Giant. She used hand gestures with her words as if they were a necessary component of speech. She continued on, occasionally wiping sweat from her face, leaving new streaks of dirt to join the first. "…and we can cut our excavation time in half."

She finished with a slight flourish of the hand, her proud stance in contrast with her dirt-smeared face and clothing. A curve played on her lips as she met the eyes of her teammates. Her passion for the crystal held within the wall was obvious. She looked more like a performer finishing an emotional monologue than a dirty miner.

Ashra's gaze crawled back to Krank, reluctant to meet his stare. Her smile froze. She dropped her hands along with the smile as if some invisible line connected the two. She swallowed hard and blinked. *Crap!* Suddenly breathing seemed dangerous. She dared a sideways look

The Sound of the Stones

toward Haker to gain a source of grounding. He was watching her with an amused smirk. At least, she thought it was a smirk. *Mongrel.*

The rest of the team stood, shuffling feet and kicking small clumps of dirt, as if it was their job to do so. If the tiny cave dwelling insects had been awake this would be their cue to insert a chirp...chirp...chirp. But it was still too early for the nocturnal insects to stir, and the silence was even more awkward in their absence. A small, high-pitched fart escaped team member Pooter, so aptly named, and his face flushed scarlet. Jinka snorted. Ashra shot them a look, cleared her throat, and turned her eyes back to Krank.

"Please?" she said, trying not to giggle manically or cry as her emotions swung on a pendulum.

Krank's face twitched in some semblance of indecipherable emotion. *Amusement perhaps?* He turned his eyes to the wall, moving in her direction with an arm stretched upward and fists clenched. *Uh-oh.* Ashra stumbled back out of his oncoming path with a big-eyed stare. She heard a strangled squeak as she scrambled out of his way. It registered in some back part of her mind that the sound had escaped her own mouth. Had it been another time and place, she might have reflected on the sound and found it amusing. But under the circumstances her heart was lodged in her throat, and she had no time for the contemplation of such musings. She barely made it out of his way and slammed against the opposite side of the mine. The wind left her in a grunt as her fingers dug into the rock for support.

It took one swing for him to open the wall. A huge crystal pocket caught the light and shone in brilliant ways as rocks tumbled to the ground. Krank continued to pound his fist along the seam. Rock and dirt slipped like a waterfall under his thrashing fist. Ashra observed in a detached way the beauty of his strength, as rocks crunched and quivered at his will. The crystal lay exposed in minutes. As the last of the debris slid to a resting place, Krank dusted off his hand, looked at Ashra with a nod, and turned to walk away.

Ashra blinked. Her mouth hung open unapologetically. They watched him slip past the end of the mine wall without a backward glance. Krank had cut their excavation time in half. In fact, he made their job easy, relatively speaking. Instead of smashing his fist into the wall as other Giants might, Krank followed the seam, using a series of hard, but varied knocks against the wall to unearth the crystals. It seemed Krank understood Ashra's painstaking explanation and then used the information to perfection.

"Well, that was interesting," Haker said dryly as he picked up his pick and headed toward the exposed crystal. He brushed a hand down his beard, knocking loose specks of rock fragments, and inspected the exposed vein of crystal with appreciation. All eyes were still fixed in the direction where Krank had left. Haker's comment seemed to break the trance and they began to mill around.

"I'll say!" Jinka said, then punctuated her declaration with an indelicate snort. Scoot and Pooter stood with pickaxes thrown over their shoulders, their heads bobbing in agreement. Haker shot the group a sidelong glance and grunted a noise intended to move the crew. If they moved quickly they could have the crystal cleared out by tomorrow. They were safe for now. Their job would be finished in time. Ashra had never seen crystal exposed so precisely, so quickly. A grin pulled at the corners of her mouth as ideas began to form in her mind.

In a Far-off Place

He smelled rich earth and moisture in the dark, musty air. Muffled noises gave way to a crack...crack...smash. A glimmer of light appeared from the darkness. Blurred colors filled his vision. He heard distant screams. Then silence fell and dark eyes looked in his direction. Emotions of intensity and confusion swam on her face. She opened her mouth then stopped as if choking on her words. She stared intently and leaned in closer. She was so close he could see the amber facets in her chestnut eyes. She tilted her head, blinked owlishly, then disappeared.

"Wait!" He reached for her but it was too late. She was gone.

Bazine sat up, breathing deeply from the intensity of his dream. His arms were stretched into the darkness of his room as the last of the dream vanished. He could still smell the foreign air, still see her eyes. He stood and made his way to the carved stone opening of their home, shaking his head as if he could shake the intensity of the dream from his mind.

Outside the night gave way to dawn, and the tree line was just now visible. The air was still cool and damp, and the birds were quiet, still nestled in slumber. The open-faced home in the cliff looked out over the land of the Nonsomni people. In the distance, a lucent spring flowed over a natural rock wall damn, bursting with vegetation. The water escaped, making hundreds of small waterfalls that emptied into the ocean below. The half-sphere cliff face was dotted with hundreds of similar dwellings, carved out long ago by the humans that first settled this land. The cliff was tucked into the mountains, which gave way to barren desert for hundreds of miles.

The Nonsomni were protected in this hidden land from dangers they knew little about. They were a peaceful people. The height of the mountains trapped the ocean evaporation, making the climate warm and humid. They had all they needed and seldom left the cove. Bazine should have felt safe and settled but he didn't. Dreams plagued him night after night. At first they were sparse and pleasant. Lately they came often and with more intensity.

The cove seemed especially made for the Nonsomni, secreted away at the edge of the world. They were protected, but legends of old kept them from wandering far. The legends were filled with fearful things.

The Sound of the Stones

But life was good and people were happy. The Nonsomni hadn't seen another human in centuries, with the exception of one.

Bazine knelt at the large water catch barrel and turned the sprocket handle with a heavy heart. A stream of clear rainwater filled his kettle. Small drops overflowed with a pit...pat...pit onto the stone ledge overhang. *Shhh.* It sounded loud to him in the early morning silence. He walked inside and reached up to the metal nest attached to the carved stone wall. He tilted a blue crystal until its tip touched a white crystal. The white crystal glowed with increasing intensity from the point at which the blue tip touched it. The light grew brighter and expanded to the length of the whole crystal. He repeated this process several times in various parts of the room where other light fixtures were mounted. He was careful to let the back room remain hidden from the light as not to disturb his mother.

It was always the same vain attempt. A ritual adopted as the days melded together. A strange feeling bubbled within him and grew stronger with each passing day. He didn't know what to do with his dreams or the feelings they left. So, for lack of a better option, he continued on with his daily routine.

He moved to the area used for preparing food and dropped a red crystal inside a low-sided stone bowl, poured a bit of the kettle's water, and sprinkled a hand-ground reactive powder in. The red crystal glowed hot, transmitting the heat through the bowl. Then he placed the heat-conducting lid on top. He set the kettle on top and waited for the water to come to a boil. The water heated quickly but he shifted from foot to foot, running his hands through his tangled black hair. The struggle to understand his own dreams left him impatient with menial tasks.

"Couldn't sleep, Bazine?" Ratha said with a sleep-thickened voice as she emerged from the back room. Her feet shuffled on the stone floor as she rubbed her eyes against the light. He woke her. *Drat.*

Bazine's lips tugged up at one side and he shrugged a shoulder. "I dreamed...that dream again," he said tentatively, as he added various herbs to his cup of steaming water.

Ratha matched his smile, took a seat, and stifled a yawn. He stood for a moment assessing her. The air seemed heavy with unspoken thoughts. Bazine shook his head and sighed. He retrieved another cup from a carved stone shelf and poured steaming water into it. He added a precise mixture of herbs to hers, just as she had taught him.

"Be careful talking about that, Bazine. The others would not understand." Her words were gentle but she gave him a knowing look that only a mother can give. It held a hint of reprimand mixed with love. "Old legends talk of danger in dreams, my son."

Bazine's eyes blazed angry for a moment but it was gone just as soon as it lit. The older woman looked into her son's troubled eyes. Eyes the colors of ocean and violets looked into a mirror set of eyes.

He dropped his gaze to his steaming tea. "I know, Mother, but they're getting stronger. I could see a face this time." He held his cup in one hand while gesturing with the other as he groped to find words of explanation. "It's...like I'm seeing something." He made several inarticulate gestures. "Something unfolding right in front of me."

He moved to the table and slumped youthfully into a chair, releasing a heavy sigh. His other hand continued to work the tangles from his long dark hair. His eyes were focused in a faraway place. "But I only get a glimpse and then nothing." His voice trailed off. He watched the steam rise from his cup as if looking for something, but if it had answers it wasn't giving them up. Bazine grunted, half amused, half frustrated.

Ratha drew in a long breath and mulled over unspoken words that urged to break free. "Son, you mustn't tell a soul. I'm afraid of what they will think if they find out." Those were not the words that beckoned to be released. She remained silent for a moment and studied her hands with a painful expression. Her long hair, streaked with silver, tumbled down around her face, its lean angles full of tension. "People fear what they don't understand." Her words came out as a whisper. She was a beautiful woman and had aged gracefully, but this topic made the lines around her eyes and lips deepen.

Bazine looked up and searched his mother's face, hoping for a way to draw her back from the dark place she went when they spoke of his dreams. It always happened this way. He would wake urgent to discover what the dreams were about. He would stop at nothing to flush out the secrets. Then he would see the distress on her face, hear it in her voice, and his resolve would melt away.

She was his only parent. He never knew his father. Ratha had been found in the desert, not too far from their cove, pregnant and near death. She stayed in a coma for some time, only waking at the beginning of labor to find she was with the Nonsomni people. She didn't know who she was or where she came from. The only thing she remembered was her name. The Nonsomni took her in and accepted Bazine as one of their own. They thought she might remember who she was eventually. She claimed she never did.

Clashing Ranks

The room vibrated with tense silence. Krad leadership gathered together in the inner chamber. Shemma sat, surrounded by his council, his fingers pinched on the bridge of his nose in irritation. The Krad ruler knew he would be challenged soon. But he had never worried about it before. He was a ruthless fighter and no one had ever come near him in battle, but Perditus was giving him cause to worry. Shemma had kept a close eye on him as he grew. Fleuric had taken great interest in Perditus as a young child, spending many hours of one-on-one time with him. Shemma had never known Fleuric to favor one Krad over another. As the creator of Krad, Fleuric had fathered many children, as all ten great Glasne had.

The Glasne dwelled in the second universe, only able to reach the first through mental manipulation or dreams. Fleuric had laid claim to many women while they slept. He had infiltrated their dreams and forced them to bear children. The women who bore fruit gave birth and died. The women he did not sense carried his seed, he killed. But Perditus seemed different. Shemma himself was a son of Fleuric! It angered him that Perditus should receive such special attention.

"There is something about him," he mumbled under his breath.

Shemma had gotten away with slighting Perditus to some degree. He gave him the lowest quarters and glowered at him when he spoke. As Perditus grew older he took notice and became closed off and withdrawn. He was socially awkward and kept to himself. He spent his days training, and spent long hours in commune with his father. This was odd for Krad. They communed with the Glasne, but only together as a group and not as often as Perditus. It was mentally and physically draining to slip into the state of mind necessary to commune with the Glasne. But Perditus didn't seem to have any aftereffects from the experience. Shemma wondered if it was practice, or some secret Fleuric shared with him that allowed him to accomplish the task so effortlessly.

"But why?" he asked no one in particular.

Shemma took his hand from his face, releasing the bridge of his nose from its tight grasp. He looked around at the group gathered, one or two Krad for each section, a total of six council members. They were a ragtag group but they were the most ruthless Benders. He had chosen among the Krad some thirty years ago with two things in mind, his ability to

The Sound of the Stones

control them, and their ability to enforce his orders without qualm. The result was a leadership of Krad who were strong, quick, and not too bright per Krad standards. They were still bright enough by half to rule over humans. Shemma had enough brains for all of them as far as he was concerned. He shook his head and grunted.

"With blood to break the bind I call our brotherhood to order." Shemma stood and took the golden cup filled with humans' blood in his hands. He dipped a finger and licked the blood from the tip, savoring the flavor. He dipped his finger once more and drew a line from his forehead to his chin in blood, then passed the cup to his left. Each council member took the cup and repeated the words, licked the blood, and drew the symbol.

As the last member of the council performed the ritual, a mist began to form. The room shifted as the mingling of universes took place. Shemma felt the familiar pull on his body as the first dimension attempted to maintain its hold. The pull released, snapping like a band. He could still feel his bones vibrating from the force as the mist settled. The weight in the second universe felt heavier. Shemma and his council kneeled in the large room as Fleuric took shape before them. His knees felt the weight of his body in double, and a dull throbbing pain emanated up his thighs.

Fleuric stood at the head of a large oval table. Nine other Glasne flanked him, seated on either side. Krad were large by human standards but Glasne were impressive, standing close to eight feet tall. They had varying facial features, all sharp and strong. Hair color varied, worn shoulder length and free. But each of the Glasne shared the same black eyes, rimmed in an eerie yellow band. They were bound in brotherhood as original beings, superior to humans and Krad. The Krad bridged the universes, sharing blood of both human and Glasne.

Fleuric's presence seemed larger than the rest. His sharp eyes scanned the council and came to rest on Shemma. Shemma raised his head to meet Fleuric's stare. Shemma could hide his resentment no better than he could his disgust of humans. The corner of Fleuric's lips twitched.

"Rise, my sons. Join us at the table." His voice was warm but firm. It commanded obedience. It dared challenge. Shemma struggled with conflicting emotions as he interpreted those intonations. Fleuric made a sweeping gesture to the empty seats at the foot of the table, and raised one elegant blond brow.

Shemma cleared his throat and rose. The other council members followed his example. Shemma sat at the counterpoint and the others filled the empty seats around him. Shemma raised his own brow.

"My Lord, what will you have me do for you?" His voice was smooth enough, but he couldn't help the grudge bleeding into his tone.

Fleuric chuckled and settled himself into his seat. He steepled his hands and narrowed his eyes. "There is nothing more you can do for me." He spoke as a matter of fact. There was no anger in his tone. It was only an observation born from long centuries of living.

Shemma swallowed hard. A cold hard fear settled in the pit of his stomach. He grappled for a reply, something he could say to change Fleuric's mind. But he knew it was futile. Nothing he said could change the Glasne ruler's mind.

"Will you have me step down, my Lord?" Shemma asked with little hope. If Fleuric would order him to step down, he might escape with his life. But no Krad ruler ever stepped down. It simply wasn't done.

"No, you will accept the challenge from Perditus, just as all rulers before you accepted theirs. It is the way. It is honorable." A tight smirk played on Fleuric's lips. He eyed Shemma appraisingly. Shemma felt the weight of his eyes and shifted. He glanced around the table. The eyes of the other Glasne were cold and bored. His council stared at Fleuric with a variety of blank expressions. *Useless mongrels..*

"Very well, my Lord. I will accept the challenge, and I will win, just as I did the last five times." He spoke as loftily as he could muster, trying to stifle the fear and doubt that swelled within him.

Fleuric laughed, amusement gleaming in his eyes. Some of the other Glasne joined him in their shared joke. Shemma pinched his lips and stared at a point behind Fleuric to avoid his mocking expression. The other council members turned their attention to Shemma, and heat crept up his neck as his face flamed red.

"You will try, I have no doubt. But you will fail. You may go now."

Fleuric's words severed the bond between the universes, and mist rose up between the Krad and Glasne. Shemma could still hear the echoing laughter as his own inner chamber materialized.

Destiny Calling

"It is time, my son." Fleuric's yellow-rimed eyes studied his son with curiosity and hope.

Perditus nodded his acceptance, looking back at his father with weary violet-blue eyes. He had eyes like his mother. It was the only thing human about him. His frame and features mimicked his father, only inches shorter than Fleuric's eight-foot height. Perditus's 7'2" frame was a perfect likeness. They could have been brothers with the same chiseled bone structure. Perditus was in his early twenties and Fleuric showed no signs of aging past thirty, though he was as old as time. Perditus would also keep his youth. Krad could live unlimited life if they could avoid being killed. The same bronze skin and the same white-blond hair flowed in thick locks just past the jaw line.

"You will defeat Shemma and take the throne," he ordered. "Through you, my son, the Glasne will be freed."

Fleuric spoke of the bounding of himself and the other fallen Glasne to the second universe. He had failed to find release in the thousands of years they had been trapped. He knew it had something to do with vibrations, but he had not found the proper mixture yet. It was the same as his failure to create in the first universe when he broke the protective seal and invoked time.

He held hope that Perditus was the key. It was hope filled with secret knowledge. He had waited for the perfect woman, the perfect bloodline to sire his chosen son. Fleuric looked at his son with fatherly pride and Perditus felt the weight of his responsibilities pressing down around him. He had known this day would come.

"Today I will take what is ours. I will stop at nothing to free you, Father." Perditus managed to sound more confident than he felt as he lifted his chin and met his father's gold-rimmed stare.

Fleuric lips twisted amused. "You are my finest creation, son. Go. Fulfill your destiny."

Perditus changed his breathing and concentrated on bringing himself out of the place between the universes. He opened his eyes and found himself back in his sleek humble dwelling. He gathered his spear and headed for the door.

A King Threatened

The weight of today's events draped around Shemma like a yoke. He had been the Krad leader for three decades, had fought and won five challenges from others who sought the throne. But today he would face Perditus.

"How would you propose defeating Perditus in battle?" Shemma asked his council. They exchanged brief looks.

"Move fast and strike hard," the largest Bender said. His face held an empty expression.

The others nodded with the same empty eyes. Shemma's lip curled in disgust. It was simple. He would have to be quicker than Perditus to win. They all knew what Perditus was capable of. Shemma's eyes traveled over his advisors nodding like yes-men. He shook his head and rubbed a hand down his face.

"If this is all the advice you have for me, then I will definitely be replacing you after I defeat that mutt today," he bit.

They did not flinch. They were used to his surly behavior. He often berated them. He was a nasty-tempered Krad who treated his advisors horribly and his servants even worse. The only thing keeping him in power was his ability to manipulate the situations through fear. He killed with little proof of dissent and surrounded himself with the slimiest Krad. Wealth and favors moved those around him. He had enough of both to keep the masses placated. No one would mourn him if he fell today and Shemma knew it.

A New Heir

Ashra was tired. She was also grimy and not in a particularly good mood. She wanted nothing more than to go home and wash, but the evening would not be hers. Humans were required to attend the Death Bowl today. She blew stray hairs from her dirt-smeared face and trudged forward. This evening Krad would show off their strengths by killing dissenters. Giants would fight Giants as a form of sick entertainment for the Krad, and tonight the Krad leader would fight to keep his position.

This was the topic of conversation as the humans made their way in to the dusty oval bowl where slaughter would ensue. Would the leader keep his position? Would the young Perditus take his place? If he did, would things change under new leadership? Tittering speculation about the outcome filled the air. These questions were almost enough to lend hope to the tired human race. But as people crammed into the stifling arena and sat on the hard stone benches surrounding the dirt floor of the Death Bowl, any hope ceased to remain as the scene unfolded.

Dirty, ragged humans stood helplessly in the center of the arena. They had a smattering of weapons. They clutched spears, and blades of various sizes, in grubby, tired hands. The looks on their faces ranged from horror to stunned complacency. The large stone doors at the far end of the ring opened slowly. Stone ground against stone, sending up puffs of dust that hung stagnant and low over the arena floor.

The noise sent shivers down Ashra's spine as she watched from the crowd. She was separated from those she knew in the rush to enter the Death Bowl and found herself nestled between two large sweaty strangers. The uncomfortable seats were all the more uncomfortable next to the smelly men who grunted, scratched, and ate stale nuts. Ashra scrunched her nose. The nuts were a sad offering to the humans, as attending the killings was mandatory. She had no appetite and politely refused a bite from the filthy hand of the man to her right, then felt a slight twinge of guilt for her disgust as he offered her a warm brown-toothed smile. She returned her attention to the action on the floor.

Twenty-one Gravity Benders entered the Death Bowl from the open stone doors. The half-human, half-Glasne creatures stood about a foot above the forty-seven trembling humans in the center of the dirt,

The Sound of the Stones

awaiting death. The Krad Benders were going to fight the humans, and the humans would surely die. Ashra's stomach knotted as she scanned the faces of those about to meet death. She recognized a man in the midst of the crowd. *The man from Mine Central!* He held a lone dagger, and trembled at the sight of the approaching Krad.

The Krad Benders held no weapons, and were outnumbered by the humans. Sure the humans were armed, but when you fight creatures that could repel gravity, what odds did a normal person have? Ashra struggled to breathe less foul-smelling air as she sat sandwiched between the two reeking men. She leaned forward and caught sight of her own dirty hands. She had ripped a hole in her pants and dust clung to every inch of her body. She was no better off than the dirty men next to her. She sighed and leaned back, embracing the filth.

Neither Ashra nor any other human could remember a time when it was any different. The Krad made sure they repressed any inkling of memory of a time before oppression. As far as humans knew, it had always been this way. It was a dark sick world full of thankless exhaustive labor. Yet, humans still found love and made families. It was the only sense of joy left to the human race, it would seem. But too often families were ripped apart by the cruel nature of Krad ruling.

Wailing caught Ashra's attention and she turned to see a small group of people huddled by the edge of the arena. A tired-looking woman held a small boy and restrained by the arm a young girl who struggled to reach her father in the center of the Death Bowl. The man from Mine Central looked to the girl and shook his head, willing her silent. The young girl's eyes were full of tears and she choked on a whimper as she strained against her mother's grasp. The boy was too young to understand and he stared wide-eyed at his sister.

If wishes could save her father, then the little girl would be powerful enough. But wishes were not enough, and the little girl would be powerless as she watched her father die today. The memories would mar her young mind. She would most likely become a shell of a person after this horrific affair.

No! Ashra had seen it enough in her short years to know the glazed look of defeat. Children who lost a parent in this manner held themselves differently. Their innocence and hope were stripped from them, never to return. Ashra's eyes stung in anguish. If she had to go on

50

year after year watching these horrors, she too might become a glassy-eyed girl, just a shell of her former self.

Loud regal music trumpeted from brass horns, signaling the beginning of events. Ashra jumped though she knew the sound was coming. Twenty-one Benders shot into the air in sleek form, as if choreographed. The crowd held their breath as the creatures soared toward the cowering humans, weapons held at the ready with unsure hands. Benders came down in streaks of motion and clashed with the humans. Some weapons found homes. Benders didn't yield to an impaled arm or shoulder. They ripped the weapons from their bodies unfazed, and turned them on the smaller humans. Humans dropped by twos and threes. It didn't take longer than ten minuets for the last to fall, slumping to the bloodied dirt, gasping one last breath. Twenty-one Benders stood over the dead humans with mild abrasions in comparison. Bile crept up Ashra's throat. She swallowed hard.

The brass horns blew unsettling music as a human crew scurried to clear the carnage from the arena floor. The little girl, so vocal before, stood silent. She watched with a blank expression as her father's broken body was tossed on the heap aboard a wooden cart. The irregular blackened stains of dried blood against the aged wood of the cart was a vivid reminder of its past riders. Ashra recognized the look in the little girl's eyes. Though she had seen it all before it never got easier. She had never developed the numbness some humans seemed able to adopt. This would never be okay.

The next phase of the Death Bowl brutality was the Giant battle. One Giant faced another to the death. The winner faced other Giants, time after time, until another winner took the title as ultimate Giant fighter. Once that title was in place, the reigning Giant faced the one Giant who had never been beaten. Long ago they stopped fighting Krank in normal matches. Krad got tired of seeing the same Giant win Bowl after Bowl. Instead, they saved him for matches with a proven fighter. They had yet to find a Giant who could overcome him.

Kursh entered from the far side of the arena through the same heavy stone door that was used not fifteen minutes before. He ducked through the door and stood to his full seventeen feet. He dwarfed the Benders standing guard. His sick gray skin glistened in the evening sun and his deep-set black eyes twitched from place to place like a wild animal. His

The Sound of the Stones

breathing was ragged, and his body swayed as if standing still was painful. His wide cracked feet splayed into the blood-stained dirt as he walked to the center of the arena. He had won the last seven Death Bowl matches. It was time for the ultimate test.

With another blaze of brass, the stone door on the opposite side of the arena ground open. Dark shadows hid Krank's form. Kursh grunted rhythmically with anticipation. The horns came to a stop on cue as the door reached its zenith. Krank stepped out from the shadows, dressed in the same tattered rags he had worn earlier in the day. He walked with purpose toward the center of the Bowl and stood only feet away from his opponent. Ashra was struck immediately by the height difference. Kursh stood two feet taller and was wider in the chest. She wondered if this would be the end for Krank, at last outmatched in strength. She felt a strange sense of dread for him. It was a new emotion, Ashra never having felt empathy for a Krad before.

Kursh's barrel chest rose and fell noticeably as he swayed back and forth. His eyes darted and his hand twitched in anticipation. Krank stood like stone, his eyes unmoving. A low guttural growl escaped Krank. It sounded loud in the silence that followed him onto the arena floor. Ashra could feel the vibrations from the growl ripple through her body. A collective gasp from the humans punctuated the intensity of the scene.

Without any noticeable indication, Kursh rushed forward swift and low, aiming for Krank's legs. Krank anticipated his movement. He moved to the side as Kursh neared, and landed a solid blow to the back of the charging Giant. The blow sent Kursh tumbling. He quickly recovered and got to his feet, swiveling to face Krank in a cloud of dust.

Kursh huffed, annoyed, and swayed his head back and forth. He threw his head back and let loose a scream. It was a loud ear-piercing sound that echoed off the arena walls. Ashra jumped. Spittle flew from his lips and hung in strands when he stopped to take more ragged breaths. Krank once again stood still, his eyes never leaving their target. His only discernible movement was a slight twitch in his right hand as he continued to assess the threat.

Kursh sprang forward with twice the speed as before and managed to make contact before Krank moved to the side. He slammed into Krank headfirst like a ram. Kursh lunged for Krank's throat, having pushed him back a few steps. As his hands neared their target, Krank blocked him with a sweeping left arm and brought his right elbow into the top of Kursh's head. His head and neck scrunched upon impact and air left him with an *oomph*. Ashra cringed. Krank disengaged and stood back to assess the damage. Kursh scrambled back a few steps and shook his head, spit slinging. A small trickle of blood seeped from his flat gray nose and he ran his tongue across his upper lip, smearing the blood. He bared brown, jagged teeth and grunted in opposition. Krank made no effort to return the gesture. He stood casually, his arms at his side, and sniffed.

Ashra didn't know much about fighting, but she had watched enough Death Bowls to realize Krank had the upper hand with the last blow. Why didn't he take advantage and finish Kursh? Was he merciful, or did he enjoy the fight? The crowd grew loud with cheers and jeers. Ashra was jostled between the two smelly men as they picked sides and waved dirty arms in the air. The man to her right called out to the feared favorite Krank, while the man on her left threw slurs at Kursh to man up and fight. *Man?* Ashra snorted.

Having some small basis for Krank's personality, Ashra began to search the Giant's face. Kursh showed no emotion, other than frustration and rage. Those were the only two emotions, besides complacency, she had ever seen expressed by a Giant. Krank had a different look though. If she didn't know better, she would almost believe she saw sorrow there in his deep black eyes. Could it be wishful thinking on her part? Could she be imprinting her own emotion as a way to feel better about the gruesome circumstance? She found herself rooting for him. She had never cared before. She simply endured these matches, averting her eyes as much as possible. But she couldn't take her eyes off the puzzle standing before her.

With nurtured frustration, Kursh struck out again, this time landing a solid blow to Krank's chest. Krank lost footing and fell backward. Kursh lunged, landing on top, and trapped Krank's arms with his powerful legs. The crowd went wild and Ashra watched in horror as Kursh wrapped his hands around Krank's neck. She rose to her feet and screamed, but it was swallowed by the crowd's maniacal noises. Krank's veins bulged under the crushing weight of Kursh's strangle. His eyes were wide and his feet dug into the ground as he tried, in vain, to gain

The Sound of the Stones

footing beneath the larger beast. Ashra's heart sank as the moments ticked by. The crowd continued to cheer and it seemed the moment of defeat was imminent.

Krank went still. Kursh barked laughter and raised his hands in the air in celebration. The moment Kursh's hands left his neck, Krank brought his knee up, in a bucking blow, to Kursh's most sensitive parts. Kursh doubled over onto Krank's chest and Krank managed to pull one hand free from between Kursh's legs. Without further ado, he smashed the stunned Giant's face with an elbow.

Kursh's body went still. Krank pulled his other arm free and threw the Giant off. Kursh rolled twice, landing face up, his arms and legs bent in an unnatural way. His face sloped inward, distorting his naturally gruesome features. Kursh was dead. Krank pulled himself to his feet and stood sullenly in the center of the arena, casting a shadow over Kursh's lifeless body. He did not look triumphant. He did not look complacent. He did not look angry. He looked...sad.

The horns played again, breaking through the wild cheers of the crowd. Krank grabbed Kursh's arm and walked toward his exit, dragging his dead opponent behind. The crowd chanted Krank's name, but Ashra had no words. She went very still as she watched Krank pause. His eyes traveled from the dirt to the crowd. They moved swiftly, searching, and stopped when they found their target. His eyes locked with hers for a few brief moments, then he turned and exited. The arena was empty, and the drag marks in the dirt cut directly through the bloody mud left from the slaughtered humans.

The crowd settled back into their seats. There was movement in the plush seating reserved for Krad leadership. Humans and Krad alike fawned over the Krad ruler as he readied himself for the next event. He swung from the ledge, jumping from the two-story-high seats with little effort. His white linen clothing billowed regally as he descended to the dirt floor. He landed in a puff of dust and glided to the center of the arena with an air of confidence brought on by decades of experience.

Shemma was a Gravity Bender who had taken the leadership from another before Ashra's time. He had been Krad leader for thirty years and didn't look a day over thirty years himself. He was tall and lean, with sinewy muscle and shoulder-length chestnut hair. His skin was clear and bright, and his dark eyes cut through the crowd as he surveyed from his new perspective. Horns played an elegant tune to accompany his claim to the arena floor. His leadership style was harsh even by Krad standards. More humans had been found guilty of infractions under Shemma than any other Krad before him, or so Ashra had been told.

Shemma clutched a staff in his right hand and removed the silver fob with his left to reveal a sharp spear tip. He tossed the silver knob to a Bender standing near the arena wall without a sideways glance. He had faced five opponents in his years as Krad leader, and defeated them all. Attempts to take the leadership were legal, and once a Krad reached the age of twenty-one they had the option to challenge the ruler to take over. Only the very brave and well trained dared to do so. Shemma himself had challenged a Krad ruler, and won, thirty years ago. Ashra dared to hope a new, less cruel leader might take his place today, then mentally kicked herself for the ridiculous thought. Hoping for something better was fool's thinking.

A door slid open to the right and the crowed held their breath, waiting for the challenger to appear. The entrance remained empty. Perhaps the challenger changed his mind. Perhaps he wasn't ready. It had happened before, a young Krad second guessing his decision and opting for life, rather than challenge a great leader and face possible death.

The crowd shifted in their seats. A shout to the left caught Ashra's attention and she turned to see a tall figure standing at the top of the stone arena. He stood motionless, a breeze blowing his white-blond hair. He shouted again. Shemma heard him and looked up, shielding his eyes from the evening sun. He looked as confused as the crowd felt.

"I am Perditus. Know my name, for I am the rightful heir to the crown of all," the blond-haired Krad proclaimed from his lofty position. His face was stone, and his eyes like knives.

Shemma dropped his hand to his hip and barked a laugh, beckoning Perditus with his spear. Perditus's lips turned up at the corners, and his eyes sparked wild. He bounded from his seven-story perch, landing on the dirt floor. The dust was not disturbed by his landing, as if he were weightless.

The two Krad wasted no time. They ran toward one another with lightning speed. Just before they clashed Shemma jumped, his linen garb making graceful lines as he twisted in the air above. Perditus

The Sound of the Stones

swiveled low to the ground, making a half circle with his left leg in the dirt, then came to a stop facing Shemma. Shemma landed with a thud, his spear at the ready, facing the crouched Perditus. Perditus rolled the spear in his right hand playfully as he assessed Shemma. They were only feet apart. Perditus rose, and now that they were close, Ashra noticed Perditus's height. He stood a full head taller, and outweighed Shemma by at least thirty pounds. Shemma didn't blink, nor did he flinch. He stood quietly at the ready.

The crowed was silent. There was an unspoken rule when a Krad leader fought; no one wanted to make the mistake of cheering for the wrong Krad, for fear of being found a dissenter. The two stood, face to face, assessing one another, and the air grew thick. Ashra could hear muffled coughs and nervous breathing coming from the crowd.

When, at last, Shemma moved toward Perditus, it was with a prowling motion. Perditus remained still, waiting for his strike. Shemma jolted forward with his spear, aiming at the center of Perditus's chest, but just as the spear reached its mark, Perditus lifted upward as if pulled by an invisible force. He twisted above Shemma's head, and sliced at his back as he came down on the other side. At first glance it didn't appear to have touched Shemma, but as Shemma swung around to face Perditus, Ashra noticed a slice in his white shirt. The open garment revealed a long gash, seeping blood. The blood trickled down his back, leaving stains of red where the blood touched his clothing. Shemma seemed unaffected, standing at the ready against the younger Krad.

Perditus was the next to move. He strode over, his spear held loosely to the side. Shemma's muscles tensed. He wielded his spear in a lunge toward Perditus, but Shemma moved slow in comparison. Perditus plucked the spear from the lunging Shemma's hands. Shemma looked stunned. He blinked, then eyed the taller Krad clutching two spears, one in each hand. Realization dawned on Shemma's face and he stumbled back a few paces.

Perditus's expression had been one of quiet concentration, but a smirk spread across his lips at Shemma's reaction. He lunged with both spears. Shemma tripped backward, falling to the ground in a cloud of dust. Perditus stopped just short of driving the spears though the Krad leader. He tossed the spears aside, crossed his arms and sneered wickedly. Perditus leaned forward and whispered something. Shemma's face went white, his eyes wide. He jumped to his feet, revealing his bloody backside to the crowd. Perditus tipped his chin in invitation.

Shemma popped his neck and rolled his shoulders in an attempt to regain control. Perditus dropped his arms to his side. His smirk faded, but his eyes still held a playful spark. Shemma feigned a move to the left, then quickly went right, in an attempt to reach the spears. Perditus intercepted before Shemma made it halfway to the spears. He grabbed Shemma around the neck with one hand and raised him several feet in the air.

Perditus's muscles bulged beneath his simple black shirt. Shemma's hands and feet flailed and his linen garb flapped in desperation. His dark eyes went wide, and his mouth worked to scream, but no words escaped. Perditus's lips twitched at the corners. He used his free hand to twist Shemma's head swiftly to the left.

Ashra heard the snap and her stomach lurched. She swallowed hard. Shemma's eyes were open but they were empty. His body, flailing moments before, drooped lifeless from the clutch of Perditus's outstretched arm. Ashra shivered. Perditus dropped him in the dust with a thud of finality. He removed a cloth from his low-slung cotton pants, and wiped dust from his hands judiciously.

The crowd roared. Ashra was jostled as the people around her rose to their feet. Ashra rose too, but remained silent, a sick feeling settling into the pit of her stomach. A new Krad leader was born. For the first time, she had witnessed the toppling of leadership. This unknown was somehow scarier than familiar oppression. It was filled with a darker blackness than she had ever sensed.

Assisting Darkness

It was deep in the bowels of the Death Bowl where Smirah finished treating the last of the Bender wounds. The pleasantly plump middle-aged woman packed her cauterizing crystal and the rest of her medical supplies into her worn leather bag. She looked up with a start as a barrage of Krad and humans followed Perditus into the room with a clash of noise. He acknowledged none of them. He looked distracted as he glanced around the room. Her heart jumped into her throat when his eyes met hers.

"You," he pointed in her direction, "will be my personal assistant." He brushed past the chattering crowd behind him.

Smirah blinked and looked over her shoulder, expecting to see a pretty young woman. There was no one behind her. Did he mean her?

"Come. Get me settled into the palace," he barked, motioning her to follow with a tip of his head.

No, he meant her. She jumped up and fumbled with her medical bag. Her fingers went numb. The crowd hushed, blinking in confusion as she left. She followed him out the back door to the sounds of murmured speculation, and climbed aboard the ruler's carriage. Sitting across from him as the carriage pulled away felt awkward to say the least. He didn't spare her a glance. He glared out the window of the crystal-powered carriage as they made their way through Krad City, leaving her to gawp. Human servants and Krad lined the streets, shouting their allegiance to the new leader, but he didn't seem affected. He was aloof and cold as he sat there in his own thoughts. Smirah couldn't guess why he had chosen her to be his personal assistant. A young beautiful woman typically held that role. This had to be a mistake. She shifted in her seat, thinking of other duties they performed.

"Women are distracting," Perditus said, as if reading her mind. His eyes were still fixed out the window. Smirah sniffed at the strange Krad ruler but kept silent. "I have no need of a female, flitting around fawning over me. It's better this way. You will serve me without the idle distractions most Krad rulers encounter. I have a job to do. I do not need distractions." He turned piercing eyes on her as if waiting for confirmation. She pursed her lips and nodded curtly. Perditus nodded as well and turned back to the window.

The Sound of the Stones

The comment stung far more than she would have expected. Sure she was older now, and a little more round than she used to be, but still a woman. What could she say though? She shifted in her seat again and fiddled with the handle on her bag. At least he would not expect her to service him in other ways. She could remain true to her dead husband. She sighed, clutching her bag closer to her body, and waited to find what the new job would bring. Her stomach churned and her mind reeled. Things would be very different now.

An Awkward Exchange

Blithe slinked through Krad City on glazed stone paths on his way to the palace. Intricate carved columns stretched toward the heavens, supporting domed rooftops, a wondrous architectural presence. Krad brilliance, human servitude, and Giant strength gave way to impressive designs against a blue-sky backdrop. Statues carved from marble resembled strange and wonderful humanlike creatures performing lewd acts. Young Krad played in a patch of greenery outside a building that served as the orphanage where Krad were raised.

All Krad were male. The mixing of Glasne and human genes brought forth an impressive immortal race, but they were all male and they were infertile. The Glasne spent hundreds of years building their half-breed race. Women were visited in their dreams by Glasne and impregnated. It was the only way Glasne could reach humans in the first universe. Women remained in a coma through pregnancy, gave birth, and died, their bodies too weak to support the birthing of such creatures. Humans raised the first Krad born long ago, before they knew the cause of the deadly pregnancies. But as the small number of Krad grew to maturity, Glasne reached them in dream state and turned them against the humans. The Krad waited and grew in strength. They bound together and usurped the human race. Many humans died, few escaped, and the rest were enslaved.

The world had been this way so long that humans forgot the past, a time when they were not servants. They forgot where they came from. They forgot who they were before oppression. Humans were afraid to rebel or even think of it for fear of being revealed through modicum scans. Krad killed any human who even thought about dissent. The Death Bowl served that purpose well.

Krad darted in and out of buildings, tending to their daily business. Scantily clad humans followed behind Krad carrying items. They served as personal assistants, cooks, maids, and playthings. Other luckier humans served as farmers, miners, and maintainers. Farmers grew crops and tended the animals that served as the Krad's source of sustenance. Miners mined the mineral, stones, and metal, and maintainers fabricated, constructed, and maintained all buildings and

The Sound of the Stones

equipment. Krad oversaw these daily chores and instructed the humans in harsh ways.

The soles of Blithe's boots echoed with each step as he entered the outer chamber of the palace. The Bender guards, clad in intricate metal armor, parted way for Blithe to enter the inner chamber, their faces held in serious concentration. Blithe rolled his eyes as he passed them.

Perditus faced the window, his hands resting on the sill. Blithe looked out past the new leader to glimpse his view. The Krad gates separated the human encampment from the glorious city. Mine Central, off to the right, sat on gentle rolling hills. Hills gave way to mountains that brought forth the mineral, rock, and metals. Green farmland stretched beyond the human encampment looking peculiar against the arid backdrop. Irrigation from a fresh underground water source made farming a possibility in the parched region. Centuries of refinement, borne on the backs of humans, turned the land into an oasis for the Krad.

Blithe turned his attention back to Perditus. Blithe was bitter and it showed in the set of his shoulders. He had strong feelings toward Perditus over circumstances that took place at his conception and birth. Blithe's secret forbidden love for a human that ended in tragedy was tied to events preceding Perditus's birth. Perditus didn't know his birth had lent to Blithe's biggest loss. He stood there easily and that made Blithe even angrier.

"How does my city fare, Blithe?" he said, without turning around.

Blithe jumped. The timbre of his voice was deep, resonating through the room, touching everything in its wake. He didn't act like a new leader. He owned it, wore it like it had always been his. That also irritated Blithe. He sneered at the leader's back.

"Well enough, master." Blithe made a small bow at the waist and removed the sneer as Perditus turned in his direction.

"What brings you here?" Perditus filled the room with his presence. His muscular frame dwarfed Blithe's slender build. But it was the handsome face that sealed the deal. Blithe was sure of it. He hated Perditus.

"I would like to speak with you about a human I have under my keep, master." Blithe attempted to keep his snide nature under control, Perditus's authoritative manner a not-so-gentle reminder to do so.

62

Perditus gestured for Blithe to sit. Blithe sat. Perditus walked to a metal plate affixed to the wall, covered in different-colored jewels. He pressed the auburn-colored jewel twice. It glowed briefly and then faded. As Perditus made his way to a tall plush chair opposite Blithe, a middle-aged human dressed in plain brown garb entered the room. She held a decanter full of auburn liquor and two glasses.

"Leave it," Perditus said, with a dismissive gesture toward the woman. She placed the items down, bowed her head, and left the room. Perditus stared after the closed door with narrowed eyes. Blithe wondered why he chose this older, less attractive human to be on his serving staff when he could have any number of attractive women.

Blithe waited silently. Perditus seemed distracted, as if he weren't fully there. Blithe swallowed and shifted in his chair. Perditus gave Blithe a sideways glance and made a small noise of contemplation. Blithe frowned. Perditus unstopped the decanter and poured generous portions in two glasses, then handed one to Blithe. He gave a curt smile, which made Blithe even more uncomfortable. Blithe took the glass gingerly.

"Tell me what is so interesting about your human, Blithe?" Perditus tilted his head slightly to one side, piercing him with violet-blue eyes. Blithe collected his drink and took a sip, trying to pretend their exchange was normal. The liquid seared as it slipped down his throat and his voice came out strained.

"Master, I have suspicions about one particular human." Blithe cleared his throat. Perditus eyed him nonchalantly, with perhaps a hint of amusement, then knocked back his own drink in one long swallow. He rested the empty glass on his knee.

"What suspicions would those be, Blithe?" His eyes twinkled and he flashed a grin that held just a touch of crazy. Blithe set his too-strong drink on a side table and eyed it speculatively lest it slap him. He cleared his throat again and swallowed, trying to soothe the burn.

"Well, master, I have been assigning difficult mining jobs to a particular young woman for some time now." Blithe smoothed a thin mustache over his skinny upper lip. Perditus watched him work at the pencil-thin hair on his face in quiet amusement. Blithe noticed and dropped his hand to his lap. He cleared his throat a third time. "At first I thought she was just a very bright human. She always leads her team well...too well. They always finish their tasks on time." Blithe paused and took a deep breath. Perditus sat forward from his lounging position and rested his elbows on his knees. He fiddled with the empty glass, dangling gracefully from his hand.

Blithe's right eye began to twitch and he worked at his mustache again. "I wanted to test a theory so I gave her incorrect information about a vein of crystal." Blithe eyed him warily. Perditus lifted his head and waited for him to continue, his expression impassive. "I misled her half a dozen times, and gave her impossible time limits to recover the crystals with improper information. She met her deadline every time."

Blithe watched the leader, waiting for some indication of how he felt. Perditus gave no indication that the information surprised or intrigued him. Perditus sat comfortably, looking lost between two worlds. Blithe thought perhaps he would need to expound and cleared his throat to make another go of it. As if shaken awake, Perditus stood and walked to his desk as if Blithe weren't even in the room. *He's crazy*, Blithe thought to himself as Perditus sifted through his disheveled desk while mumbling under his breath. Blithe thought he caught a piece of the mumbling, something about the "deep mine."

Blithe shifted in his chair and eyed his too-strong drink with a sideways glance. He considered taking another sip but decided he would rather have a twitchy eye.

"Ah, here," Perditus said as if to himself, as he grabbed a thin, square crystal plate with etchings. There was one green blip glowing on its surface. He studied it for a moment and closed his eyes. Blithe changed his mind and reached for his nemesis drink. But before he could swallow Perditus shoved the crystal plate in his face.

"There are faint vibrations in an ancient part of the mine. I discovered this yesterday. That part of the mine has been without vibration for centuries." Perditus paused and rubbed his chiseled chin. Blithe took a swallow of his drink as he studied the crystal plate. He sputtered a cough when the drink spanked his esophagus on the way down. Perditus ignored him or didn't notice. Blithe set his drink even farther away and gave it a dirty look.

"Send your *special* human to this location to recover a sample of the crystal making this vibration. It is unlike any vibration I have ever seen. Let us see if..." He paused as if waiting for Blithe to say something.

Perditus gestured with his right hand as if offering him the floor to speak. Blithe was thoroughly confused and his eye twitched in answer. Perditus sighed and dropped his hand to his side. "Name. What is the girl's name?" He said the words as if speaking to a nincompoop.

"Oh, Ashra. Ashra of the mines, and daughter of Sheed and Shara," Blithe said irritably, with only a hint of apology. He furrowed his brows, as if concentrating harder would help this awkward meeting improve. Perditus seemed appeased enough having received a name, and continued with his thoughts.

"Let us see if this Ashra gives any indication of its irregularity." Perditus went back to his desk, Blithe's presence seemingly forgotten, again. He waved a long-fingered hand.

"You may go," he said as an afterthought.

Blithe took his cue and fumbled as he gathered the crystal plate, nearly spilling the blasted drink! He exited with a grudging bow.

"And Blithe…"

He stopped in his tracks outside the door and turned just enough to catch Perditus's eyes. They were sharp and calculating.

"The way I run things will be different. From now on you will run all of your plans through me before you implement them. I will not be superseded." His tone was ice, full of ugly promises, and the look on his face was completely sane. Blithe swallowed hard, nodded, then left.

History Revealed

Electric light eyes scanned the horizon. It was his city. His father had given all these things into his control when he passed him his genes, making him the most powerful Krad there was. Now he could finally make his father's desires a reality. He felt that calling like a blanket of metal digging into his flesh. He didn't know if he could succeed. But he knew he had to try. He closed his eyes and took controlled breaths, coming to that tenuous place the two could meet.

Darkness became a murky muddle of pictures as his breathing slowed to a steady rhythm. A different room came into view. Slick black floors met dark stone walls. Dark, heavy velvet drapes hung from the walls, breaking the monotony of gray. It was an illusion of windows. There were no windows in this place. There were no stars or moon. There was no sun or warmth. Only an illusion of similarities to the first universe existed there. The surroundings shifted under Fleuric's demand, but it was a shell.

Fleuric had reached Perditus in his first year of life and taught him how to commune. Perditus took to it quickly. He didn't need the ritual of the cup and blood. It was clear that Perditus was strong. Fleuric didn't tell him, but it was the human bloodline that made him so.

They spent hours at a time making plans. The ultimate goal was to set the Glasne free to roam the first universe without aid of human dreams. They needed to break the barrier holding them in the second universe. They needed to find the thread keeping the universes separate and pull it loose. Fleuric knew it had something to do with vibration. Through the millennia Fleuric had tried a myriad of things to imitate and decipher the particular vibration needed to crack the universal code. It still remained a mystery. Fleuric was tired. But he could sense a shift, some change in the vibrations, that gave him hope. Something big was happening, if he could just nudge it in the right direction.

"Ah, my boy, you're looking well." Fleuric's deep voice echoed off the hard surfaces in the room.

"Yes, Father. I am." Perditus's voice matched the resonance of his father's. His smile was warm but his eyes were troubled.

The Sound of the Stones

"What is it, my son?" Fleuric asked, his forehead creasing in concern. He waved his hand and two chairs appeared. He waved again and a fireplace burst into heatless life.

"There are strange things taking place, Father," Perditus said, as he settled his large form into a chair. "Strange vibrations are present in a part of the mine that has been vacant for centuries." Perditus stopped short of finishing his thought.

"Well, in all my millennia trapped in this universe I have witnessed stranger things than that, my boy." There was a hint of humor in his tone, then a silence fell between them for a few moments.

"There is a human we suspect can hear crystal vibrations," Perditus finished, and leaned back in his chair to study his father's expression. Fleuric had not aged a day past thirty, but his eyes showed signs of tired emptiness. But as Fleuric processed these last words, a small light flickered in the depths of his eyes.

"Now this is news," he said with a quiet awe. Fleuric stared into the orb that mimicked fire for a moment, and then stood. He paced the floor for a few minutes with his hands gathered behind his broad back. The heels of his boots clicked a slow rhythm on the hard surface. He came to rest beside the fire and lowered himself into the chair, his mind's eye far away in a different time and place.

"Humans once knew things they do not know now." He began this story in a low humming voice. "Perditus, it is time to show you how it all began." Fleuric waved his hand and fragmented pictures began to form. They flickered on a misty cloud orb then grew stronger. "I can't remember what warmth feels like, son."

Fleuric lay curled and shivering on a cold hard surface, having been cast from the eleventh dimension. He was cast out with the others who followed his attempt to create. Unpleasant feelings such as coldness, hunger, and a stabbing pain in his back were foreign. His senses threatened to overwhelm his mind. Inside that dimension he had experienced only comfortable warmth. No pain, no hunger, only pleasurable things were there where the Creator dwelled. Now that he was cast out, he grappled to comprehend what was happening.

He sat up, feeling every sensation as he moved. The body he remembered was not the body he now possessed. His weight seemed oppressive, his muscles sore with a relentless searing pain. The air smelled foul. The sounds he heard were irritatingly loud as he processed moaning all around him. He looked into the blackness, trying to find the source of the noise. But the barren, cold surroundings held only darkness. He blinked in a vain attempt to see. It was no use.

Grunts of pain escaped his cracked lips as he brought his arguing body to stand. With trembling hands, he strained to gather powers once freely flowing. There was a flicker in the dark. It was fleeting. He tried again and his whole body shook from the effort. His legs were defiant and wanted to buckle, but he managed to keep himself erect by sheer will. Taking deep, ragged breaths, he struggled to succeed. Sweat beaded on his face, stinging from the cold. His efforts produced another flicker between his hands. He doubled his efforts. His legs gave out and he dropped to his knees, the hard shock sending agonizing pain through his lower body.

But he did not stop. The pain spurred his anguish, and at once a small orb of light balanced between his hands. The light held fast and glowed, sending pulses in all directions. His powers were weak, but a morsel of his greatness remained. A glimmer of hope bloomed in his chest, and he gave an anguished, triumphant growl. The sound was swallowed by the emptiness. A chorus of moans joined him from the darkness. The one source of illumination between his hands cast an eerie glow on his sharp-featured face. His teeth shone bright through gritted teeth as he sucked in each painful breath.

He rolled his shoulders in an attempt to unfurl wings, but shooting pain made him drop his orb of light. It shattered into nothing, the darkness closing in around him again. His once unmatched beauty among the Glasne was gone, having been ripped from his flesh. A guttural growl rose from his chest as realization washed over him. He turned his face upward, searching for the direction to send his agony. He cried out a fearsome battle cry, sending out vibrations in all direction. A chorus of screams was his only answer. The shattering noise sent ripples through the cold air. Only those whose moans came forth in the darkness heard his cry. There was no help for him. No second chances. No explanation given.

Using his fragmented powers, Fleuric made a meager existence for himself and the other Glasne in the second universe. They used their small powers to create illusions of comfort. They made homes and beds. But the second universe held no real comfort. Food did not satisfy their hunger, and drink did not quench their thirst. They could not sleep, nor feel warmth from the fires they created. They were surrounded by illusions.

After a time, and countless experiments, Fleuric learned he could hear human thoughts. Human thoughts traveled in slumber. The thread between the first and second universe was thin. It was held separate only by a thin membrane of energy, spoken forth by the Creator. It took great effort, but he trained his mind to step into the murky mists that blended the universes in a place only the mind could go. He could seep into the first universe in human dreams.

He killed the first human in their dreams, and reveled in the pain he caused them. He killed night after night and trained the others to do the same. Then the thought occurred to him: if he could kill humans in their dreams could he also create life through them? He found a woman and forced himself upon her, spilling his seed within. He was delighted when she never woke. She carried his child while held in endless sleep. Her body withered, as her belly grew. She gave birth to the first half-breed creature and died.

Humans were unaware of the darkness lurking in their dreams. Those visited by the Glasne never woke, having been killed or impregnated. And so, the humans raised the Glasne half-breed children as their own for a time. Some looked normal, and some were grossly deformed, growing to more than twice the size of normal men. But the humans loved, and they did not turn out the grotesque children.

Fleuric, and the other Glasne, reached the half-breed race and turned them against the humans. They discovered powers held within the half-breed race. Some could hear vibrations in crystals, some could repel the earth's magnetic force making them fierce fighters, and some grew big and daunting. Fleuric communed with them, and convinced them to manipulate the earth. Humans were enslaved and forced to serve the half-breed race.

When the humans figured out what was happening, it was too late. The damage was done. Fleuric called his new creation Krad Glasne, and through them, he planned to break the bond holding him in the second universe.

Fleuric's hands dropped to his lap. "Son, you must watch this one closely. What is her name?"

It was such a normal question. It felt out of place in light of the scenes Perditus had just witnessed. He blinked a few times and cleared his throat. "Blithe tells me her name is Ashra." He rubbed his chin thoughtfully. "Perhaps I will go down to the mines myself to meet her, and get a reading from her modicum."

Fleuric placed a hand on Perditus's knee and looked at his son. He nodded as if finding something there he had been looking for. "Yes, son, that is a wise idea. We will speak again soon."

With that gentle dismissal, Perditus pulled himself back from his meditative state. He sat for a few moments, looking around his room. It was all there, the same as before. But something in light of the new revelations changed his perspective. He let out a heavy sigh, ran a hand through his hair, and grunted. He changed into sturdier work boots and headed out the door.

***

Fleuric sat in the chair for a moment, watching the fire. He waved a hand and the room's form began to shift. The walls and floor melded into a great hall with a grand oval table. Fleuric stood and chanted a strange summons. Nine other Glasne materialized in the majestic hall. You would think them men, if not for their eight-foot height and strange black eyes with a yellow rim. A general bustle ensued as the Glasne took their respective seats at the large table. Fleuric sat at the head and began.

"My fellow Glasne, I have summoned you here to inform you that we have a human who has remembered how to listen. She hears the sound of the stones."

The room was silent for a moment, then erupted in a series of unintelligible noises and heated comments. One voice broke out above the rest.

"If this is the one, Master Fleuric, we must kill the human and do it quickly." He was a dark-haired Glasne and his voice came out as an eerie hiss. The others agreed through a series of grunts and comments that intermingled.

"Yes, that is what I would have told you myself many years ago." Fleuric's voice was low and steady as he made eye contact around the table. "But I feel we made a mistake so many years ago when we forced the humans to forget. Perhaps we can use this human, and force her to reveal the mystery which binds us to this universe."

Nine Glasne stared incredulously at Fleuric. If this human was in fact the one who remembered how to listen, they, and their Krad sons, were in grave danger. A lost prophecy told of one who would come to set the humans free from bondage, and cast the Glasne into an even worse fate than the second universe. When Glasne forced the humans to forget their gifts, they also stripped away the ancient prophecy. This was a safeguard for the Glasne in case that human ever emerged. It would seem that time had come. Action must be taken and Fleuric had a different idea in mind than the others.

"I am tired of this place. We will walk in the face of danger, and use it to our advantage. Go…it is time for us to walk in dreams and sire more children. We must have a strong army when we find our release from this universe." The other Glasne dematerialized from Fleuric's presence at the wave of his hand.

Fleuric's room shifted into a mist. No forms took shape this time. Fleuric walked in a haze of darkness, listening for a sound. He listened for human thoughts brought on by dreams. He listened until he heard what he was waiting for, and into the shifting shadows of her dream he stepped. She would never again see the light of day.

Laying Claim

The timing couldn't have been better, Ashra thought as she walked up to Central Processing. Blithe stood waiting. Ashra was certain he was thinking of other ways in which to make her life miserable. She could tell this from the sneer lingering behind a twitching mustache. She ignored the urge to snort and instead settled for an upbeat proclamation.

"The job is complete, Blithe," Ashra puffed, as she pushed the last cart full of crystal to the receiving line.

"Hmm, yes, I see that," Blithe said, with a curl in his upper lip. His slender mustache twitched ridiculously, causing an image of a fuzzy-legged worm to flash in Ashra's mind. Ashra lost control of her suppressed urge. She snorted and then coughed to cover it up. Blithe eyed her speculatively but continued. "I have another job for you. We have located vibrations deep in the underground mine. You and your team will take a Giant, locate the vein, and recover the crystals."

Blithe handed her a crystal plate, looking quite pleased with himself. It made his nose look longer. Ashra just barely kept herself from snatching the plate from his hand. Etchings in the crystal surface represented a series of tunnels in the underground mine. One spot glowed green, indicating a vibration signal. Ashra looked up through dark lashes and narrowed her eyes. She was sure of it. He was trying to get her killed.

"This section hasn't been worked in centuries. I thought it had been cleared." Ashra looked back down at the plate and frowned. Hundreds of etched lines wove and intersected, causing a spider web effect. Many of the old tunnels had been abandoned, exhausted of their bounty.

"Yes, well, it would seem we have overlooked some. Your team has been recognized as efficient. Efficiency is rewarded with harder tasks, you see." Blithe sneered with perfect teeth and shrugged a shoulder. "You may have the evening to rest. Get the supplies you need from Central, and start first thing in the morning. You have two days to locate the vein and bring the first load up." Blithe turned to leave, and was face to chest with Perditus.

Ashra gaped. He was striking, at least a full foot taller than other Krad. *Something's wrong. Why is he here?* Ashra's heart sank.

The Sound of the Stones

"Blithe, is this the human you are sending on our special mission?" Perditus asked, piercing her with his eyes. He was reading her, seeking her modicum vibrations with such strength that her barriers wavered. It was like frost creeping along the surface of a window, searching for an opening.

She struggled to keep calm, and grasped her barrier shields like a lifeline. *How can a Bender read my modicum?* He was clearly more that just a Bender. She fumbled with the crystal plate in her hands. Perditus reached a hand down in reflex to steady her. She heard him suck in air and looked up. He looked at once angry and confused in intermingled emotion. She blinked. He cleared his throat and removed his hand as if stung. He looked at his hand then back at her and his mouth tugged up at one side. The hair on her arms stood on end.

"Yes, master. She is the one who will be recovering the crystals from the deep mine." Blithe's tone spoke of both surprise and nervousness. He hadn't noticed the odd exchange between them. Blithe did not know his new leader well, but he knew he was not one to associate with humans. With the exception of his servants, whom he pointedly ignored, he seemed to have a strange aversion to women in general.

"Well, aren't you the good little girl?" The words slid off Perditus's tongue like sweet liquor as he stepped closer to Ashra.

He was careful not to touch her again, she noticed. She looked up into his violet-blue eyes, and they sparked a hint of anger. Then she sensed something else from him she didn't understand...*confusion, worry?* She felt the warmth of his breath as it moved her escaped hair against her face. He smelled of cloves and lemon. She blinked, opening her mouth to speak, but her voice caught in her throat. She bit her bottom lip and Perditus's eyes fixed there.

He flashed angry again and barked, "Speak!"

"I just, I don't..." Ashra stammered, flushing red, her eyes fixed on the ground. *Get a grip Ashra!* She stilled her thoughts and squared her shoulders. She lifted her eyes to his and cocked her head. She tipped her chin up and swallowed.

Perditus took a breath and closed his eyes. When he opened them again he was calm. "You have such pure thoughts, don't you, little one? Not a stray bad feeling or thought to be found in you. Hmmm?" His tone was soft, in contrast to the harsh bark he gave not moments before.

One corner of her mouth curled up. "I wish only to serve my purpose and do a good job." *There.* Ashra managed a complete a sentence.

Perditus studied her; his eyes narrowed. He seemed to be struggling with something. He looked angry but also intrigued. He shook his head and stepped closer still. Ashra could feel his breath tickle the top of her head. He closed his eyes, lifting his head to the sky. She looked at him and clenched her muscles against her tremble. He was so close she could feel his heat. He smelled good and she was angry with herself for noticing it again. A sneer twisted his mouth, calculating eyes looking down at her. She blinked. Her smile melted from her face.

"Carry on." Perditus turned away from her as if nothing had happened. He gestured Blithe to follow and walked away in graceful strides. Blithe, who had gaped at the exchange in confusion, scurried behind him like a rat.

Ashra felt like a brick had smacked her in the gut, and her mind buzzed from the force with which he had pried at her modicum. *What was that?*

Haker stood a few feet away, eyes like steel fixed on the departing Perditus. Ashra looked at Haker, and he turned to her. She raised a brow in unspoken question. Haker shook his head and made a low growl. She, in turn, raised both eyebrows. He grunted and turned his back to gather the equipment in a huff. Ashra shook her head while muttering a few indelicate words in frustration. *Men!*

***

"There has been a change of plans," Perditus informed Blithe as they put distance between themselves and Ashra. "You will now be responsible for keeping a visual on that woman. You will accompany her on our mission, and pay special attention to those she is close to. Look for any abnormal readings in their modicums, anything that would confirm your suspicions. Pay close attention to how she works. Look for anything unusual in her interaction with the minerals and her team."

Blithe blanched. "Must I follow those humans into the mine, master?" His voice was thick with a desperate plea. He grasped the sleeve of Perditus's shirt to punctuate his urgency.

The Sound of the Stones

"Yes," Perditus hissed, and shook Blithe's hand from his shirt. "I will end you if you fail me." Perditus's temper snapped. His eyes blazed as he stared into Blithe's intimidated face. Blithe gathered his hand to his chest and cradled it. His face was trembling, his eyes cast down in shame. Perditus took a breath and blew it out, regaining control. "Blithe…I am counting on you. She could be the key to understanding what binds our fathers to the second universe. We could be on the verge of a new life." Perditus clamped his hand onto Blithe's shoulder tightly, too tightly. Blithe jumped, blinking up at Perditus. "Can I trust you to do this?"

Blithe licked his lips and bobbed his head. "I will do my best, master." Perditus studied his face for a moment with eyes narrowed; he nodded once and turned to walk away.

A slow, seeping anger rose in Blithe's chest. He was not happy, and if he wasn't happy, no one would be.

Home Sweet Home

"Haker, will you make sure our load gets processed? I'm going to Central to put in our request for supplies. I'll meet you all in front of Central at first light." Ashra began to compile a mental list, her attention shifting from the strange encounter with Perditus.

"Mmm," Haker grunted in affirmation. Ashra turned to walk away, still compiling her list. "You know there are rock eaters down there," Haker said in a low tone, referring to the dangerous beasts that fed on mineral rock. Ashra froze mid-stride and turned to him. He was watching her and glowering with proficiency.

"Haker, no one has seen them in centuries. They have all been killed...haven't they?" Ashra said, with a false sense of hope dancing in her tone.

"Mmm," he grunted, then turned to busy himself with the load. His grunt caused her hope to wither and fall from her heart, replacing it with dread.

Ashra put in her request at Central and made her way back down to the human encampment. Thousands of small, quarried stone homes lined gravel streets like soldiers in formation. Her work boots crunched on the gravel road, alerting her family that she was home. She ducked in, stepping down a flight of stone steps. Homes were dug down six feet. The temperature in the home was resistant to the heat of day and cold of night, surrounded by constant ground temperatures.

The golden glow of their oil lamp filled her eyes, causing her heart to swell with warmth at the familiar sight.

"Hello, little bean," Sheed bellowed. He lounged on throws and pillows at the low table in the center of the room.

"Hello, Papa," she said, leaning down to kiss the top of his balding head. She kissed her mother's cheek. Her mother looked up from an awl and thread long enough to see the boots on Ashra's feet.

"Take your boots off, messy little bean. Ack!" she said, in mock disgust. Shara's lips curled into a small smile to lessen the sting of the admonishment.

"Our little bean has had a long day, Momma," Sheed teased. Shara shot her husband an authoritative look and he grinned sheepishly.

The Sound of the Stones

"It's okay, Papa," Ashra said, giggling. "Momma's right. I shouldn't bring my work inside our home."

Shara gave a full smile to that and returned to her darning. Ashra took off her boots, careful not to kick any more sand and dirt onto the floor, and placed them by the front entrance.

"Did you complete the job today, bean?" Sheed's tone took on a more serious note. His dark chocolate eyes held worry and concern. Shara looked up from her darning work to gauge her daughter's expression.

"Yes, it's complete," Ashra said, but didn't meet their inquiring eyes.

Ashra walked to the washing bowl and dipped her hands, cupping them to bring water to her face. Drops made paths in the dust on her exposed skin. It would take a more thorough job later to wash the day's work away. She exhaled into the soft drying cloth, then placed it carefully to the side. She eased herself into a sitting position next to her mother and across from her father, and gathered some flatbread. Various vegetables and meat paste served as a filling and she rolled it to take small bites. She did this all methodically and with the thorough attempt of avoiding the topic.

"Ashra, what are you not saying?" Shara's fiery eyes glinted as they searched her daughter's face for clues. Her one inquisitive brow was raised and ready for a battle of wills. Ashra chewed her bite of food much longer than necessary.

"Come now, my little bean! It can't be as bad as all that," Sheed said, gesturing to her scrunched up face. "Honestly, I've never seen someone so beautiful that could make such an ugly face...well, accept for maybe your mother," he said, through booming laughter.

Shara simultaneously slapped the back of Sheed's head and ignored him. It was a talent she had perfected over the years. She was a pro. Ashra sputtered a laugh, covering her full mouth to keep from spitting food, and for a brief moment forgot her troubles. Her parents were always good for that. Her father's larger than life heart and humor and her mother's ability to play off his teasing made their meager life worth living. Ashra hoped to find that kind of love one day, the kind of love that could make any situation bearable.

The playful air died as unwelcome thoughts from the day slipped back into her mind. "We've been assigned a deep mine recovery." Ashra's tone sounded flat. "It's a part of the underground mine system that hasn't been mined in centuries. I think Blithe is trying to get me killed, and Perditus came down to the mines today. I spoke with him." She shivered, remembering the exchange.

"Ashra, you must be very careful how you speak! You may be able to consciously hide your gift for now, but we don't know how far your abilities actually reach. We may unintentionally let your secret out," Shara lectured, afraid that a Sensitive would discover the truth.

Ashra had told her parents when she was ten that she could hear the rocks hum. It was at that age she began to feel the Krad reading the vibrations in her crystal modicum. It began as a game. She would listen to the vibrations in her own modicum. She sang notes in response to the crystal and altered its vibration. Keeping thoughts from the Krad turned out to be easy enough. But her mother was questioned about the scrambled waves and gaps in her memory. Her mother was quick. She told the Krad that Ashra had been passing out from heat exhaustion. She had just started her mine training and it was physically demanding work. It was not unheard of for children to die while mine training for lack of stamina.

This explanation satisfied the Krad. But Ashra sensed she had been playing with fire after she saw her mother questioned. It was then that she revealed the full scope of her gift to her parents. That night she managed to locate the vibrations in her parents' modicums, seeking to erase the conversation. Ashra hummed a haunting tune, careful this time to craft the vibration in a way that felt natural. It was a delicate work. As time went on she honed her gift, artfully reading vibrations and singing songs to alter her modicum. Although Ashra could hide her secret thoughts and conversations, her mother continued to warn her. She cautioned that they should not do or say things that needed modicum alteration. She feared a slip-up, and worried that her little bean would be found out.

"I know, Momma. It just seems like every time I turn around, Blithe assigns an impossible task. I think he suspects something. And today Perditus came to see me. A Krad leader never comes to meet miners." Ashra looked down at her hands. She didn't reveal the way he looked at her. The way his stare had disarmed her. The way his words slid from his mouth like dripping honey and scorching fire.

"You mustn't be so good at your job, little bean," Sheed said, breaking the silence with his none too subtle voice. "Take your mother and me, for example. We are decent farmers but not the best. You don't think I know how to grow the best crops around, hmm? I know the soil and the crops better than anyone else, but do I produce the highest yield every time? No!" He answered his own question. It was a practiced lecture and one she had heard a hundred times before. She watched him flat-faced. "We produce enough every year to blend in. The key to a decent life under the Krad is to go unnoticed." He grabbed a few morsels of food and popped them into his mouth, chewing and waggling his eyebrows simultaneously. He seemed exceptionally pleased with himself for giving such sound advice.

"I'm not trying to be the best at my job, Papa!" Ashra interjected forcefully, her irritation fueled by the eyebrow dance. "Blithe continues to give me impossible tasks. I either finish on time or we become a team who cannot meet their deadlines. You know what happens to teams who don't meet their deadlines, Papa." Ashra gave him a stern glare, looking more like her mother than she ever had. She was referring to the elimination process of humans who fail to meet productivity standards. "I'll just have to take my chances on a job well done!"

Sheed stopped chewing and reined his eyebrows back in. Shara watched this exchange in silence, processing the meaning and severity of the situation. Sheed looked to Shara for support.

Ashra at once felt frustrated and guilty for her outburst. She let out a long sigh. "I'm sorry." She pushed her unfinished food away and started clearing dishes from the table in silence. She scraped the leftovers into a stone container, taking out her frustration on the helpless bits of food. She placed the dishes in a large pot of boiling water and gave it a stern look of rebuke.

Shara studied her daughter's features. The glow in the room accentuated the lines of Ashra's face. The set of her jaw said angry, and her eyes spoke of fear. But behind the fear, pulsing from within and reflected in the way she held her shoulders, lived strength. Ashra met her mother's eyes from across the room. Her mingled emotions fought for dominance. Only a mother could discern the silent plea for answers written in her child's eyes.

Shara took a long breath and pushed herself up from the table. Her footsteps sounded loud in the silent tension of the room. Ashra watched her cross the floor and remove a stone from the wall. From the empty space she pulled a polished, black box and held it between her hands. Shara paused, her hand hovering over the lid.

The air in the room fell heavy, folding around Ashra like a blanket. A pulse of anticipation thrummed in her chest as her mother opened the lid and slid a cloth to the side. Shara touched a pendant with the tips of her fingers reverently and turned glistening eyes to her daughter.

"Ashra." Shara's voice was low and wistful. Ashra moved toward her, drawn as much from curiosity about the pendant as the tone of her mother's voice. "My mother gave this to me." Shara looked back to the pendant and pulled it from the folds of cloth.

The silver metal pendant was a circle. Seven strings of silver ran seamlessly within, perpendicular to one another and evenly spaced. On each string, seven tiny crystals slid effortlessly up or down. The pendant was smooth, with no end or beginning, as if forged from one solid piece. Ashra blinked and looked at her mother.

"This pendant has been passed down, from mother to daughter, for longer than memory can reach. It is always passed to the oldest daughter, in a time of great concern." Shara paused, the significance of the moment punctuated by the silence. She shook her head; a slight crease graced her forehead. "It has always surprised me that you never asked about the vibrations it must emit."

"It has no sound," Ashra said. Her voice was hushed awe, as her eyes fixed on the pendant. Shara made a noise of understanding and nodded.

"That would also explain why you never went looking for it, my nosy little bean," Sheed added with a chuckle. His interjection fell awkward into the reverence of the moment. Shara reached for Ashra's hand and pressed the pendant into her palm. When it touched Ashra's skin, each of the seven crystals slid into a fixed pattern on their strings. The pendant began to hum. The tiny crystals lit, sending prisms of color to dance about the room, in rhythm with its pulse. Ashra clasped her

The Sound of the Stones

hand over the pendant and whispered words that only she knew. It went silent, and the heaviness in the air dissipated.

"I've never seen it do that," Shara said breathlessly. Ashra looked up and her mouth curved to one side at the surprised expression on her mother's face.

"You could hear it too?" Ashra's voice matched the careful pitch of her mother's.

Shara nodded and looked down at the pendant, still clasped between Ashra's hands. She placed her hand over Ashra's. The warmth of her mother's hand was comfort; the cold metal of the pendant was hope.

"Well then, does it surprise you so much that your charm sings for our little bean? She is something special, is she not?" Sheed touted. Shara gave a crooked grin that mimicked her daughter's.

"No, I suppose when you put it that way, there is no reason to be surprised," Shara said with a smile in her voice. "It's yours now, my little bean. Keep it safe." Shara's eyes became serious. "And remember what I told you, so that one day, you can pass it along to your daughter." She squeezed Ashra's hand, and her eyes turned gentle. "Let it bring you peace."

Ashra tightened her hold on the pendant. "I will cherish it, always."

A Wise Man's Love

It was a clear and pleasant day. Wispy clouds drifted in the morning sky. Bazine stepped out of his home and headed down the chiseled stairs that crisscrossed down the cliff face. Bazine was not appreciating the beauty of the late morning. His mind was lost in thoughts of dreams. The same woman in various situations appeared to him every night. Her dark almond eyes with amber flecks haunted him in waking moments now as well. He stopped off at a bottom dwelling reserved for older Nonsomni who had trouble with the steep stairs.

"Abrack?" he called from the front stoop. "Are you well?" No one answered. Bazine paused for a moment and went in. He passed through the chiseled door and made his way through each room, separated by arched doorways. A leather pouch with various fishing items lay on the table in the front room. Bazine picked it up and tucked it under an arm. He left the home, descending the rest of the stairs down the cliff. The base of the cliff spilled out into a smattering of trees and shrubbery, dotted with various fruits and berries. He picked a handful of these and ate them as he followed a worn path toward the spring-fed lake. The tree line thickened for a bit, and then cleared as Bazine neared his destination. As he came into the clearing he saw an old man sitting on a large rock with a staff and line dangling in the water.

"Good morning, old man! Have you forgotten something?" Bazine teased as he approached the wild-white-haired spit of a man. Abrack shot him a sideways glance and smiled, showing a weathered grin.

"Did I?" Abrack winked as if knowing secret things was his job. "Now catch me some fish!" Abrack demanded with his grin still intact. Bazine chuckled and took the rod, affixing his preferred bait. They sat in companionable silence for a while. Bazine's mind wandered back to the dark-eyed woman.

"A wandering mind leads to wandering feet," Abrack said, breaking the silence. He brought out a carved bone pipe and packed it with dry leaves. He held two crystals, tip to tip, above the top of the bowl with a practiced one-handed grip. The blue and red crystals produced a series of sparks that rained down on the leaves. Abrack puffed a few times, causing them to glow bright orange. An aromatic smoke wafted up in the gentle breeze. Bazine watched the familiar scene unfold in comfortable silence.

Bazine hadn't known his father, but Abrack filled the role. He had taken Bazine under his tutelage at a very early age. He taught him everything a Nonsomni would need to know, and he also showed him fatherly love and discipline. He was odd and old, but also wise and kind. Bazine loved him like a father, and even though Abrack didn't say it, he knew the old man loved him too.

"Catch me some fish. I will cook dinner for you and your mother." Abrack puffed his pipe and blew a series of shapes from his wrinkled lips. He formed various spheres, then moved on to form more difficult ones. He puffed out a shape that looked like a leaf, followed by one that resembled a dashing animal. At last he blew staccato breaths that formed a fish dangling at the end of a pole. He looked over at Bazine and winked. Bazine's lips pulled up at the corners.

"That sounds good. Mother seems tired. It would be good for her to take a night off," Bazine said, watching the smoke designs fade into nothing.

"She is worried about you, and burdened with a truth whose time has come to be revealed." The fishing line pulled taut, distracting Bazine from asking what he meant.

After catching a few fish Bazine packed their tackle and tucked it under his arm to head back. Abrack stopped here and there along the way to gather various herbs and berries to add to the menu. Bazine wondered if there would be enough to prepare the meal as Abrack ate just as much as he gathered, staining his lips with dark berry juice. His lips twisted upward when he noticed Bazine's attention. Bazine laughed and shook his head. Abrack shrugged a shoulder and continued to feast as they made their way back home. When they emerged from the tree line they heard giggling.

"Good day to you, Abrack and Bazine!" a bubbly, blond-haired girl called from a group standing at the base of the cliff. Her hair and shapely figure bounced in tandem as she jogged toward the pair.

"And to you, Bisha," Abrack greeted her with a warm, berry-stained grin, eyes twinkling. Bazine cleared his throat and elbowed Abrack. He looked at Bazine boldly as if to say "What? I'm old, not blind."

Bisha looked from Abrack to Bazine. Her face beamed as she ran her eyes over him. "Bazine, will you show me how to shoot a bow again? It seems I have forgotten some of the things you taught me." She batted her eyelashes over catlike gray eyes.

Bazine froze. He cleared his throat again. "Maybe later, Bisha. I promised Abrack I would help make dinner," Bazine lied, casting his eyes to the ground.

"Oh…well, maybe later." Bisha stuck out an exaggerated, pouty lip. "I'll look for you this afternoon at the large cave." She skipped off toward the group of giggling girls. Bazine braved a glance and blew hair from his face. Abrack narrowed his eyes at Bazine but continued to move toward home. Bazine followed in silence. When they reached Abrack's home he laid the fishing equipment on the front stoop to be cleaned. He studiously avoided eye contact and proceeded to clean the fish in the large stone basin, desperate to make his lie truth. Awkward silence hung in the air.

"What is wrong with that pretty little Bisha, Bazine?" Abrack asked, raising wild, bushy brows that dared to buck the obvious avoidance.

"Nothing, Abrack." Bazine feigned utter concentration on gutting fish. Abrack would have none of it.

"How many pretty young women have asked for you to teach them to shoot a bow, trap animals, or fish in the past few years?"

Bazine flinched, then covered it by wiping sweat from his face with the back of his hand. "Many," Bazine answered irritably.

Abrack didn't let up. "And how many have you taught?" Abrack plucked another berry from his loot and studied it nonchalantly.

Bazine blew out an exaggerated sigh. "A few." Bazine arranged his face into mock innocence as he continued to gut fish. Abrack bobbed his head, popped the berry in his mouth, and licked his fingers loudly. Bazine cringed.

"Why have none of these girls become more than just your student? Do you find women not to be to your liking?" Abrack waggled his brows in an alternating rhythm. Bazine couldn't help it. He laughed despite his irritation and tossed a small berry in Abrack's direction. It only just missed his forehead. Abrack dodged it with deceptive agility for the old

The Sound of the Stones

coot he was. Bazine leaned back on the stone basin and sighed in resignation.

"I don't know, Abrack. Some of them are pretty and even nice, but I can't help feeling something is missing. I just have this urge to"—he struggled to find the words and shrugged—"I don't know, I just have this feeling that I'm supposed to do something, go somewhere," Bazine finished lamely. He had not told Abrack about his dreams. His mother had told him never to tell anyone.

Abrack crossed his arms, a look of contemplation on his weathered face. "Hmm…well, you are still young. A woman will come along and change your wandering mind one day, rest assured." He shot Bazine a pointed look. "I can remember being your age. I was so busy living. Girls were beautiful, but settling on just one didn't seem agreeable."

Abrack leaned back in his seat and took wistful breath. "Ah, but then I saw her." He chuckled and shook his head, remembering secret things. "Feya was such a spark, rest her soul. She caught my eye and soon after my heart. We lived many happy years together." His eyes grew dark and he turned to Bazine. "I was lost after she passed." His strained voice beckoned Bazine's full attention. Bazine turned sentimental eyes to the only father he'd ever known. "Soon after, your mother showed up, all alone and pregnant, it gave me something to focus on."

Abrack shrugged. "I took care of her and helped her with you." He waved a hand in Bazine's direction. His pleasant expression was back. "You became the son I never had, Bazine. I miss Feya dearly but I don't regret the fact that her passing forced me to open my eyes. The way you want your life to go is not always how it is to be. However"—he held up one finger—"it does not mean your life will not be good, even though it does not follow the path you wish." Bazine smiled and scraped the remnants of fish entrails into a separate bowl.

"I'll take this out for you. I'm going for a walk."

Abrack waved him on and followed him to the front arch. He watched Bazine bound youthfully down the stairs toward the tree line.

"Don't forget about dinner tonight!" he called after him.

"I won't!" Bazine called over his shoulder with a forced grimace, then disappeared into the thicket.

Abrack stood for a few moments, looking in the direction Bazine had disappeared. He shook his head and chuckled. "That boy is something else," he mumbled under his breath.

"He is, isn't he?" Bazine's mother said, a smile in her voice as she descended the stairs next to his front stoop.

"Ah, Ratha, I was just telling Bazine you will have dinner at my place tonight." It was a statement made into a question with a gentle *hmm*. "We caught some nice fish, and I am going to make my special recipe tonight!"

"That sounds lovely, Abrack." She leaned in and kissed his cheek. "You are too good to me and my boy. I am so grateful for you, my old friend." Abrack's mouth curled as he patted her on the arm. His eyes were warm and the familiar crinkle at the corners tugged at Ratha's heart. She couldn't help but smile back.

"You have raised a wonderful young man." He paused and looked out toward the lake. "Lately, he has become somewhat distant, though."

"Mmm, yes, I know." Ratha's smile faded. The silence that followed held hidden concerns. "Well, I will see you tonight. I have a few things to do this afternoon." She gave a quick smile that didn't reach her eyes and headed down the stairs.

"See you tonight." Abrack shook his head and scratched distractedly at his scraggly beard. It was time. But for what, he did not know.

A Gift Revealed and a Woman Scorned

Bazine followed the water's edge, his gait slow and heavy. He stopped at the mouth of the cave and looked at the familiar surroundings. An underground river fed into the lake from the mouth of the eight-story-high cavern. This was home. It felt safe, but he couldn't help an overwhelming feeling of claustrophobia. Bazine picked up a rock and skipped it across the water's surface. It skipped one, two, three times before sinking into the deep. Bazine glanced around. Good, he was alone. He took a few strides and hopped to a high jutting rock in the cave wall. Without stopping he bounded to the next rock, and pushed off its side to reach a higher peak near the top of the cave ceiling. He repeated this motion once more and landed on the topmost jutting rock. He scaled eight stories in three moves.

He had discovered the odd talent when he was retrieving crystal from a higher ledge a few years back. He had lost his footing while climbing the rock face, and caught himself by bounding upward off a rock that should have broken his legs upon impact. Instead, he had bounced off like a spring. He spent hours playing with his newfound talent. He could feel the power in his feet and hands. If you can imagine what it feels like to place magnets together with the polar ends matching, it felt much the same way. It was like his hands and feet could repel the earth and rock at will. He shifted the positive and negative magnetism in his body to match the earth and rock around him. He was far more agile than other men. Gravity did not hold the same boundaries for him. It freed him to make amazing leaps.

At first the use of his ability made him weak. But after a few months, his body grew stronger. Now he could use his gift with little effect. He only used his talent when alone, but it was harder to hide his abilities the more second nature they became. He almost slipped a few weeks back while hunting with some other men. A dasher tumbled into a ravine outside the tree line after being shot with an arrow. Bazine was tempted to retrieve the animal. But he caught himself just before bounding down after it. It was becoming instinctual.

He had grown up feeling different enough with the dreaming. He was 6'2", graceful and strong. But he was terribly insecure about his differences. He never really opened up to anyone for fear they would discover who he really was. And so, to everyone else, Bazine appeared to be a very serious, quiet young man, with piercing sapphire-violet eyes and a commanding presence. But in actuality, he was fun loving, with desires and passions. He wanted nothing more than to be who he was. But he was afraid he would not be accepted.

He crouched on the ledge at the top of the cavern. Scraps of leather and wood shavings littered the ledge, as evidence of his previous inhabitance of this spot. He could see the entire cave from this vantage point. Crystal glinted on the walls and ceiling. The river below glittered as it danced toward the lake. Looking out of the mouth of the cave, he could see the lake all the way to its edge. It stopped at a rock and vegetation dam, spilling into a hundred different waterfalls and emptying into the ocean below. He had seen it every day of his life, yet the sight of it still took his breath away.

"There you are!" Bisha squealed. "I've been looking for you for over an hour!"

Bazine froze and looked down. She rocked back and forth from heel to toe, causing an odd dichotomy between her womanly figure and girlish air. Bazine didn't have the heart to be rude to her. But she had not taken any of his hints indicating his lack of interest. She was the most persistent of the young women who had started to notice him a few years back, having grown out of that awkward state teenagers go through. Bisha seemed to have gone from girl to woman overnight that same few years back. She was beautiful, no doubt, with her feline eyes and long golden hair. But Bazine found her annoying. He couldn't put his finger on why she annoyed him so much. She just did.

"Hello, Bisha," Bazine called down. He hoped she would take the hint and leave if he stayed put, but it had the opposite effect. She began to climb the rock wall to reach him. "Bisha, that climb is too dangerous." She was already one story high.

"Nonsense…I've been climbing for as long as you have," she puffed, looking for new footing. The problem was there was no footing to get to the ledge he was on. That's why he went there. She managed to get another story up before she lost footing and dangled by her fingers. She let out a loud barking noise as her knees and face scraped the wall. Bazine watched in horror as she lost grip with one of her hands, causing her to swing like a pendulum. Bazine bounded down the widespread rocks as if they were a stone walkway. He reached Bisha just as her second hand lost grip, scooped her up, and bounded the last two stories to the ground. Bazine set her on her feet carefully to make sure she hadn't injured anything. She had a scrape on her left cheek and some pretty good gashes on her knees.

"Can you walk, did you injure a bone?" Bazine asked anxiously. Bisha stood wide-eyed and open-mouthed, staring up at Bazine. "You need to get those scrapes looked at." He bent over to get a closer look at her cheek and touched her face to examine the wound. "We wouldn't want them to get infected. They don't look deep but..."

Bisha interrupted Bazine's babbling with a passionate kiss.

What's a young man to do? Refuse a beautiful young woman's advances? No, Bazine was a normal young man. He let her shower him with passion and pull him to the ground, only stopping when he knew he could go no further without binding himself to her. He pulled away, breathing erratically, and placed a hand on her shoulder to keep her from continuing.

"Why did you stop?" Bisha whimpered through labored breaths. Bazine stood and smoothed his rumpled clothing and hair as best he could. Bisha was a messy heap on the cave floor.

"I'm so sorry, Bisha, I just can't." Bazine averted his eyes from her provocative lounge, and tore a strip from his shirt. He walked to the water's edge and wet it. She watched him with storms in her eyes. He brought it back and blotted her check and knees, wiping the smeared blood from her skin gently, careful not to make eye contact. When he finally braved a look, her eyes were brimming with unshed tears.

"Let's get you back and have your wounds dressed." He spoke softly and held his hand out to help her up. He led her from the cave with gentle care. But she was not her normal chatty self. She hung her head and dragged her feet as they neared the cliff face. She was quiet and refused to look Bazine in the eyes when he stopped in front of her home. She sniffed, then disappeared into her arched door.

Bazine felt horrible. But he couldn't bring himself to pretend, even if she was an incredibly beautiful, although annoying, young woman. He couldn't lead her to think there were feelings there he could not muster.

Breaking the Silence

It was early. Too early. Ashra busied herself with inventory checks so as not to feel the earliness as it were. The rest of the team made personal adjustments to their gear. Haker scrubbed a hand through his beard and belched. Jinka mumbled things best left unsaid. Scoot and Pooter scratched belly and head in alternating turns while yawning. Krank sat off to the side with a sack of food supplies nestled in his lap, watching. Ashra glanced back and locked eyes with him. Something unique glinted in the black depths, knowing, searching. Ashra hesitated for a moment before walking over.

"Krank, we are going into a part of the mine that no one has been in for centuries. Blithe assigned us the task yesterday. He gave our team two days to bring back the first load of mineral."

She paused, glancing back at her team. They were still readying themselves for the long trek into the deep. She looked back at the Giant. He looked impassive but remained in eye contact with her. *What are you thinking?*

"I requested you because you did such a great job with our last dig. I've never seen a Giant work as intricately as you. I hope you will help us this time too." Her mouth turned up at one corner to reveal a crooked smile. He blinked. She sighed and turned back to her checklist. What she didn't know was that when she had looked at him he had felt seen. And he could scarcely remember the last time that had happened.

"There are stories of dangers that lurk in the deep." Krank's voice was low. He formed the words slowly. They rolled off his tongue as if he were trying them on for the first time.

Everyone on the team froze mid-action, gawping. Ashra pivoted on her heels, opening her mouth to reply, but was cut short by a voice that could only be described as smarmy.

"I will be accompanying you on this mission to make sure you humans don't mess it up." Blithe paused long enough to survey the scene. He was dressed in pressed work clothes, his face pinched, eyes contemptuous. "Well, what are we waiting on? Let's go." He tossed his travel sack at Krank. It bounced off his chest like a grape. "Carry my pack, Giant," Blithe mumbled, trudging toward the mine.

The team gathered their equipment and scrambled to follow. Ashra stopped in front of Krank as he rose from the ground. A low growl rumbled from his chest, his eyes following Blithe. Ashra stumbled back a step, rethinking her decision to approach. He looked down and stopped growling. Ashra blinked.

"I'm sorry for that, Krank," she whispered, gesturing toward Blithe. Her eyes did not hold pity, but something more like empathy. *We are not so different.* Krank's usual stormy expression softened for an instant, and he shrugged. He slung his food sack over his back and picked up Blithe's pack, lacing the strap over one finger. He let it dangle in front of him, a look of disdain on his face. He ducked as he entered the mine. Ashra glanced back and her lips curled into a smile. Krank grunted and followed close behind.

Danger Lurks

It hadn't been used in ages and the metal creaked questionably under the team's weight as they climbed aboard. The large, freight-sized elevator worked on a pulley system powered by crystal energy. They would have to come up separately once the pull cart was loaded. They were pushing the fifteen-hundred-pound weight limit with Krank on board, but the group descended together for the trip down.

It took nearly an hour. The group nestled to the edges of the cage and lounged in various sitting positions. Blithe sat himself at an opposite corner, putting the cart and equipment between him and the others so as not to have to look at them. The team was appreciative of his desire to isolate himself. He was a downer, a cranky mule if you will. Even Krank's surly attitude was preferable to Blithe's slimy self-importance.

The blackness enveloped them like a thick blanket as they descended. Ashra pulled out a crystal lamp and pivoted the blue and clear ends to touch. A soft glow grew as the clear crystal lit from tip to tip. The yellow light cast strangely shaped shadows inside the metal cage. Ashra stood to hang the light from a dangling chain in the center of the cage, causing shadows to slink downward in retreat.

Jinka began to hum a familiar song. The sweet, tumbling tune was older than memory. Every human mother hummed it to her sleepy child. The tune echoed off the stone walls and metal cage, causing an acoustic effect that let her average voice sound angelic. Haker joined in with a gruff harmony. The lullaby had no words. It was hummed with a variety of haunting minor notes, and its effects were calming.

"Stop that racket," Blithe grumbled. Apparently the effect was not calming for everyone.

"Hmm," Haker grunted, in a way that could be agreement, or various curse words. The rest of the descent was spent in uncomfortable silence and the air changed temperature. It became almost uncomfortably cold, but the closer they got to the bottom the warmer the air grew.

The cage came to rest with a heavy thump. Ashra fiddled with the gate door in the dim light. She finally budged the stiff handle, releasing the door upward. Haker retrieved the light from the chain. He walked

The Sound of the Stones

with light hoisted, running it along the mine walls, then grunted when he found what he was looking for. He jiggled the handle on a metal bracket attached to the wall. It didn't budge. He grunted and put more weight behind his effort; still nothing.

Krank stepped forward and Haker moved back, presenting the handle with a formal gesture. With one halfhearted tug the handle moved. Krank slid the attached metal pulley system, eliciting an unpleasant grating noise. Hundreds of yellow glimmers dotted the mine tunnel, disappearing into the gentle slope of the passageway. Centuries had passed and the crystal light system still worked. It was a testament to the powers they possessed.

"Would you look at that? It still works," Jinka asserted.

"Of course it still works. Go," Blithe snapped.

Jinka sucked on her teeth but pressed her mouth shut when Blithe narrowed his eyes. They followed the single passage for a time, stopping as they reached the end of the lights. There was another light lever just inside the darkness in front of them. Ashra jiggled the handle. Stuck. Ashra turned to Krank and smiled.

"Krank, would you mind?"

He bent at the waist as if giving a small bow, then pulled the lever. The lights flickered on, revealing an ominous cavern. Twenty or so passage openings lined the cavern walls like a hub. Old metal scaffolding hung from the ceiling in varied states of disrepair. The air was musty and warm. Small puffs of steam leaking from fissures in the walls showed the source of the heat. But more than that, the density and vibration felt different here. Every hair on the back of Ashra's neck and arms stood alert. Jinka whistled in admiration. Blithe curled his lip and sniffed.

Ashra pulled the crystal plate from her pack, looking for the green blinking dot. It wasn't there. Her heart stuttered, hands fumbling to shove it back before Blithe noticed. It was too late.

"Give me that!" He snatched it from her hands. Ashra pressed her lips in a hard line, crossing her arms. Blithe tapped the plate several times and turned harsh eyes on her. "You must have dropped it," he said scathingly. Ashra raised her chin in defiance, but refrained from speaking. Blithe shook his head in disgust. "Never mind, I can find it from here. It's a good thing I came along or you humans would have loused it all up. Come on."

Blithe shoved the plate into her hands and stomped off toward a passage opening, the wrong passage opening. He seemed not to be able to hear the vibration down this deep, judging by the confused expression plastered on his face. Ashra felt some semblance of vindication for his disorientation but then reality sunk in. She would need to correct him, and in doing so perhaps reveal her secret. Blithe fiddled with the light lever and mumbled irritably. Ashra shifted from one foot to the other, opening and closing her mouth like a fish, but her brain refused to form coherent thoughts. *Passage, talk about the passage.*

"Blithe, if I read the plate correctly, and I remember the approximate place the vibration indicator lit, then this passage over here might bring us closer to the vibration," Ashra said, and though she spoke the words carefully they pierced the air. She could swear they hung above her head like a beacon.

Blithe stilled, turning toward her with raised brows. As a matter of fact everyone looked at Ashra with raised brows save Krank, who was too busy sniffing each passage opening to notice. The blood drained from her face and her mouth went dry. She stammered a few times and cleared her throat.

"You see, the passage you're trying to light crosses up and over at a sixty-degree angle to the right. That's the opposite direction of that passage where the light indicated. See?" She pointed to the plate and raised her eyes. If looks could kill, Ashra would indeed drop dead from the withering glare Blithe gave her. Ashra shoved the plate into her pack, wishing she could suck the words back from the air and start over.

"Sorry," Ashra said, her eyes tracing patterns on the floor. She toyed with a pebble under her boot, rolling it in small circles, and waited for the rage. *What have I done?*

"She's right," Haker interjected, splitting the venomous stare. *Thanks for sharing with me, old buddy.* "If you look at the passage map, this passage over here brings us closer to where the light was." He paused, unfazed by Blithe's eye daggers, to scratch his beard. Ashra continued to diligently roll the pebble with her foot. Jinka hiccupped, or giggled. Ashra wasn't sure. The woman did have a sick, inappropriate sense of humor, and timing.

After a few strained moments of silence Haker added dryly, "If you want to get the job done quick, we should follow this passage." He thrust a thumb over his shoulder in the direction of the correct passage. This was the most he had said, aside from grunts and a few strung together words, in a long time.

Ashra peeked up and noticed the unbroken stare between Haker and Blithe. Krank was still sniffing, ignoring the exchange. Scoot and Pooter shifted uncomfortably, looking lost. Jinka watched the exchange with a wicked gleam in her eye.

"Very well, human, by all means take the lead." Blithe gave a mock conciliatory bow. He sneered and his pencil-thin mustache wiggled, reminding Ashra of a fuzzy worm desperate to escape his face. Ashra snorted, then covered it with a cough and quickly headed to the opening of the correct passage.

"Krank, would you mind?" Ashra asked, pointing to the light lever. Krank grunted, shaking his head fiercely. "Oh, come on now, Krank. The quicker we get in and find the crystal deposit, the quicker we get back to the surface," Ashra soothed.

"Throw that blasted lever, you overgrown goat!" Blithe shouted. Krank looked dangerously at Blithe. He seemed to be considering a violent course of action. His eyes traveled back to Ashra, who was studiously backing away from their path. He blew out a breath through his nose and blinked.

Sorry. She mouthed the word to Krank, giving her best pouty face. The effect was more ridiculous than cute. Krank sighed and rolled his eyes. He threw the switch with a flick of his finger.

Ashra's mouth curved sideways. "Thank you."

Krank shrugged, stepping forward tentatively to follow the crew. They traveled for almost an hour before they came across the first evidence of a dig. Earth and rock had been moved, leaving a gaping hole that resembled an alcove. Haker halted, retrieving his water bag. He plopped down on a sheared rock. The surrounding temperature was becoming increasingly warm. Sweat trickled down his face, clinging in beads to the tips of his beard. He was not asking for permission to break. He was telling them silently that he needed one.

"Let's stop here for a few," Ashra said, diverting attention from Haker. A slight nod said *thank you* as he continued to take deep pulls from his drink. The team let gear slide off their backs with a collective sigh. Krank rustled through his sack and pulled out a bar of honey oats. He took a bite and chewed noisily.

"Give me my pack," Blithe ordered, watching disgustedly as the Giant chewed. Ashra noticed a glint in Krank's eyes as he tossed the bag. It hit Blithe in the chest, sending him backward. He made a *humph* noise as his rear end hit the ground. Stifled giggles and shuffling feet followed silence as Blithe slunk to the farthest corner. He didn't order Krank to carry his pack after that.

They traveled farther down the winding tunnel, coming upon remnants of dig site after dig site. There were many offshoots, but they kept to the main larger passage. Blithe became more frustrated with the mission at hand, and made it apparent with several scathing comments toward the group. After a few more hours of enduring the stifling heat and billowing nastiness spewing from Blithe's mouth, they found themselves in an opening of sorts. This particular part of the passage had been dug extensively.

"Let's stop here. I want to look at that crystal plate again," Blithe bit, shrugging his pack to the ground with a loud thud.

Ashra set her pack on the ground and pulled the plate out, offering it to Blithe. He snatched it and walked a few paces away to study it. It was at this point Ashra noticed the vibration getting stronger. She tipped her head to the side, closing her eyes to listen. It tugged on her mind. She glanced around at the hot tired faces of her team and resisted the urge to push forward.

"Why don't we rest here for an hour, have something to eat, and maybe even grab a few minutes of sleep." Ashra dug into her pack for a bite to eat. Krank stretched to his full height in the larger opening, moaning as his back cracked. Haker disappeared, most likely to relieve himself. Jinka, Scoot, and Pooter shared snacks in tired silence. Blithe took to a separate niche off the larger opening, sulking in irritation.

With empty bladders and full bellies, sleep called to them. Ashra's mind remained someplace between sleep and wake, and she allowed the crystal vibrations to hum its lullaby. Even Krank's incessant snoring couldn't keep her from drifting off.

The Sound of the Stones

She slipped further into sleep and found herself in a large hall with slick black floors and heavy velvet drapes the color of blood. The air felt cold and heavy; her body struggled against the weight cementing her feet to the floor. She saw a fire and walked toward the fireplace from which no heat escaped. Steps echoed behind her. She froze.

"You're a rare and beautiful human, Ashra."

The eerie voice slid over her. The sound of it elicited the hairs on her neck to stand. She could feel him just behind her and knew instantly who he was. When she turned, she was eye level with his chest. She willed her eyes upward past his chin, catching a glimpse of white-blond hair. Deep black eyes, with a thin yellow band, glinted wickedly, and he smiled at her with entirely too-perfect white teeth.

He was beautiful in the most gruesome way. He looked so much like his son, or rather, his son Perditus looked so much like him. But there was something about Fleuric's eyes that alluded to otherworldliness. At least Perditus, though possessing unnatural beauty, had human eyes. He watched in amusement as various emotions played across Ashra's face. Her eyes darted around the room looking for escape, but there was none. He would have to release her from this dream for her to leave.

"My son did not exaggerate your beauty," Fleuric purred, gesturing for her to take a seat. Her breath was ragged, sending loose hairs to dance in front of her dirt-smeared face. His eyes turned warm at her desperate look. "Come now, little one. I didn't bring you here to hurt you." Fleuric's lips twisted into another perfect smile. But his attempt to soothe her had quite the opposite effect and she swallowed hard. "I have a proposition for you." He eased into a seat and gestured again to the seat opposite his.

Ashra licked her incredibly dry lips with an incredibly dry tongue. She decided it unwise to be rude to the most dangerous evil she knew. She backed up and sat, misjudging the placement of the chair. One cheek of her rear hung precariously from the seat. A strangled squeak left her mouth and she adjusted her position so that both cheeks found a home. Her face burned hot and she squared her shoulders, pursing her lips primly. She cleared her throat.

"Nice place you have here." It left her mouth before she could filter it through her brain. She winced.

Fleuric's laughter came as a surprise. It echoed through the room and vibrated in her chest. "Oh, you are something else, aren't you?" He continued to chuckle as he leaned back, running a finger over his bottom lip with narrowed eyes. His eyes traveled over her in much the same way as Perditus's had the day before. Her stomach knotted and she focused her eyes on her hands bunched tightly in her lap. But no matter how hard she pressed her fists together or how hard she stared at her hands she felt exposed. *What do I do?* There was no playbook, no past experience she could pull from to help her now.

"If you don't mind, I have a mission to fulfill. I really must be getting back." She gestured over her shoulder, then dropped her hand, feeling incredibly insufficient to handle the situation.

"Hmm, yes, so you do." Fleuric cocked his head. He watched her for a moment and then sat up in his chair, leaning closer. She could smell strong, pungent incense as his cold breath reached her face. She blinked. His eyes lost their humor and his mouth pressed into a hard line. "My son wishes for you to be his." He took his bottom lip between his teeth, studying her for a reaction.

Ashra stared mutely. Her mouth parted and her face went numb. She began to speak when a deafening hum filled the room, penetrating deep into her mind. She clinched her eyes shut and clasped her hands over her ears, attempting to ease the intensity. It didn't help. She could feel the vibration in her chest, and realized it was coming from the charm on her pendant. She pried one eye open in time to see Fleuric's face. He wore an expression that was very much out of place for him. He reached for her as the room began to shift, but it was too late; she was no longer in his chamber.

She was in a long dark corridor. Muffled noises penetrated the darkness. She walked a distance dazed, and the thick mist began to dissipate. There was a loud crack and a scream. Someone called her name in frantic pleas. It was distant at first, and then the voice grew desperate. The corridor began to whiz by, even as her feet stood still. She felt the harsh sting of a slap and opened her eyes to find Haker standing over her. His eyes were wild and he kept looking over his shoulder.

"Wake up!" he rasped. "We are being attacked! We have to move now!"

Ashra struggled to her feet and blanched at the scene. A large gray creature crouched on all fours, swinging a cedar-sized tail. The walls shook and crumbled with every heavy blow. Blood pooled on the ground and spattered the walls. Blithe lay in a motionless heap beside the creature, his belly splayed open, a dark pool forming as his life drained out. Jinka, Scoot, and Pooter lay in the trail of gore, their limbs bent in unnatural ways. *No no no!*

Krank stood haggard, facing the creature's shell like muzzle. Its hard-plated body matched Krank's in girth, though not in height. The beast swung a thick muscled tail, clipping Krank in the thigh. The Giant yelped, clasping the gash with one hand. The beast fixed his beady eyes and charged forward. He didn't target Krank though. Ashra stood frozen, realizing her last moments were here and now. She gasped, slamming hard against the wall. Her head bounced and fingers stung as she gripped the stone harder, trying to melt into the rock.

The beast stopped inches from her. She could smell the foul stench as it blew out a breath, sending her hair back in tangles. Haker grabbed her shoulders and yanked her to the side. Krank had hold of its tail. His muscles bulged, straining under the weight of the creature as he flung it. The archaic beast slammed against the far wall, sending ripples across the ground. Chunks of rock broke from the wall, crumbling around the now still beast. Fine dust particles rained down around them, forming a thin white powder over the mess.

The creature let out a high-pitched squeal as it squirmed to get back on all fours. Krank walked over and pulled a boulder from the rubble. He lifted it above his head and smashed the beast's head. The crunch of its skull, and the subsequent body twitches, made Ashra sick. She heaved her stomach's contents directly where she stood. Her body slid down the passage wall, unable to find strength in her knees. She managed to wipe her mouth with the back of her shaking hand. Taking shallow rapid breaths, she looked around at the aftermath.

Haker huddled against the wall next to her. He too was breathing erratically, his eyes darting. The carnage was immense. They were the only humans left alive. Krank stood hunched, one hand braced on the wall. He was covered in blood, the fine dust clinging to his blood-spattered hands face and legs. He stared at the dead beast. He blinked rapidly then turned his eyes to Ashra. He walked over and crouched, laying a gentle hand on her shoulder.

"You're okay now. But there may be more. We need to leave." His voice was hoarse. He clinched his eyes and shook his head. "I could smell it before we came down here. I didn't know it would be this big." He hung his head. "I'm sorry." The apology came out as a whisper.

Ashra tried desperately to process the chaos but her mind wouldn't work. She looked at Krank's pained expression. He raised his eyes to hers, looking for a sign she was there behind the glazed stare. She swallowed and reached out a trembling hand to place it on Krank's cheek.

She noticed the gash in his thigh with blood freely flowing. "We need to get some pressure on that before you lose too much blood." Her voice wavered. Krank ripped a piece of his pant leg off and tied it tightly around the affected leg. She wondered numbly if that was how his clothing became so tattered in the first place.

A moan sounded from across the alcove. Ashra stood on shaky legs and stumbled toward the sound, leaving Krank and Haker crouched behind her. She heard the moan again and saw Blithe twitch. His entrails spilled from his open wound, and he lay in a thick puddle of his own blood. He breathed a shallow death-rattled rhythm, whispering something. He was a nasty son of a Glasne, but even a despicable cad deserved his last words to be heard. Ashra mumbled unladylike things as she moved toward him. She lost footing and slipped in his blood. Her rear hit the ground with a painful jolt. "Gah!"

"Careful," Haker offered. Ashra shot him a fierce look of rebuke, shifted to her hands and knees, and crawled closer. When she sat, warm blood soaked though her pants. Her stomach lurched again but she swallowed it back and growled.

"I can't hear it...but I think she can," he whispered, his expression like a child's. His eyes were glazed and distant as if seeing something not there. Ashra instinctively brushed his hair from his face, smearing blood onto his forehead and into his hairline. "Ratha...is that you? Don't go. He doesn't love you like I do. No one will ever love you like I do. No...no!" he screamed with the last of his breath, then fell silent. The desperate expression on his face followed him into death.

The Sound of the Stones

Ashra looked back. Haker was checking bodies. He shook his head grimly and wiped a hand down his face, mumbling something low and forlorn. Ashra noticed the loud humming again. It pulsated from one direction. She turned to look and saw a large opening. Small glints of iridescent crystal peeked from behind the rubble. She crawled away from the blood and gained footing on dryer ground. Every bump and bruise on her body screamed at her when she stood, but she pushed forward.

The crystal didn't have one constant hum like most. Its vibration had various intricate patterns. The pattern repeated, and as she approached she could feel her pendant answering in harmony. It was like nothing she had ever experienced. The vibrations were blending in her mind and she could almost make it out. It was like a story, or an answer, and there was something familiar about it. Her mind raced to keep up like a tired muscle. Just as her mind started to feel overloaded with the strain, the vibration stopped. She peered into the open wall and leaned in, listening for the sounds. There was nothing.

Coaxing the Storm

Dinner conversation was strained. Abrack and Ratha chatted back and forth in halting rhythm. Bazine sat in silence, staring at his food.

"You're going to be twenty-one next week, son." Ratha's statement of the obvious, an awkward attempt to engage her son in conversation. Bazine grunted, while moving uneaten food around his plate with a piece of mutilated flatbread. Ratha shot Abrack a desperate look. Abrack cleared his throat, swallowing his too big bite of food.

"The marking ceremony and feast should be a grand time!" Abrack attempted to sound light and cheery. It came across overdramatic and high-pitched. Bazine sniffed. "I'll be taking bets on whether you can make it through without flinching. How should I bet?" Abrack's second attempt to engage met with somewhat more success, and Bazine's mouth curved to one side. He looked up in time to see the wild waggle of white eyebrows.

"There will be no flinching." Bazine waved one hand flat to punctuate his declaration. He lifted the first real bite of food to his mouth and smiled. Ratha laughed, running a hand though her son's black hair. He reached up and grabbed her hand, giving her a start, and brought it to the side of his face. He searched her eyes. "I'm sorry I have been so out of sorts." He loosened his grip, blowing out a long breath as he sat back in his chair. "You're always so patient with my moods."

Abrack watched the pair with matching violet-blue eyes, and noticed how little Bazine looked like his mother. If not for those eyes, you wouldn't know the two were mother and son. Ratha's brown hair gave into silver years ago, and her small slender frame and narrow face contrasted with Bazine's high cheekbones and chiseled features. Abrack wondered what his father must have looked like. He must have been a tan-skinned man with sharp lines of face and build. Ratha knew. She saw his father's face every day when she looked at him. His eyes were hers, but nothing else. It was a painful reminder of the love she lost. Bazine could see that pain hiding behind her eyes from time to time. He never asked, afraid of what the answer held.

109

The Marking Ceremony

Today was it. It was supposed to be full of joy and honor. The honor Bazine felt, but the joy lay hidden. A feast followed the marking ceremony and would be attended by all Nonsomni. Even the weak and the young attended. The celebration was a chance to show off favorite recipes. Men and women alike would compete in games of running, climbing, shooting, and throwing. Children would play their own versions of adult games. Girls would dress in their finest clothing, fixing each other's hair in intricate knots in an attempt to win the attention of young men. The celebration would last well into the night until children collapsed in contented exhaustion. The eldest member of Nonsomni would deliver the marking ceremony speech to explain the custom and the reason behind it. Abrack took the role of oldest member a decade before when his predecessor died peacefully in his sleep.

Abrack stood atop a large flat rock before his people and raised his arms. The crowd fell silent. "Our memory tells of twelve families that came to this place long ago. They escaped a great oppression. They did not speak of the details, for they feared the words would open them up to the oppressor." He swept a gaze around the crowd. "The ancestors spoke of humans that once saw pictures in their mind as they slept. They called it dreaming." Bazine shifted slightly at those words but his face remained impassive. "The founding twelve families broke away from the dreaming people, for it was in their dreams that terror came. And so our story begins with twelve families, setting up a new life."

Abrack paused. His traditional leather garb threaded with blue, red, and yellow crystals glinted as he moved his arms in animated display. Wild white hair and even wilder eyes enhanced the effect. He lowered his voice in a dramatic demand for attention. Children and adults alike held their breath, straining to catch every word.

"We are the Nonsomni, the dreamless people. We are protected from evil things that would come in dreams. We are happy and safe here in our plentiful land, but we remember those who were of the dreams." He stood straight and squared his shoulders. "Tonight we honor the oppressed people with this marking ceremony. Our Bazine is now twenty-one. He is considered a man today. We recognize his coming of age, and remember lost humans by marking him with this symbol, brought with the original twelve families. Our history tells us that this symbol represents the promise of freedom. We celebrate this and remember those who were left behind."

His voice rose and fell with a practiced lilt. "The marking is placed on the left side of the chest over the heart." He pulled back his wrap to reveal his own mark, turning so all eyes could see. "The location is symbolic in remembrance of those who were left in harm's way. It is a reminder to be grateful of the life we have, and a reminder to stay hidden in our land." He turned to Bazine with serious eyes. "Let us never forget...let us always be grateful."

Bazine lay in the ceremonial circle, anticipating pain. The master marker dipped his wooden dowel into the black ink and began to tap a staccato rhythm. His practiced touch resulted in a less painful experience than Bazine had expected. The master marker's expression stayed focused as he studied the placement of each prick. Bazine closed his eyes and concentrated on breathing.

The crowd watched silently for a time. But a lone baby made a hungry cry, which stirred a toddler to comment on the noise. A few coughs and a sneeze sounded loud in the silence. The master marker finished his work by bringing a soft cloth from a bowl of herbal water to cleanse the mark. Bazine opened his eyes. The water washed the excess ink from the welted skin, revealing a circle with seven lines reaching vertically, from edge to edge. On each line a smaller filled circle sat in varied places on the lines.

Each man received this mark on his twenty-first birthday. It had been this way since the original twelve came to this place. Bazine couldn't help but wonder. Could the freedom the ancestors spoke of be more than just the freedom they had from past horrors? He longed to travel. He longed for answers. He longed to find the dark-eyed woman he saw in his dreams. The mark only served to punctuate this need, and brought him to a crossroad. He could settle down here and try to forget the dreams, or he could tell his mother and Abrack that he needed answers.

Grave Orders

"She must be controlled!" Fleuric slammed a fist on the top of his chair. "You must keep her near you at all times." Fleuric paced the floor in front of Perditus. He had never seen his father so flustered. "If I didn't think she was worth the trouble..." He stopped short of finishing his thought, turning narrowed eyes on his son.

"Yes, Father, as soon as she comes back from the underground, I will have her escorted into the palace." Perditus's attempt to soothe succeeded only in fanning the flames.

"She left my presence in a dream, Perditus!" Fleuric barked. "No one leaves my presence in a dream. It is impossible!" Fleuric's eyes turned black fury, his breathing erratic. Perditus flinched.

"Shall I bring her family in, as well?" Perditus was hesitant to speak but thought perhaps his participation in the conversation could lend to resolve.

"Kill them! Kill them so she has nothing to live for! Kill them!" Fleuric's voice shot tremors through Perditus's chest. His father's mouth turned up at the corners, his anger turning to amusement at his own idea. "Make it look like an accident. It will deflate her, and she will be less likely to try to escape or use her gift against us." His voice turned mock soothing. "You will comfort her in her time of grief. You will gain her trust and get as close as possible. You will learn how her gift works, and when you do"—his eyes went wild and he bared his teeth—"we will use it to gain access to the first universe." Fleuric's voice dropped to whisper. "Soon, my son...we will be unstoppable."

Perditus blinked. There was nothing left to say. The orders were given. He nodded curtly and left his father's presence to carry out the mission.

The Danger Pursues

The quietness was deceptive among the carnage. The smell of copper hung in the air, a reminder of the blood-soaked cave. Ashra stood, staring into a crevice made by the rock-eating beast. A warm breeze through the cracks stirred her hair. She smelled water on the warmth. In the distance, a long bellow sounded, causing the hair on Ashra's neck to stand. *That can't be good.* Another rock eater was beckoning to its mate. There was no way to know how much time they had, but probably not long. Krank leapt to his feet, causing more rocks and dirt to rain to the ground around them.

"We have to go! There is another!" Krank growled, as he simultaneously snatched his pack and herded Ashra and Haker toward the exit. An explosion of guilt and responsibility welled up in Ashra's chest.

"What about the others!" Ashra pushed against Krank's insistent hand in a futile attempt to go back for the dead crewmembers. Krank continued to prod them with little effort. Ashra screamed an unintelligible slew of words. She swiveled to the left and dodged Krank's hand, landing hard against his thigh. She growled, pounding fists into his leg. Krank stood physically unaffected, though his face twisted in confusion. Haker grabbed Ashra's wrists in mid-swing and held them fast. She looked at him with all of the contempt she could manage. Her breath came ragged. Haker's eyes were rigid, and his jaw muscles jumped.

"We have to save ourselves, Ashra. They're gone." Haker spoke through clenched teeth. Ashra blinked away tears paving streaked dirt tracks down her face. Haker's eyes softened. Ashra swallowed and nodded. He released his grip, and her arms fell to her sides in quiet agreement. Another distant howl called like a warning bell, spurring them to move with unified purpose.

They were making reasonable time, putting distance between the bellowing rock eater and themselves. They heard the shrill shrieks only an hour before, the rock eater having found its dead mate. It had been eerily quiet since. The only sound now was that of their own labored breath amongst shuffling footsteps. Moments later an earth-shattering rumble followed a louder roar. The beast was closer. Haker looked back and picked up his pace. It was a grave mistake as his foot caught a lose piece of stone. He went down, his head bouncing off the ground with a sickening thud.

"Haker!" Ashra stumbled to kneel, hands grabbing for his face. He was out cold. She licked her lips, trying to think of something she could do. She slapped him but it didn't help. Krank pulled up short, staggering to avoid them. He regained his balance and scooped the incoherent Haker up in one arm. Haker's head bobbed limply. Krank growled something that sounded like "Go." Ashra picked herself up and pushed forward, ignoring aching muscles. Strength eluded and her lungs burned, but there was no time for rest.

After some time Ashra's legs faltered. She felt her body moving unbidden toward the ground. But instead of the hard landing she was expecting, one strong arm lifted her, Krank's forward motion never stopping. She didn't say a word but lay in his arm grateful, struggling for her first deep breath in over an hour.

They were near the large open cavern that connected the passageways. Hope for escape dared bloom in her chest. Krank stepped into the larger passage and rose to his full height, stretching cramped muscles. Ashra looked up at Krank's face. His eyes darted, assessing. His breath came heavy but he showed no sign of stopping. A few strides was all it took and he crouched to continue through the passage that led to the exit lift.

That's when they heard a deep-set huff. Krank froze, muscles tensing into rock. He backed up slowly into the cavern hub, the rock eater following. His eyes searched desperately for another way, turning only to find two more rock eaters. Ashra dug her fingers into Krank, watching from the protection of his arm. Haker lay limp in the other. Ashra envied his ignorance. Krank scanned the weathered equipment bolted to the ceiling with a leery eye. The rock eaters inched closer, huffing angrily and swinging tails.

Krank's eyes went wide and jaw set firm. "Hold on." He said the words while jumping. Ashra's stomach lurched to her throat as she clambered to grasp an arm, tattered clothing, anything really. She was somewhat surprised to find she in fact did get a good grip on his shirt, though her legs flailed about. Krank managed to grab hold of the iron scaffolding and hung by one arm. The old metal groaned under his weight and his legs swung wide.

"Climb up there!" Krank ordered, his face pinched as he struggled to hold on. Haker's dead weight in one arm and Ashra's floundering grasp on the other made this task a bit of a challenge. Ashra clawed up his arm, feeling slightly bad for the boot she shoved in his face. She balanced on the high, narrow beam, limbs shaking. He waited for Ashra to gain her balance, then shoved Haker up. Ashra pulled in an effort to help and almost lost her footing. She let loose a loud whooping noise but found a place to hold. Krank himself did not whoop ridiculously, but instead grunted under his own weight.

The three beasts gathered in the center of the cavern, just below them. They circled like sharks, swinging tails and making their own sounds rather unlike whooping, Ashra thought. Krank looked up at Ashra as she dug a rope out of her pack with fumbling fingers. Her breath was ragged and she felt weak, but she managed to tie the rope around Haker's limp body.

Krank's voice came out grave and strained. "I will lead them down another passage. When I do, make a run for it." Ashra opened her mouth to protest but before she could argue, Krank let go, dropping like a sack of bricks. He landed on one of the rock eaters, its body crunching under his weight. Large swinging tails and angry screeches sprang toward him as he staggered to his feet. One tail made contact, sending him backward into the cavern wall. He hit with such force Ashra felt it through the metal beam. *Krank!* His breath left him in a loud whoosh as rocks crumbled down around him. He went still, silent. The two remaining beasts charged. Ashra watched, helpless to assist as they approached him.

Ashra screamed. The sound pierced the air in waves and seemed to come from some deeper part, a piece of her soul as yet to be discovered. All of her energy left her in that moment, a last cry of frustration.

The pendant around her neck hummed. The crystals lit, sliding into a pattern. The earth began to quake, shaking the scaffolding. Ashra's eyes flew wide and she clung to the metal beam with one hand. The other grasped Haker. Small rocks and dust falling foreshadowed two large boulders as they dislodged from the ceiling, dropping directly onto the charging beasts. They were crushed instantly.

The rocks went still and her pendant hushed, its crystals sliding back to their resting position with a gentle click. A steady rush of blood, beating to the rapid rhythm of her heart, was the only sound. Dust still

The Sound of the Stones

hung in the air like mist, casting doubt as to the realness of it all. She licked her lips, tasting salt. When she at last dared movement, the jolt of pain through her muscles erased all notions that this might have been a dream. *Must move.*

Ragged breaths made the work harder as she lowered Haker's body to the ground with the rope. Rubber arms challenged her descent but she managed, slipping down to check on Haker. He was still breathing. Ashra moved through thick dust, picking her way around rubble.

Krank was unconscious but still breathing. She let out a breath she didn't realize she'd been holding. One small hand reached tenderly to his face, brushing dust and rock away. The gash behind his ear made her wince. She pulled out her water bag and drizzled a stream onto the wound. A guttural growl indicated he was no longer unconscious.

"That hurts," he rasped, then snorted. Ashra laughed in relief, a sound like tiny bells echoing off the cavern walls.

"Come on, you big baby, let's get back up top and away from this beast-infested hole in the ground!"

Krank pulled a strained smile that looked more like a grimace. But it was beautiful to Ashra nonetheless. Haker groaned, sitting up gingerly at the sound of Ashra's laugh. She picked her way back through the debris and untied the rope around Haker's chest. He sat in silence for a moment, rubbing the bump on his head. Krank walked up behind her and looked around at the mess.

"What happened here?" Haker asked. He scanned the scene; an ashen complexion accompanied a very bewildered look on his face. "Krank, you sure did give them a thrashing," he said, as he stood, trying to balance weight on one good foot.

"I only took out this one." Krank gestured to the nearest beast. Its middle was split by the force with which Krank had landed, guts and blood oozing from every orifice.

"What happened to the other two?" Haker winced at the first bit of pressure he put on the other foot. Krank looked at Ashra with narrowed eyes.

"Rocks fell." Ashra shrugged. "Can you walk?" she deflected.

"I think so." Haker took a few tentative steps. He had a limp but was mobile.

"Good, let's get out of here." She didn't wait for an answer and they followed behind.

Not All of Them Made It

A guard entered the inner chamber and cleared his throat, waiting to be acknowledged. Perditus turned from the window slowly, leveling his eyes at the guard.

"Master, they are back, but not all of them made it."

Perditus's face went rigid. "Where is Blithe?"

"He was killed along with three other humans, rock eater got them."

Perditus pressed his lips in a hard line.

"And the girl...?" His voice was dark and his shoulders stiff.

"She went back to her home."

Perditus's face went through a myriad of expressions and he was silent for a moment.

"Very well, get a carriage out front. I will go collect her," Perditus finally said. The guard nodded, bowing as he exited the room.

Perditus turned back to the window. He looked but didn't see, lost in his own thoughts. Blithe was dead; he wasn't terribly upset about that. It was Ashra his thoughts lingered on. He thought of the shambles he had created for her to come back to. Part of him reveled in the thought of being her shoulder to cry on, but a very small part of him felt a twinge of guilt for the grief it would cause her. It was a new emotion, and it confused him. He pushed the foreign emotion from his mind and walked toward the door. It was time to discover the secrets Ashra kept.

More Heartbreak and Captivity

It was nothing but a pile of rubble strewn down the street. At first Ashra ran back and forth erratically, looking for a witness to tell the tale. But the street was desolate, save one woman who had emerged from her door. When she saw Ashra, her face had gone pale. She shook her head solemnly and ducked back into the shadows.

Ashra's home was no longer her home. Her parents…gone. Once the surge of manic dissipated, numbness set in. She stood alone.

Smashed bits of pottery mingled with crushed stone. Pieces of fabric peeked from crevices with a dust-covered filth. Ashra knelt, pulling at the fabric interlaced with rocks. It came loose from the rubble and stones rolled to the ground, nestling at her knees. It was her mother's scarf.

Suddenly the numbness was gone and a flood of emotion made her blood run cold, her face hot. Her stomach turned and hands trembled. She pulled the cloth to her face, breathing in her mother's scent. Tears washed her cheeks, her throat clinched so tight that she could hardly breathe. The pain in her chest was so intense, so real, she thought she might die. Then shock took her again. The numbness left her staring blankly, unable to process the meaning. It could have been minutes or hours that she knelt there. Moving rocks and fragments of memories aside was futile. Her parents were not in the mess.

A carriage pulled up behind Ashra. Perditus exited. He stood behind her, looking at her crumpled, desperate form. Her eyes were swollen, staring distantly. Tears, crusted with dust, covered her cheeks and neck. Ashra turned her eyes to him. They were dim shadows of the eyes he had seen before. The sight shot an odd sensation through his chest. But it was a fleeting feeling. A moment of human weakness he quickly dismissed, replacing with determination.

"Ashra, come with me. I will keep you safe now," Perditus said in soothing tones.

Something about his voice made Ashra stand. Her legs argued and her knees ached. It must have been hours and not minutes she had knelt. She clutched her mother's head wrap in her bloody fist and walked vacantly toward Perditus. He gathered her under his arm and ushered

The Sound of the Stones

her into his carriage. He felt solid and warm and she was cold, so very cold.

He climbed in after her and sat opposite, watching her as she stared out the small circle window. A Bender guard sat up front, driving the carriage through dismal gray rock homes. The desolate human camp gave way to opulent buildings as they entered into Krad City. But she didn't see. Not really, anyway. She knew where she was but it didn't matter. The only people she ever loved, and who truly loved her, were gone. Her reason for living had vanished in the blink of an eye.

Perditus's voice came from a muffled distance, barely reaching her. "It was a Giant," he said in gentle, muted tones. She turned her eyes to him and his voice became more clear. "He was angry and ran through the human camp. It was pure bad luck that it was your home he smashed. I'm sorry for your loss, Ashra."

There was something strange about his voice. She allowed the deep timbre to reach inside as he scanned her modicum.

"You ran into some trouble in the deep mine?" he inquired gently, as if talking to a wild animal.

Ashra didn't answer but instead began to laugh, whooping and snorting at the ridiculous minimization of her situation. When she stopped to take a breath, sorrow and guilt washed over again, spilling new tears. And there Perditus sat, his face stone, his eyes bright, silently watching. She sniffed, looking out the small window, and decided she didn't care what he read on her modicum.

***

Haker walked back to the human encampment. Having been questioned ruthlessly for hours and in light of the events prior, his body hurt, his ankle throbbed, and his head pounded. He lived alone. He had never found a mate or had children. He was a gruff, backward man that women didn't quite get. But he had a large heart and he would mourn the loss of his team members. Shock had, up until that moment, shielded him from this emotion. When he entered his small, one-room dwelling he slumped to the floor, letting loose the emotions he could no longer bury. He wept for the dead, he wept for the living, and he wept for things that could never be said.

***

Krank was not questioned. One look at the Sensitive appointed to question him sent the smaller Krad running. Krank sulked home and shut himself away in his dingy tent. He spoke to no one. No Giant could hold a decent conversation, and no human or other Krad wanted to. Not with him anyway. He sat there, feeling more alone than he had ever felt. His only hope was that Ashra would call upon him again with a mining project. At least then he would be seen.

Keeping Ashra

Though it was grand and beautiful, it was loathsome as well. The carriage stopped at the front entrance. The palace rose from slick paved streets, boasting intricate carved architecture. Even the domed top seemed arrogant as it looked down its nose on Ashra when she stepped out. Perditus offered a hand and she took it absently. Her boots hit the pavement, sending jolts of pain though her legs, reminding her of a time not long past. The running, screaming, gasping for breath, the fighting for a life she wasn't sure even mattered anymore.

"You will stay with me now."

Perditus spoke the words softly, but his tone said the choice was not hers. She allowed him to guide her up the grand front steps to the large double door. The doors swung wide. Servants greeted them with heads bowed. Ashra watched the scene numbly as they fawned, ushering them into the front foyer.

"Please see that she is comfortable. She will join me for dinner in one hour," Perditus ordered. His tone was gruffer as he spoke to the servants. They moved swiftly to obey. One woman escorted Ashra up a tall staircase toward the sleeping quarters. Ashra continued to allow herself to be led, dimly acknowledging the pristine artwork and lavish decor littering the halls. Her sarcastic internal dialogue would, under normal circumstances, have amused her with some derogatory reflection on the garish display. But she felt mute both inside and out.

Her room was the definition of opulence. Lush fabrics draped the windows and four-poster bed in various shades of pink. It was almost enough to elicit a mocking laugh but she couldn't quite muster the breath. The servant woman disappeared into a smaller connecting room. Ashra stood in the middle of the large chamber simply existing.

The sound of running water came from the next room. She knew there was such a thing in Krad City, but had never seen it work. She padded to the door and looked into the room where the servant had disappeared. There was a hefty copper tub, with a pipe streaming water. Steam rose from the tub. The servant turned and caught site of Ashra.

"Come here then. Let's get you cleaned up so you can be decent for dinner." The woman beckoned. Ashra entered the room and stood

The Sound of the Stones

blinking at the woman. "Off with your clothes," the servant said, as if it were a common request. Ashra crossed her arms over her chest in protest. "Come on then, you have nothing I haven't seen before." The servant chuckled.

Ashra sniffed and the servant waved her forward. Ashra sighed, then obediently stripped down, quickly moving to immerse herself in the water. She slouched so that her head sunk below the surface, letting the water curb her embarrassment. It held the sounds of a steady rush, as the stream hit the water's surface. It soothed her. She blew out bubbles of air and blinked up, studying the sleek ceiling through the distortion of the water. The ceiling was carved with decorative swirls. She could stay there and let the warm blanket of liquid soothe her pain permanently. But, just as she could hold her breath no longer, her mother's voice spoke into the deep recesses of her mind.

"Ashra, my little bean, you were made special for a reason." Ashra jolted, blowing out a breath as she sat up into the cool of the room. She sucked air hungrily while watching the servant woman lather something in her hands. Before Ashra could make a guess as to what it was, the servant began to work it through her hair. She wasn't being gentle. It smelled of flowers and spice, but her scalp stung from the vigorous treatment of the servant's hands. The servant rinsed and lathered three times before she seemed satisfied with the results, making *humph* noises under her breath. Ashra wearily eyed a puffy pink loofah filled with sweet-smelling herbs and oils. The servant picked it up and scrubbed her skin till she thought she might scream. She was no longer comfortably numb. Ashra leered at the evil servant as the woman surveyed the results. She bobbed her head, satisfied.

"Come on, out with you then." The servant urged Ashra out of the tub and proceeded to yank the tangles out of her long dark hair with a series of odd-looking devices powered by the very crystals she mined. Ashra had no idea they could be manipulated in such a way. She knew they used the crystals for all sorts of things, but humans were not privy to any of the Krad advancements, and in her line of work, she never got near enough to Krad City to see them. It took the servant the better part of fifteen minutes to brush her hair smooth.

"Such tangles," the servant said, clucking her tongue.

Ashra thought, rather indignantly, it was she that had put them there to begin with. She gave the woman a dirty look but she didn't seem to notice. When the servant seemed content with her torturous ministrations, she dressed Ashra in a simple ivory gown. The sleek material clung to Ashra on every curve with its swooping front neckline and even lower cut back, plunging down to the base of her spine. It draped in puddles on the floor behind, and came just to the floor in front, allowing her slippers to peek out.

The servant let out a low whistle and nodded. Ashra caught a glimpse of herself in the full-length looking glass and her breath caught in her throat. Her hair fell in loose waves down her shoulders and reflected bits of light, having been blown smooth. Her eyes were bright and her face was clean. Her olive complexion was stunning against the light-colored dress, and her curves filled the dress nicely. The clear gloss the servant put on Ashra's lips tasted of honey, and served to enhance their natural pink fullness. Ashra blinked. She had never seen herself in that way before. It was almost a small distraction until she noticed how much of her mother she saw staring back. Pain clutched her heart, clinching her throat closed. She inhaled a few breaths and the servant moved her out the door.

"Come on now, let's not keep the master waiting." There was a hint of cynicism in the servant's tone.

Ashra followed through a maze of hallways and down stairs to the lower dining hall. She entered into the room, her slippers clicking across the marble floor as she gawked at the posh stone-carved cathedral ceiling. It was lit by hundreds of tiny crystals. The light bounced off the walls and ceiling, casting various long and short shadows, and giving a warm glow to the room. It felt cozy, though its ceiling stood two stories high. The crystal vibrations gave comfort to Ashra, something familiar in this strange place. She wrapped her arms around herself, trying to hold on to the small piece of solace, and scanned the room.

Paintings hung about the walls. Different scenes were depicted in each. Humanlike men seduced beautiful women in many of them. Ashra blushed, having never been exposed to such things. Those paintings all had the same black floor with rich, red draping. Ashra recognized the room and shivered. Others detailed humans bowing to Krad. Krad stood in haughty poses while humans were portrayed as humble and lowly. Glasne and Krad were pictured together in the same black-floored room around a large table, looking serious and lofty.

"Admiring the art?" Ashra turned to find Perditus leaning against the arched entrance. A slow smile spread across his lips as his eyes traveled over her. He nodded and made a low growl deep in his throat. "I knew under all that mine dust there was unparalleled beauty."

Perditus's voice sounded strange. It made Ashra feel dirty, despite the vigorous cleaning she had just endured. Perditus looked intimidating now in an entirely different way. She tried to tell him to go jump off a cliff, but the words caught in her throat. He pushed himself from the doorway and walked gracefully across the room, keeping eye contact as he closed the distance. Ashra's mouth went dry. He stopped just a foot from her, his eyes lingering on her pendant. He reached out and traced his finger down her neck, following the line of the chain. Ashra stiffened. His finger stopped just below the charm. Ashra could hear her own breath quicken and her chin began to tremble. She decided that despite her recent trauma, she really did want to live. And why for the love of everything had she not taken off her pendant?

Ashra swallowed hard, the sound of her heart beating loud in her ears. Perditus watched the vein in her neck pulsate with strange fascination. His lips curved up as he raised his eyes to hers. Her fear that the pendant would react to his touch subsided, as it remained silent when he brushed his finger across it. He froze looking down, and his face clouded with confusion.

"These crystals do not have any noticeable vibration," Perditus marveled as he lifted the charm to get a closer look. "Fascinating, where did you get this?" he asked, leaning closer.

His breath was hot on her neck. Ashra made a strangled noise in the back of her throat. He looked back at her and cocked his head. She could see clearly now the violet flecks among the blue, as his eyes shimmered in the warm glow of the room. She had never been this close to a man before, besides her own father. But this was not the interaction of a father with his daughter. This was clearly intimate in a way she had never known. She had no control as her body rejected the closeness. She backed away from him and stumbled on her dress. A loud bark escaped her mouth as she fell.

Beth Hammond

Had it been another place and time, she might have seen the humor in it. But it was now, and she was careening toward the floor with a very dangerous man-beast standing over her. Perditus caught her by the arm and pulled her up before she hit the ground. He drew her close, too close. She gasped and writhed in an effort to break free. Perditus laughed under his breath and released her on steadier feet. Ashra gathered herself, jutting her jaw in anger as she moved to the table. Heat crept up her neck, and she couldn't decide which part of that exchange was more embarrassing. She plopped into a chair, hating the feel of exposed skin that the dress allowed. She scooted into the table, willing it to protect her. Perditus was plainly interested in something she was unwilling to give. She wondered how much of a choice she had in the matter.

"So, the pendant…where did you get it?" Perditus's mouth twisted amused, and slid easily into the seat next to her. Servants bustled in and placed dishes on the table.

"My mother gave it to me," Ashra answered shortly, not trusting her voice to be steady for a long explanation.

"Mmmm…and where did your mother get it?" Perditus asked, with a fraction less gentleness than before.

"It has been handed down for as long as anyone can remember," Ashra countered softly. She toyed with the napkin on the table, avoiding eye contact. "My room is nice," she said in an attempt to change the subject. Ashra braved a glance to judge his mood.

Perditus smiled insincerely and took some bites of the first course. It was a cold soup. Ashra followed suit and found the cold soup less than appealing. She waited for something else to eat. Perditus eyed her curiously as he finished and dabbed the corners of his mouth with a napkin. The next course was salad topped with various berries and cheeses. Ashra ate the familiar food with relish, not realizing how hungry she had been. She tried to remember the last time she had eaten. It must have been twenty-four hours since her last bite of food.

Ashra hadn't noticed Perditus watching her eat, so engrossed in the salad and her own thoughts. When she glanced up he was studying her intently. She was suddenly very self-conscious and dabbed the corners of her mouth with a napkin as he had done.

"So, my little one, what did your mother tell you about the necklace that comes from further back than anyone can remember?" His tone held a hint of sarcasm, and he wasn't smiling anymore. Ashra chewed slowly, trying to figure out what she could say. Perditus raised one brow, tapping fingers on the hard table surface. She sighed.

"She said it was to signify strength in character," Ashra lied, and then took another bite of salad while holding Perditus's stare. She raised a brow of her own and chewed. Frustration began to settle onto his face, but she held steady, committing her expression impassive. His fingers stopped drumming and he laid his hand flat.

"I see. Well, no one could argue your strength in character with the amount of good work you do in the mines," Perditus said with a one-shoulder shrug.

Ashra continued to force herself to eat, though she had lost her appetite. She knew Perditus was baiting her. She chewed her food, politely nodding in acknowledgment of his compliment. In the silence Perditus pried into her mind by way of the modicum. Ashra stayed calm, breathing steadily, and attempted to look casual. She wondered how she was doing. Perditus was persuasive; his beauty and something about his deep, resonating voice almost made her want to confide in him...almost. There were several more moments of awkward silence.

"Where are my parents' bodies?" Ashra bleated. The words hung in the air and echoed back into Ashra's mind.

Perditus sat back and cleared his throat. "When I heard of the incident I had some guards go down and recover their bodies. They were badly mangled, so I had them sent for incineration." Perditus spoke casually, lifting a shoulder in a matter-of-fact way. "Then word came back that you had returned with only one human. We interviewed Haker and read the incident on his modicum."

The memory of the last days came flooding back, punching her in the chest. Perditus held Ashra's eyes, and she fought to keep the tears from welling. Perditus's hard expression softened, and he reached over, taking one of her hands in both of his. "I came down to get you. My father tells me he shared my intentions toward you, but you were pulled from the dream before he could finish speaking with you. Can you tell me what happened?"

Ashra had almost forgotten the dream for all of the chaos. She shook her head, chin trembling.

"I'm not sure," she admitted. "I was speaking with him and then I was being shaken. The rock eater was attacking. It's all a blur." One tear dared escaped, trailing down her cheek.

"Mmm...Yes, your modicum does indicate a blur," Perditus said grimly.

Ashra sniffed and straightened her back, wiping the tear hastily from her face. "When will I be going back to Human Camp?" Ashra braved the question, trying to take advantage of his tender side. Perditus's mouth curved warmly, though his eyes held a glint of something else.

"You will be staying here in the safety of my home for a time." Perditus traced the path down her cheek where one tear had fallen. He followed the lines of her jaw and her neck. Then played gently with her pendant, brushing fingers against the low neckline of her dress. All the while his eyes stayed fixed on hers. Her mind saw the beauty in him, but her heart rebelled. It took a great deal of control not to push away, afraid of what his reaction would be. She cleared her throat and settled for using words to break free, thinking scratching at his face or spitting unwise.

"I'm tired. I would like to sleep now."

Perditus's eyes lit angry before settling gentle. He smiled and stood, leaving his napkin on the chair. He held out a hand and she took it.

"Of course," he said.

Ashra allowed him to lead her in the direction of her room, leery of the flash of anger that had lit his eyes the moment before. They walked up stairs and down the hallway in silence. His grip on her hand was gentle but unyielding. She wanted to pull away but didn't. He slowed to a stop at her door, turning to face her. He tipped her chin, lifting her face to his. Her heartbeat quickened, and her knees became weak. His eyes were full of something unfamiliar though there was no doubt what it meant. It scared her to her core.

"I'm right across the hall." He meant it to sound reassuring, but instead it made her feel trapped. She nodded silently, not trusting her

The Sound of the Stones

voice. "Your servant is in the room to help you prepare for bed. Send word to me at any hour if you need anything."

He leaned down and placed a kiss just to the side of her mouth, his lips barely grazing the side of hers. Heat rushed to Ashra's cheeks. "Anything at all," he said against her lips, then opened her door swiftly, his eyes lingering. She backed into her room and began to shut the door, peeking at him through the crack. Once closed, she leaned against the door and blew out a long sigh of relief. Mixed emotions overwhelmed her. She felt empty and alone. And while she felt allegiance to her own suppressed people, she also felt strangely safe here in the confines of Perditus's palace.

The servant sat at the fireplace watching. When Ashra turned, she stood and gathered up nightclothes, helping Ashra remove the gown to slip into her nightdress.

"What is your name?" Ashra asked, stifling a yawn.

"Smirah," she answered, her pursed lips indicating a reluctance to say more. Smirah was a middle-aged, slightly plump woman with short, brown hair. She was dressed in a simple brown linen pantsuit with a white rope belt tied around her waist. Her face was soft and warm but her eyes were weary.

"Do you have a family, Smirah?" Ashra continued, so lonely for human comfort that Smirah's reluctance to speak seemed unimportant.

"Not anymore," she answered quietly. Her face wore pain as she turned to hang Ashra's dress.

"I'm sorry," Ashra said, feeling guilty for making her speak of painful things. Smirah bobbed her head primly and turned down plush blankets. She patted the mattress and Ashra slid into bed.

"I will be right down the hall. If you need anything press the red crystal." She gestured to a metal panel on wall to the right of the bed. There were various colored crystals on the metal plate. "The blue crystal will reach the master. He said you may use it if you wish." Smirah's eyes held pity with those last instructions.

Ashra simply nodded. Smirah left the room, dimming the lights as she went. Ashra lay in the silence, surrounded by the soft hum of stone. She began to cry, making warm puddles on the pillow beneath her face. Sleep took her, and even in sleep the tears did fall.

On the Other Side of the Lands

He knew the direction the wind would blow even before it brushed his face. Rucain stood atop a ledge that led to the elders' sacred cave, waiting. The wind caught strands of his white-blond hair as he listened. His sister had turned thirteen years just one week past, and since then the wind felt different. He had always found comfort in its fickle dance, but the urgency with which it called now stripped comfort from his chest. Inner turmoil roiled in his stomach but you couldn't tell. His emotions were a hostage that his face would not betray.

Akira climbed the jutting rocks to meet her brother. They would go in together to meet the elders. The two always had an unspoken bond, these strange people with odd inward personalities. She tried desperately to mimic Rucain's impassive expression, but her inner light prevented her from hiding the emotions on her face. She hated that about herself. She wanted nothing more than to be like him, to gain his approval. Criticism ran deep and his compliments were few and far between.

"You're late," he scolded with a cool demeanor, a slight edge of irritation in his voice.

Akira winced, then regained her bearing, holding her face steady. "Training took longer than usual. New youths came of age, and I was expected to help instruct." Her voice was cold, matching her brother's tone. Her ice blue eyes meet his and she pretended to be unaffected by his admonishment.

Rucain assessed her for a moment. While Akira saw a cold stone expression, what she couldn't see was warmth spread in his chest. But instead of a smile to ease her mind, her brother simply grunted. "Come. They are waiting." He turned toward the sacred cave. Akira took several breaths and donned her best stoic expression before following.

Ten weathered men sat cross-legged in a circle. A fire heated the cave from its center. Some of the men smoked pipes, and the air was thick with the aroma of dried leaves. Akira eyed their serious expressions as they turned to look. She didn't want to be there, and fought of the urge to flee. But she didn't want to shame her brother, so she walked forward and stood next to him.

The Sound of the Stones

Most of the men wore flat faces, assessing the pair. The cave felt stifling under their heavy stares. At least one set of eyes was comforting. The man farthest back watched Akira with a warm, familiar face. Racka, her grandfather, always looked as if he knew a secret when he smiled. He was her favorite person in the world, and he made her feel as if she were his too. Rucain looked so much like him, only time separating the likeness with weathered age. But he was still a strong man, despite long years of living, and held great respect from their people.

"The time is upon us," Racka began. He stood, using his staff as leverage. Rucain and Akira waited at the back of the cave like statues. The nine other elders remained seated, but turned their attention to the standing man. Racka pulled a small crystal from the depths of his cloak, holding it aloft. It twinkled iridescent, casting irregular light about the cave. Waves of prisms bounced off smoke, making the cave feel crowded.

"This crystal began to change upon Akira's birth." Racka's serious expression turned warm for a brief moment as he met his granddaughter's eyes. Akira's lips pulled up at the corners. "It has grown stronger with each passing year." He held the stone up further and turned his eyes back to the other elders. "Now it pulsates like the beating of a heart." He clasped the stone tight and tucked it back into his robe. He turned grave eyes on his grandchildren. "It is time."

Truth Be Told

Dry tear streaks lined her face, staining the pillow she rested on. He could almost reach out and brush her cheek with a shaking hand. She was alone; the fire in her room was dim. This was not like the times he had seen her before in his dreams, her eyes filled with fire, wonder, hope. Now her eyes were clinched shut against pain, some horror he could not understand. He felt a pull toward her unlike anything he had ever known. She was his reason for being, yet he didn't even know her name, didn't know where to find her. There was one thing he was convinced of. She had to be real, or life was not worth living. He had to find her. He had to know.

Bazine woke too early, as he did every night he dreamed of her. He sat up from his sleeping mat, scrubbing his hands over his face. He considered lying back down, but noticed light coming from the front room. His bare feet padded lightly on the stone floor as he walked to the front room. His mother sat at the table, head resting in her hands. She looked as if the world pressed down around her. A sinking feeling settled into the pit of his stomach. He placed a hand on her shoulder as he neared, desperate to ease the pain. She lifted her head and covered his hand with her own. Her eyes were pained and weary. She smiled weakly but it wavered and fell.

"My sweet son, I have some things I must tell you," Ratha said, taking a deliberate cleansing breath. "Make us some tea. We have much to talk about."

Bazine nodded, swallowing at a lump in his throat that refused to budge. He prepared the hot drinks, lingering in the moments left before unknown things would be revealed. Realization pierced his heart. Time could not be turned back, and it was time to know things that would never be forgotten.

"Tell me what's on your mind, Mother," Bazine prodded carefully as he eased into a seat across from her. He put the drinks between them and gripped his own as if to protect himself. She looked more troubled than he'd ever seen, and he silently wished to take away her pain. She took the steaming cup and sipped, her eyes avoiding his.

"I have not been completely honest with you, or anyone for that matter." Her voice was timid as she brought her eyes level with his, a

The Sound of the Stones

look of regret riddled within. He remained silent, nodding a small sign of encouragement. His face was calm though his heart worked in overtime, pushing blood through his veins that had seemed to run cold. She took a deep breath, then blew it out slowly.

"When the Nonsomni found me, it is true I was in a coma. I didn't wake until I was in labor." A slight curve graced her lips as she reflected on her only child's birth. "You were such a beautiful baby, Bazine, such a strong little thing." The lines around her eyes eased and she reached for Bazine's strong hand to give it a squeeze.

"You know where you come from." It was a question and statement in one. He searched her eyes for confirmation; her frozen expression told him the truth.

"Yes, I know where I come from." Her eyes dropped to the table. She pulled her hand back slowly and gathered it to her chest. "I thought I was doing the right thing by keeping it a secret. I thought I could protect you from our past if no one knew the truth." She shook her head, squeezing her eyes tight in memory. "I was afraid they would send us away if they knew who you were." She choked on the last word and rested her head in her hands. Bazine felt torn between comforting her and his desire to pry. He reached his hand across the table and brushed loose hair from her face.

His tone was gentle but firm. "Who is my father, where did we come from?"

Ratha lifted her head and straightened her back, showing conviction to finally tell her son what he deserved to know.

"You are so much like him, Bazine. I miss him every time I look at you." Her chin trembled. Withheld tears trickled down her cheeks but she forced herself to continue. "I come from a land far to the north, over the mountains and through a great desert full of nothing but death." She spat the word death, scrubbing tears from her face angrily. "Humans were once free all over this world, but a strange creature called Glasne came through dreams and made women have children. The women never survived the birth."

She pressed her lips in a line and shook her head before continuing. "The half-human, half-Glasne are called Krad Glasne. The Krad took over, and ruled the humans ruthlessly. I was a slave for the Krad, a farmer along with my mother, father, and older sister." Her eyes took on a faraway stare as she recalled details of the life she left so long ago. "My sister, she…"

Ratha began to tremble. Tears welled up again, threatening to brim over. Bazine moved closer. He had no words of comfort, so he simply held her hand, waiting for her to finish. "My sister and I were very close. Oh, Bazine, she was so lovely." She smiled through bleary eyes and sighed. Then her expression twisted into pain. "One morning I couldn't get her up. It was time to go out to the fields, but she wouldn't wake. She was alive but not responding." Ratha closed her eyes, shaking her head in defeat. "I knew then what had happened. She had been visited in her dream by one of them." She made the word "them" sound like a curse.

Bazine was beginning to see his mother in a new light. She looked younger, vulnerable, scared. It was so different from the strong, unmovable woman he had grown up knowing.

"I had seen a few other families lose daughters giving birth to Krad. It was always a possibility but we tried to take precautions." Ratha took hold of her cup, bringing it to her lips to take a sip. "There are herbs that help suppress dreams, a recipe passed down from before anyone could remember. It worked most of the time." She set her tea down, tracing the lip of the cup in silence for a moment, then shrugged a helpless shoulder. "But every once in a while a dream slips in. Her drink must not have been strong enough. Maybe the herbs were old and lost their potency. Maybe she didn't drink enough. She always hated the taste of it." She looked at Bazine, eyes wide. "Whatever it was, they found her."

Bazine studied his mother's weary face. She was still a very beautiful woman. He wondered what her sister had looked like. Perhaps they had the same eyes, eyes like his. But the rest of him, the dark hair, tan skin, broad face, was that from his father?

"What happened to her, and what of my father?" Bazine asked, sounding more like twelve than twenty-one.

"My sister was taken into Krad City to be monitored during the pregnancy. There was one Krad, in particular, who was assigned to our farming sector to read our modicums."

"What's a modicum?' Bazine interrupted, sounding twelve again. Ratha tipped her head and continued.

The Sound of the Stones

"It's a small piece of crystal the Krad placed in our brains at birth. The crystal holds vibrations of thoughts and memories. Some of the Krad can read those vibrations. That's how they knew if humans were thinking of rebellion. They always had the upper hand."

"Do I have a modicum? Do the Nonsomni have them? Why didn't the tea work for me?" Bazine blurted.

Ratha giggled despite herself at her son's peppering questions and patted his shoulder.

"No, you do not have a modicum and neither do the Nonsomni. They are free from the Krad and the Glasne creatures. For some reason this group of people do not dream. I don't even think the Krad know the Nonsomni exist. As for the tea"—Ratha shrugged—"I don't know why it doesn't work for you."

Bazine frowned. "Do you have a modicum?"

Ratha shook her head, her jaw tensing.

"How?" Bazine countered quickly.

Ratha took a deep breath, settling in to tell the worst of it.

"The Krad that was assigned to our sector seemed to care for me. He would sneak me into Krad City, to the orphanage where they kept my sister. It was a small comfort to sit by the bedside and speak of things from our past. I knew she would never wake, but just being with her those last few months was something at least. I thought maybe she could hear me, take comfort in the fact that she was not alone."

"Did the one who snuck you in remove your modicum? Is he my father?" Ratha shook her head.

"No," Ratha said emphatically. Her mouth worked in silence, searching for words. "There was another Krad...he guarded the pregnancy section of the orphanage. Simion." Ratha whispered his name, her hand hovering over her lips as if to recapture a lost moment in time. Her trance was broken when Bazine shifted in his seat. Her secret moment dissipated like the steam rising from her tea. She dropped her hand to the table and cleared her throat. "He was what they call a Gravity Bender. All guards are Benders. Their abilities in movement and fighting are unparalleled."

Ratha's eyes lost focus, drifting to another time, a land far away. Her voice became wistful. "Simion would stand at the door and listen to my stories as I spoke them over my sister. Gradually he became more interested, inching his way into the room. Eventually he began to ask questions, and shortly after began telling me stories of his own. I can't quite explain how it happened, but we fell in love over those months."

Ratha turned to Bazine. His expression was stone and she placed a hand on his jaw. His eyes reflected pain as realization crashed down around him. The weight of her secrets shattered the dim hazy reality he had clung to as a child. He could choose to be angry, or he could lend understanding. Her eyes held love, a vast dialogue asking for forgiveness, acceptance, understanding. The small lines around his eyes and lips eased, if slightly.

The deep lines around her mouth relented and she smiled. "You look so much like him."

"What happened? If he loved you, then why did you end up here and all alone?" Bazine's tone was riddled with anger and edged with guilt. He gripped her hand protectively as if he should have been there to help. As if he were some how responsible for the pain caused all those years before.

Ratha placed a reassuring hand over his. "We were in love, Bazine, but our love was very unorthodox. Krad had relations with humans, but loving a human was forbidden. Humans were not thought of as equal, we were possessions." She flipped a hand to the side in dismissal. "Playthings at best. The Krad Sensitive who snuck me in had his own intentions with me too. He thought he loved me. I'm sure of that, but his love for me was warped with twisted jealousy and ownership."

Ratha pursed her lips and sniffed. "I became pregnant with you during those last few months." She looked down shyly at her hands, her voice softened as if to hide behind the subtlety of her tone. "Your father was the only one I had ever been with in the way a woman and a man come together to create new life. I loved him and it felt right." She shrugged and fiddled with her cup, embarrassed for the intimate details.

Bazine felt a slow burn creep up his neck, coloring his cheeks and ears bright red. He shifted and cleared his throat, seeking to change the subject.

"Then why did you leave? Where is my father?" A touch of anger tinged his voice and he immediately regretted the way it sounded when

The Sound of the Stones

his mother looked up with big eyes. "Tell me what happened," he amended with a softer tone. Ratha blinked, then nodded.

"When Glasne come together with human women, those women can bear their children at the expense of their life. But for some reason Krad could not have children. They were infertile. At least that's what everyone thought. But when I became pregnant it was an anomaly no one had ever heard of. When I told your father, he was afraid for me. He wanted to take me far away from Krad City, to find a secret place, and live a life with me where no one would ever find us. He knew we needed to remove my modicum so that no Krad Sensitive could find us once we left. We could only think of one Krad to turn to. So the Sensitive who snuck me in, Blithe, became our only confidant in the matter."

Ratha pinched the bridge of her nose and closed her eyes against the memory. "I should have known it was a bad idea." Her voice held belated cynicism. "He seemed very taken with me, and Krad can be so possessive. He did help by removing my modicum, but he tried to sway me to leave with him instead." She dropped her hand to the table and opened her eyes. "He said he didn't care if the child was not his, that he would raise it as his own. It was almost pitiful how he begged. I felt so bad for him. I never thought he would try to harm us."

She barked a laugh, then looked up suddenly with tormented eyes, begging wordlessly for forgiveness. "The day your father and I left, we took enough to keep us watered and fed for a long trek. We decided to head south and look for green land to forage from. We got several days away before Blithe caught up." She gripped her hands into fists and swallowed. "He took your father's life while we slept under the desert stars. When I woke to find the horror of what he had done..."

Ratha's voice cut short and she swiped a hand over her face where new tears ran. She squared her shoulders and continued. "I held your father in my arms for hours as Blithe looked on. I said awful, hurtful things to him and he left me there to die." The room went silent as she stared into the empty space remembering. Ratha stood; the chair scraping the floor pierced the stillness.

Bazine watched his mother walk out. The room felt hollow. He ran a hand over his face and rose to follow. He stood for a moment, watching his mother's shoulders shake from silent sobs. He placed an arm around her in place of words of which he had none. She sniffed and wrapped her arm around his waist. They watched the rising sun and dancing colors in the sky as they bounced off the water below.

"I stayed there, next to your father's body, for a long time." She was silent for a few more moments. "As I drifted in and out of consciousness, a vision came to me soft in the night. A bright light danced before me, and a small voice told me to move on. It told me that you would be safe and that you had a purpose, and that one day you would know what it was." Bazine felt his mother shrug, her face still pressed against his chest. "So I got up, and kept walking south. I walked so long…so very far." Her voice was weak remembering. "I was tired and thirsty. I don't know how long it took me, or how far I'd traveled, but I finally collapsed." She sighed wearily, as if she had taken the trip all over again.

"The next thing I knew I was here, and Abrack was speaking soothing things over me. You were born just a few hours later and that is where your story begins." Ratha pulled away and looked up, waiting for him to realize. Bazine blinked and looked out over the land.

"You know what my dreams mean, don't you?" he asked, still looking out into the dawn.

"I think only you can know that, son," she said, bracing herself for his revelation.

"I must find the girl." His voice was soft but when he turned his eyes to his mother they were passionate, asking for her to understand.

"I know, son. Your dreams, the surroundings you describe, are where I come from."

Bazine closed his eyes, relieved that he wasn't crazy, grateful that his drive to find the girl wasn't based on his own imagination. There was a long silence between them, their eyes focused in the distance.

It was peaceful here. Ratha had always felt sad for all of the people left behind when she tried to escape with the love of her life. She had left the only home she had ever known, her sister who had not yet given birth, and her loving parents. They were left alone having lost two daughters. Ratha had lived with that guilt for so long, it was a long overdue relief that Bazine would be fulfilling his purpose, and perhaps some good could come from the sadness of the situation.

"I am so proud of you, Bazine."

The Sound of the Stones

He looked at his mother with the realization that she was letting go. She was giving her approval to seek what he needed to find. Neither of them understood why, but they trusted that the purpose would show itself in time. Bazine had one other person he needed to speak with before leaving.

He packed a few things in a travel sack, a water bag, some food, a few crystals for various purposes, and his knife. Ratha brought out the only possession she had from her lost love, Simion. She had torn a piece of his shirt when she left his lifeless body those twenty-one years ago, a small memento to keep by her side in remembrance. It was muted red with small crystals sewn into the rich fabric. She pressed it into Bazine's hand.

"This is the only thing I can give you of your father's. It came from his shirt. I want you to keep it, and remember that you came from love. Go find what it is you need to find. Fulfill your purpose so that our love and his death were not in vain."

Bazine took the cloth and tucked it close to his heart. He kissed his mother, gathered his things, and took one last lingering look at the brave woman who had escaped for love, who had pushed on when it would have been easy to give up, who had been strong as he grew, keeping secrets to protect him.

"I love you," he said, and turned to leave. She watched him descend, so strong and beautiful like his father. He took more than his travel sack as he left. He took her heart as well.

Blurred Lines

The room mocked her. Ashra spent a lot of time in her too-pink chamber. She looked forward to meeting Perditus for dinner, desperate to escape the staring walls.

"You are beautiful," he would say.

She watched him, leery. A subtle gaze held a little too long, brushing hair from her face indications of his intent.

"It's just a simple charm," she would tell him when he asked again about her pendant.

His eyes were troubled at times, as if he were struggling with something. He was strong and willful but underneath that she saw...more. She was lost.

"You are the sun," he would whisper, then close his eyes in pain. She could say nothing in return.

Everything that mattered was gone. In the absence of her family she began to feel dependent, whether on Perditus or the routine she wasn't sure. It wasn't a longing for him per se, but a need for comfortable familiarity. This was her life now. *I want to go home.* What home?

"Your home is here," he would tell her when she asked to leave. He became angry in flashes, then soothed her with sweet, empty words. It didn't feel like home, so barren, so cold. She drifted.

"You are mine," his eyes would say.

"I want to leave," hers would answer.

He could have forced himself on her with no consequences but he did not. It did earn a small amount of trust from Ashra, further confusing the lines that once were so clear.

Tears fell every night though sleep took her. She had no dreams and for that she was grateful. Perhaps it was a gift from Perditus. She was on the verge of revealing her gift. If she could please him would he let her leave? Something held her back. A small quiet voice spoke in the recesses of her mind urging her quiet. She waited.

The First Defiance

Fleuric walked the misty corridor, searching. Having met with Ashra once before, he should have been able to find her with ease, but she continued to elude him. He growled and ran a hand through his hair. The tittering stream of other human dreams flooded his mind, making him angrier.

"Father." A distant call broke the stream of human thoughts. Fleuric took a long breath and turned toward the call of his son.

His father stepped out of the mist. His eyes were weary, and his gait heavy.

"Son, what news have you? Why have you waited so long?" His voice matched his expression.

"I have the girl." As the words left Perditus's mouth, his father's face settled into subtle relief. Perditus wouldn't tell him he waited because he wanted Ashra to himself.

"And what of her parents?" Fleuric asked, narrowing his eyes.

This was the real reason he had avoided his father until now. "I staged their deaths." Fleuric's eyes blazed angry but Perditus continued. "They are hidden for now. I believe they know more than it seems. But I need time to extract information from them before they are disposed of." What he didn't tell his father was that he hadn't killed them because he couldn't. When he thought of hurting Ashra his resolve left him. No. He couldn't tell his father that.

Fleuric looked ready to burst. His jaw clenched as he rubbed a hand over his face. Perditus braced for impact as the room grew heavy. Then Fleuric's expression softened, turning to resolve. "Perhaps that is best, as long as the girl thinks they are dead."

Perditus released a breath he didn't realize he was holding. "She wears a pendant with strange crystals that do not vibrate," Perditus said. It sounded more like a question than a statement.

Fleuric's eyes flinched briefly and he sniffed. "And the crystals from the deep mine?"

Perditus shook his head. "They met with trouble. Blithe was killed. Two humans and a Giant survived. They did not bring any back."

The Sound of the Stones

Fleuric waved a hand flat. "No matter. The girl is the key. I'm certain of it. What do you know of the pendant?" Fleuric asked as he lowered himself into a chair.

"Not much, she's guarded when I ask about it. Nothing in her modicum reveals anything of use." Perditus remained standing, unease settling into his chest. Something had changed. The way his father interacted with him was different since the girl was discovered. Perditus shook his head and rubbed at the back of his neck. He looked up to find him watching.

"Son, you must win her trust. Find out what she is hiding, where the pendant came from. What it has to do with her abilities. If she learns what she is capable of…" His voice trailed off and he narrowed his eyes. He hissed, "If you sense anything is wrong, kill her." He stared at Perditus as if waiting for a reaction. He did not flinch, though the words "kill her" echoed in his mind, clenching his heart like a vise. "Do you understand me, son? She must not be allowed to use her gift for humankind."

Perditus met his father's eyes unbending. "Yes, I understand." Perditus was careful not to let emotion bleed into his tone. Fleuric watched him a moment longer.

"You must do what is necessary, no matter what." He leaned forward and pointed sharply.

"I will." Perditus's tone was clipped. Before Fleuric could respond, Perditus began to detach himself from the trance. His father's eyes looked surprised as his face dissipated from view. Perditus did not feel sorrow for that. He was filled with a strange kind of rage he did not understand.

He walked to his door, his hand hovering over the knob. He pulled back and ran his hand though his hair. He paced the room a few more times, stopped in the middle of the floor, and looked at the door angrily. He cursed under his breath, gave in, and walked out.

The door creaked as he opened it. He held his breath and listened. The sounds of gentle breathing and crackling fire filled the room. He stepped over the threshold of the door and crossed the room. The soft light of the fire traced the outline of Ashra's sleeping form. She had kicked off the covers and pulled herself into a ball. There were tearstains on the pillow. The tear tracks on her face still glistened.

He closed his eyes and clenched his jaw. He looked down, reached a hand toward her, and stopped, hovering just above her. His hand trembled and he found himself both angry and amused. He reached past her to grab hold of the blanket and pulled it to cover her, then held his breath. She sighed and mumbled something. He let out his breath and rubbed a hand over his face. He stood for a moment more until her breathing settled, then left the room quietly.

A Love Unrequited

Ashra peered over her glass of spirits. Perditus was quiet this evening. He hadn't scanned her modicum or asked any clever questions. Nor had he told her she was lovely. He watched her silently while forking his food. It felt like the quiet before a storm.

"Why do you keep me here?" Her question hung in the air, pregnant with anticipation for his reaction. She braced herself for the irritation that was sure to follow. It always did when she pressed him on such matters. But his eyes didn't flash angry and that too made her anxious.

He rose from the chair and moved closer, all the while holding her eyes with a seriousness that unnerved her. He knelt down on one knee at her feet and took her hand in his. She would have preferred his irritation over this reaction. She shifted in her seat.

"My little one." It was what he called her when he was in a good mood and it quite frankly made her skin crawl. "Do you know what you make me feel?" His eyes were sad, his voice less sure than she had ever heard. Ashra swallowed hard. "I am not who I once was. I thought I knew what to do, but then I saw you, spoke with you, touched your skin." He reached up with his other hand and touched her cheek. Ashra's blood ran cold and her mouth went dry. "Could you love me? Could we change who we are? Would it be enough?" It was the last thing she wanted from him. She could no more love him than she could love the sharp edge of a spear as it sliced her skin.

Ashra sighed and dropped her gaze to their hands. His grip tightened as if that act could reach a part of her that lay hidden from his view. Ashra's mouth worked to form words but her mind was blank. How do you turn down someone who holds your fate in his hands? How do you say no to the sun when it provides both the necessities of life and the ability to burn you? Did she have a choice? Would he force her to pretend she had feelings she could not? Her silence stretched long, too long. Her breathing seemed loud in her own ears. She looked up in time to see the realization pierce his eyes. Where there was hope and tenderness now lay stone and steel.

Perditus dropped her hand and stood. He turned and walked toward the door, his footsteps clicking slowly over the floor. Without

The Sound of the Stones

looking back he said, "I could give you a better life." He paused, his shoulders tense. "I could be a better man for you."

His voice was quiet but it carried a vibration through the room, hovering around Ashra like a veil. He hesitated as if waiting for a reply. Ashra didn't move, didn't breathe. She braced herself for something. Anything would be better than the silence. Ashra opened her mouth but it was too late. Perditus left. With him he took the veil of vibration, leaving Ashra alone in the grand dining room, feeling empty, alone, confused...*relieved*.

A guard entered shortly after to escort Ashra back to her room. Perditus didn't send for her for days and relief turned to loneliness. She needed hope. But hope was like the wind. She could sense that it was there, but could never grasp it in her hands.

Searching for Hope

Ashra pressed her ear to the door. The guards were quiet. They looked slightly startled when she flung open the door.

"Oh, hello," Ashra said with mock surprise, batting her eyes with ridiculous innocence. The guards shifted uncomfortably and Ashra found she very much liked to make them feel that way. She was bored and desperate to find a way out. Perditus had left her to her own accord having made his feelings blatantly clear and her having blatantly not returned them.

"You shouldn't be out wandering the halls by yourself. You could get lost," the taller guard stammered, trying to figure out how to get Ashra back into her room without touching her. Her lips pulled up at the corners.

"Oh, well then it's a good thing you're out here. I'm hungry and I don't know where Smirah went. Let's go to the kitchen." She raised her chin, defiant, and set off down the hall. She didn't much care anymore about rules. Throwing caution to the wind seemed a much more enticing endeavor.

The guards looked at each other and the shorter guard shrugged. The taller guard rolled his eyes and followed.

"You need to turn around. The kitchen is the other direction," he said, walking briskly to catch up. She continued to walk in the wrong direction. The Bender jumped, flipping above her head, and landed on his feet in front of her. She stopped and put her hand on her hips.

"You really don't want me to go in this direction, do you?" She narrowed her eyes. The guard held his spear close to his chest, trying to appear something between menacing and gentle. Ashra snorted. She blew a strand of hair from her face and turned in the other direction. "If you don't mind, I'm hungry. I don't feel like playing games right now," Ashra called over her shoulder flippantly to the guard still standing in his awkward position. He pushed ahead and took the lead.

"This way, but you get the food quickly and we go straight back to your room," he said with conviction, as if that would make this breach of protocol okay.

The Sound of the Stones

Ashra was already taking in the subtle details of the hall and chamber doors, noting lights, locks, and windows. The walls and lights, statues, and various stone structures all put off varied vibrations, most of which congealed into a subtle hum that marked this place as someone's home.

The guard led her down a series of halls and down a smaller back stairway. It was a different staircase than the one she used to have dinner with Perditus. She mentally mapped the turns they took to get there. She had counted the doors and windows and even the lights as they made their way toward the kitchen. Her years training in the mines had taught her how to map in dark, unfamiliar places. You became good at your job or you died. The Krad had unknowingly trained Ashra for this. Her attention to detail was polished. This asset would come in handy if she could find the right opportunity to use it.

The guard did take her to the kitchen. She wasn't really hungry but took enough food back to her room to feed all of Krad lest she look like a liar. On the way back, they passed another Bender. His hazel eyes met hers as she walked toward her room.

"Mesheleck," the Bender guard greeted the hazel-eyed Krad.

Mesheleck tipped his head in greeting, never taking his eyes from Ashra. She got the strange sense he was trying to tell her something. She stopped. Mesheleck kept walking but looked back over his shoulder before turning down another hall. The guard cleared his throat. She moved again but went back to her room with a strange sense that something big was about to happen…but what?

A Reason to Rebel

Ashra woke in darkness. A faint light broke through the window but it didn't reach her bed. Smirah bustled around, preparing a morning meal. Ashra smelled toasted bread and heard water pouring slowly into a delicate cup for tea. Her stomach growled in answer. She lay watching Smirah for a few moments. So purposeful were her motions, shoulders taut with heavy burdens, moving as if these gestures were her only escape.

"I lost my parents, you know." Ashra said this softly as much to herself as to Smirah. Smirah jumped, startled by Ashra's voice.

"Oh, I didn't know you were awake yet." Smirah recovered and diligently fiddled with the breakfast tray. Ashra slid from under the covers and wrapped a blanket around her shoulders to ward off the morning chill.

"Have you lost much in your life, Smirah?" Ashra asked, desperate to find comfort with another who had suffered as she.

Smirah stilled as if frozen by her words. "It isn't proper to speak of such things, young lady," Smirah scolded gently, then rearranged the breakfast tray though it needed no attention.

"Don't you wonder how it happened?" Ashra asked, frustration bleeding into her tone.

"How what happened?" Smirah's hand went motionless above the tray.

"This." Ashra gestured around the room. She walked to the window, jerking the heavy drapes open with quite a bit more force than necessary. Sunrays burst in, reflecting off the dust motes stirred by the force with which the drapes had been abused. Ashra pointed to the edges of Krad City and then back toward human camp. "And that." Ashra spat the words. She stood in the rays of light, eyes blazing. Billowing dust flitted around her head like snow.

Smirah blinked indignantly. She opened her mouth and closed it. No words would come, and in her silence Ashra continued. "How is it that we became slaves to these beings?" Her voice grew softer but the passion in her tone remained. "Where do the Glasne come from? Can we ever be free? Is there a way to stop them?" Ashra's hand hovered in

The Sound of the Stones

the air as she stared bold-faced into Smirah's dumbfounded one. She dared to ask the questions no one else would.

"Are you trying to get me killed, Ashra?" It was the first time Smirah had addressed her by name and she whispered it in desperation. "Are you trying to get yourself killed?" Her voice trembled as she sat heavily into a chair, shaking her head in disbelief.

Ashra relented with a sigh and joined Smirah in the adjacent chair. "I don't know...maybe. Is life worth living without the ones you love to share it with?" Ashra said this as a matter of fact and with little emotion. Smirah raised her eyes to Ashra. The look in the servant woman's eyes changed from fear to pain. The same pain reflected in Ashra's, and for a brief moment they were connected in grief. *You know.* Ashra broke the stare and cast her eyes to the floor, startled by the intimacy.

"What if I told you that the ones you love are not truly gone." Smirah's voice was small but steady. The words tumbled around the room until Ashra could piece them together to form meaning. She pulled her eyes from the floor and searched Smirah's face. Mingled guilt and fear touched her eyes but her jaw was set firm in defiance.

"What do you mean, Smirah?" Ashra whispered fiercely. Her heart pounded and her lips went numb. She forced herself to stay seated by digging her fingers into the arm of the chair. Her body wanted to jolt, lips wanted to beg. Smirah looked toward the fireplace where small flames danced in a dying fire. The silence was maddening. Ashra dug her nails deeper to keep from shaking the woman. Smirah's lips pressed into a thin line and she shook her head.

Ashra took a long breath through her nose, abating the urge to scream. "Please, Smirah, I can help you. I can make it so this conversation never shows on your modicum. They won't know you told me." Ashra's voice pitched high with cut-off tears. She moved to the edge of her seat, releasing her grip from the chair. Her hands rested palm up on her lap in desperation.

Smirah looked at Ashra and gave her a tired smile. "I'm not even sure I want to hide from them anymore. They took my husband; they took my children." Her chin trembled, eyes glistening in the firelight. "You're right, there is no real point in living without the ones you love."

Ashra licked her lips and leaned forward, inching her hands toward the woman who seemed to be holding a lifeline. "Smirah, please, do you know something about my parents?" Ashra held her breath, hanging on to a small sliver of hope that her parents were not really dead. Smirah's eyes flashed fierce and her jaw tensed. Ashra's heart began to sink but then Smirah spoke.

"I overheard some guards before you came here. Talking about a woman and man they brought into custody. They were working out plans to make their home look like a Giant destroyed it. Some of the other servants were talking about what happened to your parents. It all seems odd, doesn't it? I mean why would they want you to believe your parents are dead?"

A cold chill ran up Ashra's spine. She felt a strange mixture of relief and overwhelming fear. If her parents were still alive and here in the palace, why were they being held? Ashra took a deep breath as realization dawned. If they could make her dependent, make her feel that there was nowhere else to turn, then she would reveal her gift. It had almost worked...almost. The air fell still and Ashra played the scenario over in her mind. She had nearly given in to him, let him be her refuge. The air in the room moved again, shifting, tugging, urging Ashra forward.

She placed a hand over Smirah's and began to hum. The delicate song was music but more. It filled the empty spaces in the room, moving in invisible waves that could be sensed but not seen. If you closed your eyes you could almost see the waves, as if human sight was a hindrance. Smirah's eyes lit with wonder when Ashra's pendant began to glow. The pulsing light, soft at first, grew brighter, thrummed faster as the song reached its peak, then lay still. Silence filled the room once more. There was a sense of purity in the air like the peace that comes after a raging storm.

"You will be fine. No one will know what we have talked about." Ashra's voice was soft. Her face held peace if only for that moment. Smirah nodded silently. There were no words. There was no doubt. The primal awareness in Ashra's song touched a place Smirah knew, remembered but had never realized she'd forgotten. Smirah stayed quiet while helping Ashra get ready for the day, mulling over the path her life had taken. She started to understand that even though horrible, unspeakable things had happened to bring her here, something larger was on the horizon. She was a part of it, even if it was a small one.

An Emotional Farewell

His heart was heavy but his mind at peace. Bazine paused outside of Abrack's home. This was it. He would say goodbye to the only father he'd ever known, not sure if he would ever make it home again.

"Are you going to stand there all blessed day or are you going to come in and say something to this old-timer?" Abrack called from the dimly lit front room of his home. Bazine stepped inside and lit a few more crystals so he could see, his eyes having already adjusted to the morning sun.

Abrack assessed his demeanor and the travel sack. "So, my son, what is it you've come to tell me?"

Bazine smiled to himself. Abrack knew.

"I must leave." They were three simple words that held both deep-seated truth and a call to action.

Abrack searched Bazine's eyes for a moment and tipped his chin in agreement.

"Yes, I thought you might." Abrack held up a finger and disappeared into the back room. Bazine heard him rummaging, muttering to himself before a coherent declaration broke free. "Ah, here we go." Abrack returned with shuffling feet, his lips pulled upward in satisfaction. He held a wad of pelt in his hands. He held this out and unwrapped the fabric, revealing a small, odd crystal.

"Where did that come from?" Bazine's voice was hushed and his brows drawn as if that particular expression could help him understand the foreign object.

"Well now, that is the question of the ages!" Abrack answered. His face turned serious, eyes flashing knowledge of a secret past.

The crystal was small, fitting in the palm of his hand, and easily concealable in his fist. It pulsed a subtle glow of colors, the spectrum of which went beyond the scope normally seen.

"This is a piece of our history that even the original twelve families did not understand." He shook his head and looked up from the stone. "Our history goes back even further than the original twelve. This piece of rock has been passed down from leader to leader since before the

The Sound of the Stones

Nonsomni found this land, and it is said"—he lowered his tone, his eyes twinkling—"when time has come to remember how to listen, the lucent stone will show its colors and remind us how to hear."

His voice was full of aged wisdom, eyes full of boyish wonder. "Bazine, this stone began to pulse the night you were born." The words hung in the air; the hair on the back of Bazine's neck stood stiff. "It was not hard for me to come to love you." He looked down at his hand, closing it over the stone. "I must confess there were times I wished it was not meant for you. That I might keep you here…safe." He shrugged an easy shoulder to acknowledge consent. One aged sinewy hand released the stone into the palm of a young ready one. He closed his hand over Bazine's with a firm grasp. "You have a purpose far greater than I can imagine. I have always known that, my son. Follow your instincts and take this with you. I am certain you will find your way."

Bazine looked into Abrack's familiar, weathered face. Emotion overwhelmed him and one tear escaped, slipping down his cheek despite his effort to fight it. The tear was one of regret for leaving the people he loved, but also relief for understanding and validation.

"I don't know if I will be back." Bazine almost choked on his words and cleared his throat to cover it. "Thank you for everything, Abrack."

Abrack's face was serious as he also fought off tears, but a slow smile spread across his lips. He gripped Bazine's shoulder and gave him a firm shake.

"Ah, my strong boy, I have a good feeling I will be seeing you again. Do what you must, and I will take care of your mother. Now go; time is wasting." Abrack folded Bazine in a strong embrace and led him to the entrance of his home. Bazine looked out over the sweeping landscape, the safety he had always known. A piece of his father's shirt was tucked close to his heart, the stone nestled firmly in his pack. He stepped down from the cliff face in the direction of the desert and didn't look back.

Abrack watched him until the arduous desert swallowed him. He kept his eyes there as if watching could lend safety to the boy. He imagined smooth travels, and sent silent thoughts to someone or something above, in hopes that his wishes were heard for the child he loved like his very own.

A Glimmer of Hope

Smirah shuffled down a dark hall toward the holding chamber. In her hand she held the meager food provided to prisoners. She had added two extra stale bits of bread and some ale to wash it down with. Getting in trouble for that small gesture was a possibility, but she was in the mess and figured she may as well be in it all the way. The heavy cell door boasted a small opening covered with a metal plate. She slid it open.

A ray of light spilled in. It illuminated Sheed and Shara where they huddled, falling in and out of restless sleep. Smirah placed the tray into the slot, looking for signs of life. Shara woke first. She crawled across the cold hard floor, dragging chains behind her. One grubby hand grasped the tray, her eyes squinting into the hole.

"Hello?" Smirah whispered.

"Who's that?" Sheed bellowed, clanking metal chains as he scooted toward the door.

"Shhhh," Shara scolded.

"Sorry." Sheed tried to whisper the apology but it still came out loud. Shara slapped him on the arm and leaned closer to the door.

"Are you there?" Shara's voice trembled and she licked dry lips. "Can you tell me anything, why we are here, what we've done?" Her question met with silence for a moment, the only sound the clink of metal as Shara shifted to get a better look.

"Do you have a daughter?" Smirah asked this so quietly they could barely make it out. But the word "daughter" was clear enough.

"Yes!" They spoke in unison, shifting this way and that to gain sight of the woman. Their faces pressed together like a vise, trying to see out a too-small hole.

"She is safe." Smirah pressed her hand to the door like a prayer before turning away.

"Please don't leave us here!" Shara's voice cracked as she fought back tears. She pressed hard against the slot in the door as if she could somehow manage to fit through.

The Sound of the Stones

"Have you seen our little bean?" Sheed asked. The words echoed in the cell but silence followed. Shara choked back a sob and pressed still harder to the door.

Smirah was almost to the foot of the stairs but paused when Shara cried. She swallowed hard, turning back. "Perditus has her. She was told you were killed." The cell stayed quiet. "Perditus thinks you have answers for him. Something about your daughter. About her gift." She whispered it, but the word "gift" sounded loud in the stillness.

Clinks of metal shifted but no words answered. Smirah continued. "Ashra knows you are here. She"—Smirah stammered for words, not sure what to call it—"fixed things so I won't give her away." She went silent for a few more moments. "I've done what I can. I'm not sure how safe I will be now. You may not see me down here again."

It was then Shara reached through the slit in the door, fingers searching.

"Thank you," she said.

Smirah touched her hand and leaned closer. "Life's not worth living without the ones you love."

Smirah left but did not close the slot. A small dash of light washed in, a sliver of hope.

A Giant Plan

Weeks went by with no word. Krank was summoned to help on the dig. Haker was there and Krank was glad to see a familiar if not friendly face. The team leader, however, was a stubborn old man with no regard for anything but himself. He gave orders to Krank harshly. Krank gave him only what he asked for and nothing more. He smirked inwardly at the mess he left behind.

Before Krank left, he knelt down near Haker and asked quietly, "Where has Ashra gone?"

A shadow crossed Haker's eyes and he shook his head solemnly. "It isn't good...a Giant smashed her parents' place. They were killed and Ashra was taken to the palace."

Haker's words were matter-of-fact and they felt like a slap across Krank's face. Krank shook his head.

"No Giant has been inside the human camp." Anger rose in his chest. Something was wrong.

"I'm just telling you what I was told. That's why I got reassigned. Ashra doesn't work the mines anymore, hasn't for weeks now."

Krank lifted himself to his full height, dwarfing Haker in his shadow. "She's in trouble." His words mingled with a growl. He looked down at Haker. "Come find me later. I will need your help for what I have planned." Krank left Haker standing there, scratching his beard.

Haker pressed his lips in a hard line and sighed. "This might get ugly."

Strange Strangers

It was everywhere. A monstrous expanse of almost bleach-white sand, sloping in dry waves as far as the eye could see. By day three in the unforgivable desert, Bazine decided to travel by night and rest by day, crafting a makeshift lean-to with his meager belongings. Temperatures reached near 120 degrees during the day and sank to a frigid 50 degrees by night. Moving by night seemed the only way to keep from freezing. He found sparse patches of succulents once or twice a night, breaking open the ripe fruit to drink from liquid trapped within. He had several welts on his hands and quickly learned how to handle the fruit, pain an ever persistent teacher. The liquid wasn't nearly enough, but it kept him alive. He would have considered turning back on day two if his fitful daytime sleep wasn't riddled with visions of the dark-eyed girl with a strange man. The strange man put his hands on the dark-eyed girl. She looked frightened. It drove him on.

The brightest star guided him. Ratha had told him his dreams were visions of the place she came from, Krad City. All he knew was that it lay far to the north. So he trudged on, fingers sore, lips chapped, and a nagging desire to lie down and sleep.

On the night of day four he noticed large grooves approximately ten feet across in various places in the sand. He would see them for twenty feet or so and then they would stop, punctuated by a large sunken divot in the ground. Thirst and exhaustion muddled his mind. Instead of wondering what made the patterns in the sand, he played a mental game, tracing the lines with his eyes like connecting dots.

Over a dune he caught sight of a small orange light in the distance. The light flickered, hovering above one groove in the sand. It looked like a tall, thin man wearing a glowing ball for a head. The groove wiggled back and forth as if dancing. Bazine grunted a laugh, then ran a hand over his face. He winced as a welt on his palm scrubbed his stubbled chin. That's when he felt it.

The sand moved. It was subtle at first so he thought his mind was playing tricks again. When the sand began to sway like an ocean wave he realized he was either crazy and done for, or lucid and still done for. Whatever could make the sand move in that way was big. He veered to the left in an attempt to gain steady ground. The movement stopped. A

169

The Sound of the Stones

few minutes later the ground moved again and Bazine dodged further to the left. This happened on an off for the next twenty minutes like some sort of demented game.

"Come on!" His voice cracked. "Do something!" He felt like an idiot screaming at the sand in the dark. Nothing happened. He pushed on, following the fading North Star. The sand stayed quiet.

He was just about to break and make camp when the sand began to shift again. He scrambled back but couldn't find a hold as the ground undulated. That's when the thing crested, rising from the depths with an eerie moan. Sand slid from its body like falling water as it rose farther and farther into the air. Slick tan skin glistened in the dawn, seeping foul mucus. Once it reached its peak, some twenty feet high, it screeched, then crashed to the ground, barely missing Bazine. He let loose a string of unintelligible expletives while seeking a place from which to spring. But there was none to be had. He sank further into the divot, toward the massive ugly worm.

Loud moans gave way to a wailing cry. Sand sprayed him in the face as the creature writhed. Bazine scrambled back, futilely scrubbing at his eyes. He fumbled blindly at his side. Numb fingers found his dagger and pulled it loose from its sheath. With trembling hands and blurred vision he stood ready, squinting at the beast.

The creature freed its back end, slapping a tail to the ground. Sand fell like rain as it turned toward Bazine. A gaping mouth boasted three rows of teeth, dripping slimy goo from their razor edges. The mouth pulsed opened and closed, a promise to devour. It moved toward him though it had no eyes. It seemed to sense Bazine's wild shifts and hooting commentary.

Bazine stilled himself, shutting his mouth, afraid to breath. The beast lunged. Bazine swiped at the creature with his too-small weapon and nicked the side of its mouth. The creature recoiled for a small moment, allowing Bazine to scramble back a few steps. But those few steps were not nearly enough as the thing lunged again with a vengeance.

Bazine braced for impact, squeezing his eyes shut. Something sliced through the air followed by a sickening thud. He braved a glance. A long wooden spear sprouted proudly from the beast's head. It writhed in pain, a flapping tail sending sprays of sand in all directions. Bazine shielded his eyes and continued to back away. Its last moan was a sad muffled trumpet. It submitted to its fatal wound and lay still, seeping into the sand. He spit sand from his mouth and turned. A small white-haired girl not more than twelve or thirteen stood a short distance away watching, eyes the color of ice. A man stood behind her in a hooded cloak. The three watched each other in silence. Bazine was the first to move.

"You there...I want to thank you for your help." He held his hands up and stepped forward. The little girl blinked at him expressionless and scurried off to the north. The cloaked one walked toward him. As he approached he took down his hood. His hair was as white as the girl's but his eyes were a darker gray. He was probably close to Bazine's age, with a slender build and narrow face.

"I am Rucain." He motioned for Bazine to follow with a jerk of his head, then turned in the direction of the girl and went swiftly.

Bazine paused, weighing his decision. He decided to follow, wagering he could take the slender man and small girl if they posed a threat. They walked about fifteen minutes before reaching a small rock outcrop that seemed out of place in the middle of the desert. The girl sat, stoking a fire with a stick, her eyes as wide as the moon. Bazine stood quietly. The man took off his cloak, revealing a surprisingly muscular build for his slight frame. He was lean and cut, wearing cream linen pants tied with a red rope belt. He wore no shirt but had arm cuffs on each bicep, enhancing the impressiveness of his strength. Upon closer inspection, Bazine saw each leather armband bore a familiar symbol.

It matched the mark Bazine wore on his chest.

Fearful Inquisition

If he couldn't have her then it didn't matter anymore. Perditus walked the dank corridor, his heavy footsteps echoing the emptiness in his chest. He reached the thick metal door and held a crystal chip under a beam of light coming from the metal box affixed to the wall. The door clicked. He opened the door, allowing a dim stream of light into the cell. Sheed and Shara huddled together in the corner. The light glinted from their troubled eyes. Perditus was backlit and his facial features were hidden in the shadows. He paused in the doorframe for a moment and studied the two. He scanned their modicums.

As he stepped into the cell just a hint of light caught his violet-blue eyes and they were fierce. Sheed and Shara had been brought in by guards weeks ago, and this was the first time either of them had laid eyes on him. But there was no mistaking who he was. The heavy scent of incense followed him into the cell.

"I believe you have information to share with me." Perditus's voice was deep and penetrating. Both Sheed and Shara could feel the persuasive pull of his veiled command, but their love for their daughter was stronger.

Shara came to her feet first, her chin raised and face proud. There was no doubt where Ashra's beauty came from. She had a timeless look with strong bones and bright chestnut eyes framed by thick dark lashes. Her eyes glimmered in the low light and her full lips pressed together tightly above a set jaw. She looked unmovable, defiant. Sheed stood next. He took his place by Shara's side. He was a large-built man but a full foot shorter than Perditus. They all stood silent, eyeing each other for a few moments.

"If you wish for your daughter to live, you will tell me. You will tell me everything or I will make her suffer and before I'm finished she will beg for death," Perditus hissed through clenched teeth.

Sheed continued to stare. His eye twitched and nostrils flared. Every muscle in Sheed's body tensed like a coil ready to spring. Shara dropped her gaze, the pride falling from her face.

The Sound of the Stones

Shara's lips moved silently as she struggled to form thoughts. "She can hear the crystal like the Sensitives." Her voice trembled. She looked at her husband. He was still tense, staring. Perditus ignored him.

"Go on," Perditus prompted.

"She was about ten when we discovered it. She told us she had always heard the vibrations." Shara's voice was steadier now.

"What about your modicums? Why do they not reveal this information?"

"She can"—Shara made an inarticulate gesture with her hand searching for the right words—"change the modicums, tell them not to record certain memories."

Perditus frowned. "How?" he asked softly.

"I'm not sure," Shara said, her eyes flashing fear. "Please don't hurt our little girl. She has never tried to harm anyone with this gift. We have been good workers. Please!" she finished, her voice pinched with restrained tears. Sheed put a hand on Shara as if to silence her. Perditus watched them for a moment.

Sheed could stay silent no longer and his voice came out slow and deep. "If you harm my daughter in any way I will end you." His body trembled not in terror but in seething anger. Shara gasped.

Perditus narrowed his eyes and began to laugh. It was soft at first but grew louder as he turned to leave, echoing off the walls of the cell. The heavy metal door shut behind him, cutting them off from the world.

Shara crumpled into Sheed's arms. He held her silently. Again, they were left in the dark, wondering about their daughter's fate. It was a dark and empty place in the heart and mind. Hopelessness nagged. The smallest glimpse of hope they had was overshadowed by the darkness. They were reaching, arms outstretched, clambering to grasp the tip of the shred of hope that remained.

Convincing a Mercurial Heart

"She has the gift. Her parents admitted it," Perditus said. He felt like a shell, empty, wavering. It didn't feel like a victory to know this.

"What have you done with them?" Fleuric asked, searching his son's eyes for clues.

"They are still alive." He didn't care that it would make his father angry. He also couldn't meet his father's eyes. He still couldn't bring himself to hurt Ashra, though she crushed him with nothing but silence.

"They must die! If she can read vibrations, what makes you think she doesn't already know they still live? You fool!" His voice boomed, penetrating Perditus's chest. Fleuric's yellow-rimed eyes radiated fury. Perditus did look up then but his expression stayed cold. It felt good to feel something other than despair.

Fleuric's eyes softened, as did his tone. "Get rid of them. Force her to lean on you, to need you. Only then will she reveal her gift."

Perditus didn't tell him he had failed at that too. She would never lean on him. Never let him in. He thought about these things and barked a cynical laugh. Fleuric eyed him curiously.

"What can you tell me of her gift? Is it like our own?"

Perditus paused before he spoke, remembering the fear in Shara's eyes, the tremble in her voice.

"It is like ours in some ways, but more."

"More. What do you mean more?" Fleuric leaned forward.

"She can manipulate them, alter them to her will."

Fleuric's eyes went wide.

"How?" he whispered. "Have you seen her do it?" He sounded desperate, pathetic.

"No, but there are no vibrations on her parents' modicums to indicate they know of her gift...but they know. That had to be her doing."

Fleuric's jaw clinched and he drew a hand down his face. "How are we to know that she has not altered others as well?" There was no way for them to know, of course. His expression turned imploring. "You

175

The Sound of the Stones

must kill anyone she has had extended contact with. The fact that she could leave her dream, and now this...I believe we are in grave danger."

Perditus nodded once and pulled himself from his father's presence. He sat for a while, looking at nothing in particular. For the first time, he considered leaving his father alone with no further contact. What would it be like if his father was free from the second universe? Did he really want him to be free? He could leave, go into hiding. But then what? He shook his head and laughed. No, he just needed to give it some time. If he could just go through the motions he would probably forget the pain, be himself again. He stood, rolled his shoulder, then walked out the door to get the job done.

The One

Bazine eyed Rucain. They sat silently around a small fire but Bazine would stay silent no more.

"Where are you from?" Bazine asked, glancing at the familiar marking on Rucain's armband.

Rucain looked at Bazine as if judging his trustworthiness then glanced over his shoulder toward the west.

"We come from the west." His answer was short, and he appeared not to want to share any more than that.

"That marking on your armband..." Bazine gestured to his arm but didn't finish his sentence. Rucain absently reached up and touched the cuff. Bazine untied the top of his shirt, peeling back the left corner to reveal his mark. Rucain and the girl watched with blank stares. Bazine cleared his throat, not knowing what to make of the two. He tied his shirt back and fiddled with a small twig at his feet.

Bazine glanced back up and found the two still staring at the place where he had tied his shirt back, as if they could still see his mark.

"You are the one then," the strange girl said in a hushed tone. It was the first time Bazine had heard her speak.

"I'm sorry?" Bazine asked. Rucain shot the girl a stern look. At least that's what Bazine assumed was a stern look. It wasn't much different from his normal look. The girl ducked her head and looked to the ground. Rucain looked back to Bazine with narrowed eyes.

"What does she mean, I'm the one?" Bazine asked more forcefully.

Rucain shook his head.

"Forgive my sister, she speaks silly things. She is still a child."

Bazine sighed, irritated, and looked back to the girl.

"What is your name?"

The girl lifted her chin a bit, trying to shake off her brother's rebuke. Bazine offered a warm smile.

"Akira."

"I want to thank you both for helping me out back there." Bazine gestured over his shoulder toward the south. "I'm not sure my small blade would have worked against that beast." His mouth twisted, embarrassed.

"It was a sand worm. You're lucky you haven't come across more. They come out at night," Rucain said with no particular inflection in his tone, as if killing sand worms and meeting strangers were everyday events.

"I've been traveling by night to avoid the heat. I'm on my way north," Bazine said, in an attempt to keep up the conversation.

Rucain twisted his face disapprovingly. It was the first real change in facial expression Bazine had seen from him.

"Nothing but trouble lies to the north. You should turn back." Rucain waved a hand flat as if forbidding him to go.

Bazine shrugged his shoulders, gesturing helplessly with one hand.

"I must," Bazine said. The pair stared at him.

Bazine rummaged in his pack and pulled out a cloth drawstring bag. "I don't have much, but I want to show you my appreciation for saving my life back there." He pulled some dried Etrog fruit, dusted with sugar, from the bag, and offered it to the white-haired siblings.

Akira gasped. Rucain looked at Bazine's outstretched hand and slowly took the fruit from his hand.

"Then it is so," Rucain said, looking at his sister. "Akira, it is he."

Akira smiled wide and took the offered fruit as well. She clasped it in her hand, holding it to her heart.

Bazine stared at them stupidly. "Will someone please tell me what 'the one' is?" He dragged out the words "the one," verging on irritability.

"The one who bears the mark and offers the fruit of goodwill," Akira said with a ridiculously giddy look on her face and not at all perturbed by Bazine's obvious annoyance.

Rucain gestured to his armband. "We are of the Fugashi people. We live in the mountains past the desert to the west." Bazine was still staring stupidly. Rucain continued, "Our elders sent us to find the one. You have fulfilled both signs. You are the one." He gestured at the fruit and then to Bazine's chest.

"The one that what?" Bazine's voice pitched high. His face pinched and he gestured wildly with both hands, a further indication of his growing irritation should they need it.

"The one that will take us to her," Akira chimed in, smiling as if his display of irritability was nothing to be concerned about.

The Sound of the Stones

"To the girl who wears the sign around her neck. She will reveal things to us that we have forgotten." Rucain finished where Akira had left off. He said it in an offhanded way, as if this information was commonplace and, in fact, Bazine should probably already know this.

Bazine sighed and rubbed his nose. He looked toward the north. "I know no woman that wears the sign. Only men bear the marking." He started to gather his things. "I am traveling north and as you said it is not a safe place to travel," Bazine said, hinting that he would be on his way without them.

"Then we will go with you," Rucain stated, as if it were already decided.

"But the girl could be harmed. It's too dangerous," Bazine answered, not entirely sure he wanted to travel with them.

Rucain gave a hardy laugh, startling Bazine. It was such an odd expression coming from him and it changed the shape of his face and eyes, making him appear almost friendly.

"Who do you think threw the spear that saved your life?"

Bazine turned to look at Akira. She blushed and dipped her head.

"Akira is a trained fighter. She is the best in her age group. Not even the males can defeat her in duels!" Rucain's face came alive, making him look younger all at once. Akira blushed still further. His expression went from excited back to stoic in an instant, rendering him older again.

Bazine couldn't think of any polite arguments. *No, you're weird and you make me flap my arms too much* didn't seem like something he could say and still remain cordial. He nodded a quiet thanks to the girl. It would be good to have the company even if they were strange. They might prove to be an asset once he reached Krad City. He wasn't sure what to expect but he was sure it wasn't going to be pleasant.

"All right, should we be on our way then?" Bazine asked.

"Let us share a meal before we go," Rucain countered, reaching inside his own pack to pull out a package. He opened it to reveal some dried meat and flatbread. Bazine watched as Akira dug in the sand with her hands. She made a hole about two feet down and then pulled two stone cups from her pack. She looked back at the small pit. As she stared, the hole began to fill with water. Akira dipped the first cup in, filling it with sandy water, and set it on the ground beside her. She placed a cloth over the empty cup and held it firm with one hand. She picked up the filled cup with the other hand and carefully poured the water through the cloth. When all of the water was drained the second cup held clean water, the cloth having filtered the sand. She offered the first drink to Bazine. He took it and drank deeply.

"I have been thirsty for days, only drinking from an occasional plant." He smiled wide, wiped his mouth, and handed her back the cup. "Thank you."

"You just have to know where to look," Akira said, with another big-toothed grin, eyes twinkling.

"Yes, I can see that now," Bazine said, with a friendly laugh. They ate and drank until their bellies were full.

Bazine was tired, having traveled the night, but he was eager to keep moving and ignored the urge to sleep. He didn't want to run into another sand worm, and decided that Rucain's advice to move during the day was sound. Rucain fashioned a head wrap for Bazine and showed him how to soak it in water for protection from the searing sun. Bazine was appreciative of the new technique. Rucain seemed pleased to help. At least Bazine assumed that he was. They moved at a decent pace. It was a much better pace now that he was hydrated and they had water when they needed it. Bazine decided he was grateful having run into them.

The great desert expanse didn't hold much to look at besides the seemingly same sloping sand hills over and over. It left the mind to wander. Bazine started thinking about where Rucain and Akira came from.

"Tell me of your people, Rucain. How did they come to live in the mountains to the west?"

Rucain nodded as if he'd been waiting for the question.

"The elders speak of ten families that escaped a terrible fate long ago. They hid away in the mountains. We wear this symbol"—he gestured to his arm that was covered by his white linen cloak—"to remind us to keep looking for the signs. It is said that one day we would need to find the girl with the sign around her neck."

Bazine cleared his throat. "What exactly is this girl supposed to reveal to you?"

Rucain shrugged. "I'm not sure," he said, shifting his travel pack to the other shoulder.

"Then why is it so important to find her if your people are already safe?"

The Sound of the Stones

Rucain took a swig from his water bag. He wiped his mouth and looked at Bazine, narrowing his eyes. "Have you ever felt pulled toward something so strongly that you couldn't ignore it?"

Bazine's lips curved knowingly. "Yes." It was a simple one-word answer, but with it, an unspoken bond was formed.

They continued to walk, only taking small breaks until the sun dipped behind the horizon. They repeated this same pattern for thirty-six more days. They learned much from one another on their journey. Bazine learned that Akira was a brave and competent girl on the verge of womanhood. He learned that although Rucain was often stoic and a man of few words, he was very intelligent, and passionate about their purpose in finding the girl. He believed deeply in a greater meaning to life and their purpose here on earth. They spoke often of the elder traditions and the vague memories that remained of time before the tribes had hidden away. Rucain and Akira learned that Bazine was a kind and easy-tempered young man who was easy to smile and generous of heart.

At about the thirty-day mark Bazine finally trusted them enough to share his dreams. His talent of gravity bending remained a secret, but he shared his desire to find the dark-eyed girl whole-heartedly. They decided that they might indeed be pulled toward finding the same girl, albeit for different reasons. They hunted for small game, and Akira dug for water. They fought off several more sand worms and became a good team for survival in rough terrain. They learned tribe techniques from one another and became genuine friends.

It was the morning of the fortieth day a picture came into view. They stood at a distance for quite some time taking in the scene. The buildings soared high, a silhouette against the sky. None of them had ever seen structures so incredibly fashioned. It seemed almost impossible that such great works could be created with mortal hands. Bazine got a sinking feeling that they would never find who they were looking for, let alone make it in and then back out alive. They could only hope and trust that whatever or whoever had pulled them there would show them the way.

They looked at one another with a quiet understanding. Energy was high and the tension palpable. They did the only thing they could. They started walking toward the outer limits of Krad City, toward the massive human encampment with row upon row of small stone homes.

Breaking Free

Ashra woke with a start when Smirah walked in the room. A sinking feeling settled in the pit of her stomach, and a dim fire revealed the look on Smirah's face, verifying her feeling. Smirah closed the door and leaned against it. She looked at Ashra, clearly struggling to find the right words.

"What is it, Smirah?" Ashra struggled against the blankets to sit up and braced herself for the worst.

"I overheard one of the Bender guards. Your parents are to be killed immediately."

Ashra sucked in a loud breath and stood. The blanket on her foot wouldn't let go and she struggled to unwrap it, eventually breaking free and throwing the cover across the room. It floated rather unsatisfactorily to the floor. She grabbed a pillow and threw that too. It landed with a more gratifying thud. Smirah watched this all while still pressed to the door, her expression never changing. Ashra stood in the middle of the room trying to organize some semblance of thought. She had to do something. She must.

Smirah wasn't finished with her bad news. "They have also been ordered to find and kill anyone you have had extended contact with over your life.

Ashra's blood ran cold. She thought of Haker and the few close friends she had gathered while growing up in the human encampment. She thought of Smirah and wondered if it meant her too.

"We have to do something," Ashra said firmly, her eyes flashing with fear and then anger. Smirah shook her head and lowered her gaze. "No!" Ashra cried, "I will not lie down and wait for my family and friends to die because of what I am!" Her voice broke and tears welled up in her eyes. Smirah's face held defeat. Ashra tried a different tact. "I will die trying then." Her voice came out in a resigned hush. "Will you show me where my parents are?"

Ashra crossed the room to where Smirah stood with her gaze still fixed on the floor. Ashra knelt at her feet and took her hand in her own. "I know your life is on the line, and I have no right to ask for your help, but please, please give me a chance to save them. If nothing else...die

The Sound of the Stones

with them. Give me one last chance to tell them I love them, that I'm sorry for what my life has brought them." Her words came out in a desperate sob.

"We have to hurry. It may already be too late." Smirah's voice was soft and held little encouragement.

Ashra threw on her mining clothes and pulled her hair into a quick bun. She pulled on her boots and threw her pack over one shoulder. "Let's go."

Smirah glanced out the door and turned to Ashra. "The guards are out there. Hide behind this door. Do you remember how to get to the kitchen?" she whispered. Ashra bobbed her head. "Go down that way and I will meet you there outside the kitchen door. Don't get seen," she said, as she walked to the one window in the room. She picked up a small chair and smashed it through the glass, then screamed loudly. Ashra pressed against the wall. The door flew open, barely missing her face. Both Benders rushed in, their staffs at the ready.

"What is going on in here?!" the taller guard demanded, scanning the room, then fixing his eyes on the broken window. Both guards moved toward the shattered glass. Smirah pointed outside, muttering a slew of incoherent words. Ashra slipped carefully from behind the door, out into the hall.

She moved quickly, her heart racing. She willed her boots silent, as they seemed incessantly loud. She counted the lights and doorways as she made the turns that would lead to the kitchen. When she got to the base of the stairs she heard someone walking toward her. She pressed her body against the closest wall and held her breath. The footsteps turned and went in the opposite direction. She waited, her heart beating loudly in her ears. She listened until the footsteps were gone and took a small breath, trying to slow her heartbeat. Just as her breathing got back to almost normal, she heard footsteps coming down the stairs. Her eyes darted and her pulse quickened as she looked for a place to hide. In front of her was the kitchen door. To her right was a dead end and to the left was a hall leading to the unknown. For all she knew she could walk right into a bunch of Krad if she went that direction. *Oh, hey. How's it going, fellas? Nothing to see here.* She was torn. She opted for the dead end, pushing hard against the wall in hopes that she might become one with it. The footsteps came faster. They were only a step or two away. She

184

caught the first glimpse of a foot coming down the staircase. They were plain brown work shoes under brown linen pants. It was Smirah. Ashra sucked air, relieved. Smirah came down the last step, her eyes wild. Ashra pulled from the shadows. Relief washed over Smirah's face.

"We don't have much time. Follow me." She immediately turned, heading down the hall to the left. Ashra followed on her heels. They turned right, down another smaller hall, and Smirah stopped in front of a stairwell leading down into a darker place. They shuffled down the small, poorly lit stairs with quiet, hurried steps.

At the base of the stairs, several metal doors lined a dark hall. Ashra shivered at the thought of her parents trapped there. They stopped at the end of the hall. Smirah opened a small rectangle opening by sliding a metal handle and peered inside.

A small sliver of light flooded into the dark cell and Shara opened her eyes from fitful sleep. Sheed jolted and stood. They crawled toward the opening, clanking their chains behind them. Ashra pressed her face to the slit and sighed.

"Who's there?" Shara's voice trembled.

"Momma?" Ashra called, her voice thick with emotion.

"My baby!" Shara cried.

"Little bean, is that you?" Sheed jockeyed for a position, desperate to catch a glimpse. Their hands reached out of the small slit and Ashra clasped them tightly. Shara mingled a laugh and cry into one strangled sound.

"Can you open the door?" Ashra looked to Smirah expectantly.

"I don't have the key." Smirah's own voice was pinched as she held back tears.

Ashra's eyes darted around for an answer. She recognized the metal box that could be triggered by a crystal key. It was the same kind of technology used to summon Giants. She immediately began to scan the crystals with her mind. If she could change the vibrations in the crystal light sensor would it release the lock? She concentrated. The vibrations she used for modicum modification played over and over in her mind. A series of clicking noises indicated the release of the heavy metal door.

The Sound of the Stones

Rushed footsteps and garbled conversation preceded two guards as they clambered down the stairs. Ashra looked at Smirah, a desperate fear mirrored in their eyes. There was no time for a warm family reunion now. Ashra shoved Smirah into the cell. She closed the door and darkness enveloped them, save a small sliver of light. The guards were getting close. Ashra concentrated on the sensor again, willing it to lock. It did. She glanced over her shoulder at her mother and father, jerking her head toward the darkest corner. They nodded understanding and moved themselves back to their spots, chains dragging. The guards were at the door. Ashra concentrated on the lock mechanism as the guards held the key under its beam of light.

"What's the problem?" one guard asked.

"The lock isn't opening," the second guard answered, his voice pitched in confusion.

"Give me that," the first guard spat. There were a few silent moments, then mumbling curses.

"See?" the second guard said crossly. The first guard let out an exasperated breath.

"Okay, we need a Sensitive to reset the lock."

Their footsteps grew quieter as they climbed the stairs to the upper floor. Ashra let out the breath she was holding.

"They will be back soon, Ashra," Smirah said. The light fell in such a way as to highlight the sadness in her eyes.

Ashra nodded and moved toward her parents. She fell at their feet and they held her. Great heaving sobs, muffled words she could not speak. Unspoken grief for the situation was apparent enough without them. Tears stung Smirah's eyes as she wrapped her arms around herself, rocking gently. They continued to hold one another with the knowledge that those last moments were fleeting and the end for them all. Loving silence would have to be enough.

Meeting Fate

Bazine waited until dusk. The camouflage of night would give them a better chance of slipping in unseen. They prowled the perimeter of the human camp, quietly observing the comings and goings of other humans. He noticed a stark difference between the humble homes of the humans and the soaring palace-like buildings in the distance. It helped him better understand his mother's disdain for the place.

They skirted the entire camp as night fell. They watched, agape, as the Giants came and went from frayed tents. The creatures were unlike anything they had ever seen. Bazine held his breath as a man approached a Giant. They hung on the edge of camp just yards from the scene. Bazine struggled to hear their conversation. He crawled closer.

"We must move now," the Giant growled. He crouched next to the human, his eyes shifting uneasily. Bazine pressed harder into the shadows.

"What do you want me to do?" the man asked, in an equally gruff tone.

"I know what area they keep prisoners. You need to be the lookout. Just let me know when I can make it from the wall to the palace without getting seen. Cause a distraction if need be while I find her."

The man stood quiet for a moment, then shook his head.

"That's not going to be easy." The man said leveling his eyes at the Giant. He sighed and ran a hand down his face as if struggling with a decision.

"She's in trouble. We move tonight. It may already be too late." The Giant stood, dwarfing the man, and looked out toward the soaring buildings in the distance. He walked away without an answer. It was clearly not a question but an order. The man followed.

Bazine closed his eyes. How was it he had happened upon two that would go against the Krad? Could he enlist them for his own cause? He looked up as if to search for an answer. With a nod of his head he went back to gather Rucain and Akira, who were leaning against a fence a few yards away.

"Let's follow them," Bazine whispered and then turned to leave.

The Sound of the Stones

They struggled to keep up and remain hidden. The Giant and the man dodged outside the fence, cutting around the mines to the right. They were two lumbering silhouettes, one tall and one short. The Giant walked hunched, using shadows as a shield. The man walked in front, pausing ever so often to let a Bender pass. He would wave to the Giant when the coast was clear. They continued this pattern until they reached the outside wall of Krad City. Bazine kept his distance, following just close enough to keep them in sight. When they stopped, he stopped. A tall stone wall rose high, surrounding the inner city. They followed it, stopping at the tallest building. Bazine and his two companions waited in darkness a short distance back.

The trip took just under an hour, giving the night time to take full form. He watched as the Giant grasped the twenty-foot wall with his hand and lifted himself so just his eyes peered over the top. He dropped back down and motioned to the man. The man walked over and the Giant lifted him easily to sit atop the wall.

Bazine glanced toward Rucain. His expression was flat but he leaned his head to the side as if asking *what are you going to do?* Bazine shrugged one shoulder, smiled crookedly, and jumped. He landed soft, crouching low. There were crystal lights affixed every ten feet on the inside of the wall, dimly illuminating the courtyard. Bazine maneuvered into the shadow just out of reach of either light. He looked down at his friends. Rucain and Akira watched plain-faced. If they noticed the oddity of his jump they didn't show it.

The other man was also strategically placed between the lights, cloaked in shadow. Bazine signaled for his friends to wait with the wave of a hand. They had no choice in the matter because the wall was too high, having no foothold for them to scale. Slight movement caught Bazine's eye. The Giant pulled himself up and over the wall in one swift motion. He landed quietly, low to the ground, his eyes scanning the yard. The Giant looked up and made eye contact with the man and tipped his head.

In four long strides the Giant made his way across the open courtyard, pressing himself hard against the palace wall. He moved slowly along the wall with his ear almost grazing its surface. He snuffled grunts and sniffed. Bazine watched curiously when the Giant stopped, sniffing between two different spots.

The Giant glanced back toward the man on the wall. He was hidden in the shadows but the Giant seemed to be able to see him. He scanned the courtyard and then the wall again. His eyes glowed an eerie green in a reflection of light.

That's when he saw Bazine. Bazine went stiff and he held his breath. The Giant's eyes narrowed as he stood looking at the unwelcome guest. Sweat trickled down his back and a chill pricked his spine. Bazine tipped his head and motioned with a hand, hoping it was the universal sign for "go ahead." The Giant snuffed a breath, sweeping the yard with his eyes one last time.

Bazine let out a haggard breath and watched. A large, tight fist attached to a bulging arm smashed into the palace wall. Bazine thought that he would very much not like to be on the receiving end of that fist. The hard blow caused a fissure in the wall about five feet high. The Giant pounded again in a different place. He swung two more times and the wall fell. The Giant had landed his blows in such a way that the wall defied its natural tendency to fall away from the assault, instead falling toward him, leaving whoever was inside safe.

Then he saw her. Bazine's mouth hung open and his heart forgot to beat. He could tell, even from this distance. It was the way she moved, her hair, her small frame. But most of all he could feel her when his heart remembered to beat again. There she was. He decided right then and there that it must be, had to be, something guiding him. He did not get here on his own.

The Desperate Flee

They were huddled together in the dark recesses of the cell when they heard a thundering crash. They scrambled back, leaning hard against the inside wall. Three more shuddering quakes gave way to a large crack, gaping at the bottom and thinning as it crawled up the wall. It went silent for a moment and then the wall fell away, landing in the courtyard.

When the dust settled Krank stood just outside, a dark figure. His eyes glowed green as he searched the cell. Ashra stepped forward and relief washed over his face. She thought she very much liked that face, green glowing eyes and all. She looked over at her parents, their faces fixed in disbelief, chains still attached making straight lines toward the fallen wall. Smirah gawped, mouth wide and eyes even wider.

"I know him, I think he's come for us." Ashra said this even as she moved in his direction. She stepped over the toppled wall and scanned the courtyard. No one else was out there as far as she could tell. She surged forward and Krank took a knee. She wrapped her arms around his neck. "Thank you," she said. Krank brought hands to her carefully lest he crush her. She pulled back, tears brimming, and brushed both hands along the sides of his face. "Have you come to help us?" Ashra choked on her words as tears streamed down her face. They were different tears than the ones shed before.

"Yes, but we have to go now. We'll have company soon." His voice was thick with emotion.

Ashra moved to follow but looked back. "My parents are still tethered." Ashra gestured to the fallen wall. Krank reached down and snapped the thick metal chains with one jerk. Smirah and her parents stepped gingerly from the cell and over the broken wall, gathering their chains to keep them from clanking.

"Let's go." Krank turned toward the wall.

They followed him clumsily, struggling to keep up. When they approached the wall, Krank lifted them one by one. Haker was perched on the wall, his arm stretched toward them like a lifeline. His eyes met Ashra's and he nodded as if to say "I'm here for you." Warmth spread in her chest even as the fear of getting caught still lingered.

The Sound of the Stones

Haker helped each of them down the outside of the wall by holding their hands as far as he could lower them. They dropped the remaining ten feet. Shara and Sheed let their chains fall first so they could grasp Haker's hands. Haker anchored his body by allowing his lower half to dangle inward toward the courtyard, distributing his weight toward the rear. It was an awkward display and quite likely amusing to watch with Haker's rear stuck up into the air like an apple, but it worked.

Ashra insisted on going last. She would not leave her parents behind again. Sheed, Shara, and Smirah made it over safely and just as Krank lifted Ashra into Haker's waiting arms they heard shouts. Six Bender guards rounded the far left corner of the palace. They were headed their way, wielding spears and shouting an interesting slew of obscenities.

Haker moved quickly, lowering Ashra to the ground. She hit the ground hard, her teeth rattling. Painful jolts shot up her legs, a not so gentle reminder that she was still alive. Krank cleared the wall, grabbing Haker as he went. A solid thwack and tremors through the ground boasted his arrival.

The first guard bounded the wall in a single leap. He flipped in the air, easily clearing the wall. The guard's landing was softer and not quite as impressive as Krank's, Ashra thought, but the spear pointed toward them was intimidating. She would give him that. Five more guards followed, pointing spears and trapping Ashra and crew against the wall.

"What is the meaning behind this, Giant!?" the first Bender shouted. He inched closer, pressing the tip of his spear to Krank's stomach. The other Benders followed suit. Krank had spears pressed in various places from his neck down. One of the spears rested a little too closely to Krank's more sensitive parts. He jostled his hips, trying to will the spear to move. Though the awkward shimmy was a valiant attempt, it didn't work. He huffed, irritated, and instead reached out, plucking the most offensive Bender from the ground. He dangled there like a worm.

The other guards shifted uncomfortably. Having never intentionally tussled with a Giant they seemed at a loss for what to do next. There were a few more moments of hesitation, giving Ashra time to think inappropriate, but also humorous, things about the Bender wiggling like a worm. It was her downfall. Humorous daydreams often preceded trouble. Another guard slipped behind Krank and grabbed Ashra by the hair, pulling her forcefully from the protection of Krank. Ashra yelped.

Krank flung the worm Bender in his hand, knocking two guards to the ground.

The remaining two Benders jumped simultaneously, aiming spears at the top of Krank's head as they descended. Bazine launched from the wall, intersecting the two airborne guards. The unnecessarily rough guard holding Ashra jerked her hair sideways. She buckled and her knees hit the ground hard. She distractedly acknowledged the pain, but her eyes focused on the stranger who was flying through the air.

Bazine sliced his blade through the air, nicking one Bender on the shoulder. He caught the other Bender in the face with a backward thrust. One guard landed on his stomach with a heavy thud, his arms and legs splayed motionless. The other guard landed on his feet and looked at his affected arm indignantly. Blood seeped from the sliced flesh, appearing black by the light of the moon.

Bazine landed on his feet opposite the two guards, his legs bent at the knees and knife at the ready. The worm guard that Krank had thrown only moments ago was back on his feet charging. He moved quite a bit faster than a worm now, Ashra thought. The guard holding Ashra by the hair seemed distracted as he watched the scene unfold.

Time to move. Don't just sit there. Do something! She reared back on her haunches and with as much force as she could muster at the awkward angle, slammed her head into the guard's nether regions. She heard the air leave him in a pained *oomph*. He doubled over, but managed to keep hold of her hair, using her bun like a handle. His head was within reach so she swung an elbow back, catching him in the face. She felt a satisfactory crunch and the guard let go, stumbling backward into her father's firm grip. Sheed held the guard's arms and Haker grabbed his head, snapping it quickly to the left. The guard went still and slumped to the ground.

Ashra looked back in time to see Krank smash two more guards together. They crashed like cymbals. And then there were two more people fighting for their team. Ashra wondered if they had somehow manifested from the wall.

Akira pressed a spear to the neck of one guard, the cut on his face dripping blood down one cheek. He held Akira's eyes assessing. She stared back impassive. Rucain stabbed his spear toward another guard, but the Bender jumped and his spear caught empty air. Rucain stumbled, unable to stop his forward momentum.

The Sound of the Stones

Bazine pursued the airborne guard, burying his knife in the Bender's neck. Ashra opened her mouth to scream as the last functioning Bender aimed his weapon at the back of Bazine's head. The spear launched with a Bender attached. As he was about to reach his mark another spear pierced the air, impaling the guard in his arm. The Bender dropped his spear and fell to the ground like a brick.

Bazine landed, turning just in time to see Akira drop her arm. She walked over to the stunned guard as if taking a leisurely stroll. As she removed the spear from his arm she kicked him, eliciting a pained yelp. All of the Bender guards were now on the ground either bleeding or dead.

One guard tried to crawl away, leaving a trail of blood on the ground as he went. Krank walked over and without hesitation crushed the guard's skull with a stomp of his foot. The sound of the crunching skull made Shara gag. Smirah grabbed Shara's arm to steady her as she heaved. Sheed turned to Ashra. His eyes were wild, blinking rapidly as he checked her over with clumsy hands. Krank eyed the humans cagily. Then he turned his stare on the strangers. Krank opened his mouth as if to speak but was cut off.

"I don't mean to break up this party, but we need to move." Haker glanced over his shoulder. "Now."

Ashra swatted her father's hands away, assuring him she was, in fact, okay and can you please tend to mom while she's puking. She turned toward the strangers. The girl looked young. The white-haired man looked to be related and quite a bit older. Then her eyes met his, the one who moved like a Bender. He was looking at her. Even in the moonlight she could see the violet-blue hue. The familiarity of that color felt like a smack in the face. She opened her mouth to say something but nothing came out.

Krank was already moving and grunted for them to follow. Sheed and Shara gathered their chains and began an awkward shuffle. Bazine tore his eyes from Ashra and noticed. He placed a hand on Sheed's shoulder and knelt at their feet. With three solid taps and a wiggle of his blade the shackle fell loose. He repeated the motion three more times, releasing Sheed and Shara from the chains. He glanced up, his mouth turning up at the corners as he stood. He looked to Krank.

"Lead the way, giant one." Bazine gestured forward with one hand.

194

Krank narrowed his eyes at the stranger for half a heartbeat and sniffed, then moved swiftly into the dark of the night, seven humans following close behind.

The vibrations from the modicums of her parents, Smirah, and Haker were very readable, like glowing beacons of the night's events. She couldn't, however, read any vibrations from the three strangers. She thought perhaps the violet-blue-eyed stranger was Krad based on his movements during the fight, but there was no doubt whose side he was on. *Why?*

The other two white-haired strangers did not have modicums. That was the big question swirling in Ashra's mind. How was it possible that these humans did not have modicums? She pondered these things between stumbling steps as they skirted the perimeter of the human camp, moving toward the mines.

The modicums were an issue. She needed to fix them so their vibrations weren't sounding like warning bells. She had never attempted to quiet a modicum completely. Only once had she silenced a crystal and the result lay nestled on her chest and hung from a chain.

They moved painstakingly slow, dodging like an accordion through the shadows. She was torn in concentration as questions nagged. With her mind pulled in three directions, she attempted to fix the modicums, keep from falling, and most importantly avoid getting captured. She focused inward, concentrating on her own modicum. It was no easy task. She sang the necessary mixture of vibrations in her mind. She stumbled on a rock and lost her tenuous grip on the modicum. She bit her lip, muffling a yelp as her knee hit the ground, then picked herself up and kept moving. After the third attempt she felt her modicum surrender and lay quiet.

Having a bit more confidence that it could be done, she focused on her mother. She was successful on her second attempt with Shara. She followed the same pattern of concentration three more times. All modicums lay perfectly quiet, giving off no readable vibrations. She felt somewhat giddy at the accomplishment and grinned stupidly in the dark. If she could do this for herself and four other humans could she do it for the others? Perhaps not today but in the future. If she could, the humans might stand a fighting chance.

Descending into Darkness

They paused just short of the back entrance to the mine. They crouched in the shadows and scanned the mine grounds. There was no activity. Krank looked back and pointed toward a passage in the mine that led to the deep. He made his way toward the opening. They followed quickly and glanced around, feeling exposed despite the cover of darkness.

Ashra was the second one to reach the mine and Krank ushered her inside, placing himself in front, ready to receive the rest. As they filtered in, Krank placed them each behind his sturdy frame. Bazine, Rucain, and Akira entered last and found Krank forming a barrier between them and the others.

Krank's voice came out eerily quiet. "Who are you?" There was no doubt he was prepared to kill three more to protect the ones behind him.

"Bazine." His voice matched Krank's quiet confidence. "This is Rucain and Akira." He gestured toward his travel mates. Rucain and Akira stood stoically, seemingly unaffected by the whole ordeal. "We mean you no harm." Bazine swept his gaze from the Giant to the people behind him.

Ashra watched, her dark eyes narrowing in curiosity. His eyes lingered on hers perhaps a moment too long. She looked away quickly, stepping forward. Perhaps it was crazy but she trusted them. Things were happening all around her and they seemed to be lining up for something bigger. Just an hour ago she knew she was done for, but now… She laid a gentle hand on Krank's arm. His body was tense and his stare didn't waver, but his muscles relaxed slightly under her touch. Bazine turned his eyes back to Krank. A moment of tense silence broke with a low growl from the back of Krank's throat. The sound of a distant shout changed the subject.

"Let's move," Krank gruffed, herding them further back down the tunnel. They moved with stumbling urgency until they reached the deep mine lift. It was as good of a plan as any in the dire situation. They piled on board without question. Krank threw the lift initiator and they began a slow descent. The grinding metal was entirely too loud, Ashra thought. She held her breath, hoping the guards had not heard. It was futile though; of course they heard. Shouts and footsteps grew louder as they

The Sound of the Stones

entered the mine tunnel. They continued to descend, the darkness enveloping them.

They listened to the muffled shouts from above, but the heavy metal clanking disguised their words. Ashra began to think they might actually get down to the bottom without interception when the lift came to a jolting halt. *This isn't good.* They sat, trapped and completely at the mercy of the guards above. The lift controls were at the top or at the bottom. Nothing in the way of control lay within the lift itself. That was an unfortunate design, Ashra thought.

She bent to retrieve a light from her pack so they could see, but her hand stopped when she realized it wasn't there. It was still back in the cell at the palace. *Well, of course it is.* The cards were stacked against them and Ashra's hope began to wane. Then a small light filled the lift. Bazine held in his hand a small piece of iridescent crystal. Its vibrant glow allowed Ashra's hope to wax again.

Then it happened. Metal crunched up above and the lift began to rise. It wouldn't be long and they would be face to face with a plethora of angry Bender guards. They had fought off six altogether. That was hard enough even with a Giant. They were done for.

Krank bent the metal screen that protected the occupants from the outside lift chains and gripped them in each hand. The gears moaned in protest as the lift continued to rise. Krank's arms pressed hard against the top of the opening. The metal bit into his skin and Ashra winced as a small stream of blood trickled down his arm. Krank's face showed no sign of struggle, though, and his grip held steady.

The moaning gears screamed high and mournful before relenting. A crunching noise indicated Krank's success as the lift came to a jolting stop. It jogged when the chain slipped through his fits. He tightened his grip and the jarring motion stopped. After a few tries, Krank succeeded in equalizing the pressure to keep their descent relatively smooth. The lift weight was immense, but he managed to lower it slowly to the bottom. It wasn't safety he was lowering them to. He was giving them all a fighting chance to survive.

It had been weeks ago they had turned them on, but the crystals still emitted a yellow glow. It was possible more violent rock-eating beasts lurked somewhere in the passageways. The stale air triggered images. They pranced through Ashra's mind contemptuously, but there was no time to second-guess. They had to chance that danger to avoid the more imminent peril up above.

"We have to go where it happened, Krank." Ashra's voice echoed in the deep as if confirming her statement. She trained a defiant stare on Krank. He snuffed out his nose and wrinkled his face, obviously not on board with that suggestion. "Krank, when we were there, the wall was cracked during the struggle. I saw the crystal pocket."

She paused and looked at Bazine. "It was like the one you hold there, like these on my pendant." She touched the pendant with a gentle hand. Bazine looked from the pendant to the crystal in his hand. A curious emotion crossed Akira's and Rucain's faces; Ashra noticed but continued anyway. "I felt a warm breeze from the cracks in the wall." She glanced down the path, then said with a tone that managed to sound both hopeful and anxious, "It could be our way out."

"It won't be long before they find another way down," Haker interjected.

"He's right, we have to move now to stay ahead of them," Bazine said forcefully, then made a placating gesture when Krank shot him a withering glare.

Krank motioned an *after you* gesture to Ashra, conceding to her plan. Ashra snorted. They moved quickly, making much better time than her mining crew had. A life on the line was an excellent motivator and a great distraction from the pain of moving faster than your body wants. They didn't stop for breaks. They pushed on, their bodies aching and lungs burning from the speed with which they moved. Ashra felt the crystal calling. It was more intense this time. It was reaching out, seeking her, and each painful step was an answer to its call.

The Way Out

They traveled three hours before stopping. They slumped heavily to the ground, panting, eagerly waiting turns for one of the three water bags the strangers had. They sat in sweaty, gasping silence. Krank walked down the path in the direction they had come. Without warning his fist met the ceiling with a loud crack. Everyone watched in stunned silence as he made his way casually back toward them. As he approached, a rock separated from the ceiling and fell to the ground behind him with an emphatic rumble. Everyone stared at the obstacle and then looked at Krank for explanation. Krank shrugged.

"Just giving them something to do when they get down here," he said, with a defiant glint in his eye.

Ashra giggled despite the situation. Bazine's lips turned up at the corners. He offered Krank a drink. He refused the drink politely, Ashra thought, in that he didn't growl. She suspected he was saving what little water they had, knowing his stamina could outlast any of theirs. Ashra watched Bazine, enjoying the smile on his face. She realized in her enjoyment a smile lingered on her own lips. *Why am I smiling?* Then he looked at her. His expression turned serious. She felt a strange flash of emotion and it wasn't clear if it was transferred from him or of her own accord. She glanced down at her hands, studying the dirt smears.

"What's your name, dark-eyed girl?" he asked, and sat next to her.

"Ashra," she answered lamely and braved a glance. His smile was back. He leaned against the wall and stretched one leg, keeping the other bent. He rested one arm over the bent knee, dangling the water bag from his hand. His demeanor was so disarming that she found herself relaxing.

"Ashra." He tested her name. She liked the way he said it. He hadn't yet taken a drink but offered her the bag instead. "It suits you."

She noticed a dimple on his left cheek. *Why are you noticing that?* She took hold of the bag and concentrated hard on not thinking about the dimple. His fingers brushed against hers, sending a slow tingling heat up her arm. *What the heck?* She inhaled a small breath and tugged at the water bag. He didn't let it go but neither did she. She looked up from her hand. His smile was curved to one side now and he lifted one dark

The Sound of the Stones

brow. She quirked her own brow and pursed her lips, willing herself not to care that she found even his eyebrow intriguing. He chuckled softly and released the bag.

"Well, of course it suits her. We named her that," Sheed stated irritably, from the other side of the tunnel. Shara thrust a water bag at her husband and smiled sweetly at Bazine. He took the water and drank deeply, one big eye glued to Bazine.

Haker grunted and stood, making much more of a production at brushing dust from his backside than necessary. "Let's go."

At the pace they were keeping they would reach the destined spot in a couple of hours. At Haker's insistence they pushed ahead, each of them concentrating on the next step and their next breath. After another two hours of a grueling pace, the smell of death assaulted them. They were close. They all slowed in quiet understanding. As they approached, the scene of the gruesome tale unfolded. The blood puddles, splatters, and smear-stained rocks had turned brown and crusty. The slain bodies had been trampled, leaving them crushed and rotting. The remaining rock eaters had obviously been there to investigate. The rock eater carcass was pushed several yards, in what Ashra assumed was a futile attempt to revive it. Ashra suppressed the urge to puke. Shara gasped and covered her mouth with her hand. Smirah clucked her tongue. The others looked on with varied expressions of disgust, except for Rucain and Akira, who just stood there.

"What happened down here?" Sheed bellowed, his voice echoing in the stillness.

Krank moved toward the rock eater carcass.

"We ran into some trouble," he said. He poked the dead creature with his toe, his lip curling in disgust. Ashra walked toward the far wall that contained the imploring crystal, trying desperately to avoid the carnage. She leaned in and felt a warm breeze brush her face. She moved loose pieces of rock carefully to reveal the crystal. Its colors seemed to dance, matching a vibration that only Ashra could hear. Everyone watched silently as she ran her fingers along the various crystal shards.

Her voice was hushed and somber. "Krank, will you open the wall?"

Krank nodded and with several cracks of his fist the wall tumbled away, revealing an opening to a tremendous cavern. Crystals dotted the walls and ceiling of the newly opened cave, causing an effect much like glowing bugs in the night sky. Ashra leaned over the edge. Colored lights reflected from an underground water source in a colorful display.

"Oh," was all she could say at the breathtaking sight.

She hadn't felt them all approach until Bazine stepped up beside her, sending that strange warmth up her arm where he brushed up against her. Their collective silence held wonder at the scene but also questions, as the base of the open cavern was at least one hundred feet down.

"How will we get down?" Ashra voiced the question everyone was thinking. She glanced at Bazine and he grinned. He scratched the back of his head sheepishly, shrugged a shoulder, and then bounded into the cavern. She watched gape-faced as he scaled the wall from one jutting rock to another, crisscrossing as he descended. When he reached the bottom, he ascended just as easily. He perched on the ledge and held out a hand to Ashra. It was then that she realized her mouth was hanging open and closed it.

"Oh, no you don't," Sheed said, placing himself between his daughter and Bazine. Shara tugged on her husband's arm and cleared her throat meaningfully. He grumbled something under his breath but allowed her to pull him sideways.

"I won't let you fall." Bazine's hand trembled slightly and his eyes were serious. Ashra cocked her head to the side. She looked him over, peered over the side of the opening, and shrugged. She took his hand, and in one fluid motion he swung her around to his back. He felt sturdy and warm and she wrapped her arms around his neck. "Don't let go," he whispered, while stepping off the ledge.

Ashra felt like a bird. Her hair caught the wind and she felt a moment of pleasurable weightlessness. But this was quickly followed by a ridiculous urge to climb upward as her stomach crawled up her throat in a desperate attempt to escape her mouth. She wrapped tighter to his neck. In doing so, her nose inconveniently clashed with the back of his head. She whooped a yelp and pulled his hair. He gurgled something that was not quite a word. They landed at an awkward angle but Bazine managed to keep them upright despite Ashra's ever so helpful foot lodged in his thigh. She slid from his back and made her own production of brushing dirt from her backside while studiously avoiding Bazine's eyes. Bazine turned and placed his hands on her shoulders.

The Sound of the Stones

"Are you okay?" His eyes twinkled with amusement. He managed not to smile too wide when she sniffed and touched her nose to make sure it was still attached. It was, in fact, still there, though throbbing and likely twice the size it was before.

"Yes, thank you." Ashra said this primly, as if some semblance of dignity could be mustered from her tone. That brought a full-fledged smile to his face. He threw back his head and laughed. She wanted so badly to be mad at him for laughing, but she couldn't due to the fact that she enjoyed the sound of it. She smirked.

"We survived, didn't we? I told you not to let go. You were perfect." He winked and bounded back up the cliff. Even though he was teasing her, and even though her nose still hurt, she stood watching him with a stupid grin fixed firmly to her face.

The Underground River

Krank proved to be an asset as well. He shared the task of transporting the crew down the jagged steep wall. Sheed proved something else, to be stubborn.

"A little help?" Bazine asked, eyeing Sheed's large frame. Krank grunted amused.

"Oh, no! I'm not going down like the others." Sheed waved one hand flat in rebuke as if the gesture would seal the deal. Krank snorted, gathering Sheed in one arm. Sheed gave a startled yelp but held tight. Krank scaled the rocks with one free hand. Bazine watched the scene with a quiet smile.

Sheed's feet hit the ground and he straightened, brushing wrinkles from his clothes. He sniffed and cleared his throat. He looked at his wife. Shara's eyes danced with amusement, her mouth turned up at the corners. He sighed and returned the smile.

There were a few moments of silence as they all looked around. Sheed whistled. "Will you look at this?"

They all stood wide-eyed. The cavern rose two hundred feet into a sweeping domed ceiling. A large lake of clear water reflected the colors of the thousand iridescent crystals, which dotted the cave walls like stars. The lake narrowed to the south into an underground river. The crystals gave off enough light to illuminate the cavern in dim wavering colors. There were steep banks on either side where the lake narrowed into a river, making it impassable on foot. By water then, Bazine thought to himself. Krank busied himself sniffing out new smells. Bazine and Rucain scanned the cavern for anything that might be of use to make a raft.

Ashra closed her eyes and breathed deeply. She tilted her head from side to side. Bazine stole a glance. Even as the welt on his head still thrummed a reminder, the patterns the light made on her face, emphasizing the line of her jaw, the shape of her mouth, made him forget it. He shook his head and looked away. He couldn't keep his eyes from straying back to her even in light of the dire situation they were in. He felt like a kid, awkward and desperate. He looked up from his

The Sound of the Stones

thought to make sure she was still there. She was looking at him now, eyes curious.

"We will need to travel by water," Rucain said, echoing Bazine's earlier thought.

Bazine nodded and focused on debris lying on the bank. Odd dome-shaped objects littered the cavern floor. They were tucked into crevices and covered in silt, as if washed to shore long ago. Upon closer inspection they looked to be large shells from animals since decayed. They varied in size, ranging from about one foot in diameter to the largest Bazine saw, seven feet. The shell dipped in the center, the hard-coated surface creating what might be a watertight seal. Some of them were badly cracked, but a few remained whole. Bazine picked up one of the smaller shells and placed it on the water. The gentle current swept the shell downstream. It stayed upright.

"It could work," Bazine said more to himself than anyone. Krank, who had been sniffing all corners of the cavern, snorted when he saw the tiny shell bobbing slowly downstream. "Well, maybe not for you, big guy," Bazine said dryly. Krank pressed his lips in a hard line and grunted. Ashra eyed Krank's expression and laughed. It exploded off the cavern walls, happiness in the midst of a trial. Krank's expression softened.

Rucain moved to the edge of the water and flipped a bigger shell, grunting as he turned it. He waded in the water and tentatively climbed inside, using his spear to keep it from tipping. Once his weight was distributed, he pushed off with his spear. The makeshift boat remained stationary by stabbing the river bottom with his spear. It worked. Rucain had what might be considered a self-satisfied look on his face as the corners of his mouth curled upward fractionally. He floated there, the edges of the shell a safe distance from the water surface. Two people could easily fit in the larger shells. Sheed would need one to himself and Krank would need to follow on foot, but it wasn't a bad plan.

"I'm at a disadvantage," Bazine said, breaking the group's observations of Rucain. "I have given you our names"—he gestured to Rucain and Akira—"but I only know Ashra's."

"Krank," Krank said flatly, not taking his eyes off of Rucain, who was now practicing moving from side to side.

"Sheed, and this is my wife, Shara. We're Ashra's parents." Sheed shot Bazine a pointed look, emphasizing the word "parents" as if the word could disintegrate him that very moment. Bazine bowed his head respectfully and noticed the small curve playing at corners of Shara's lips. She dug her hand into Sheed's arm, all the while keeping a pleasant expression. Sheed furrowed two large brows and sniffed. It was abundantly clear that Shara was Ashra's mother. They had the same eyes and shape of mouth. Shara's hair was dark brown, whereas Ashra's was more auburn. Perhaps when Sheed had more hair, it was auburn too. It was no small blessing that Ashra did not look much like Sheed, especially when he made faces like the one he was making now.

"This is Smirah." Ashra interrupted his thoughts. "And this"— Ashra moved toward Haker and rested a hand on his shoulder—"is Haker." Ashra beamed at him. Haker cleared his throat and tipped his head curtly. "A bit of advice." Ashra leaned toward Bazine and pointed at Krank. "You don't want to get on his bad side," she whispered conspiratorially. Krank grunted in agreement.

"I'll take your word for it," Bazine agreed.

"Why did you help us?" Haker's voice ran cold. He leveled his eyes at Bazine, and the air grew tense. Bazine's face dropped and he glanced from Rucain to Akira. Neither of them offered any indication of helping as they stared blankly like statues. Bazine scratched the back of his neck and nodded.

"The truth is, we saw you two." He gestured to Haker and then Krank. "We aren't from around here and I figured you might be good guys since you seemed to be plotting against the Krad." He shrugged a shoulder. "I couldn't just walk away once I saw what you were doing." He glared at Haker. "Look, we helped you... As to the reason we came here"—he shook his head firmly—"that story will take more time to tell than we have to spare."

Making Their Way

Krank waded into the water, his face scrunched in anticipation. His shoulders relaxed and the lines on his face lessened. The water was obviously not so cold as he thought. Four large shells carried the rest. They tethered the vessels by holding on to the edges by hand. This was not as easy as one might think. A stretched arm against bobbing current was irritating, Ashra thought. Though probably less irritating than the Krad would be should they catch up, she reminded herself.

Rucain steadied the aquatic caravan with quiet regard. His eyes scanned as his hand clutched a spear at the ready. He'd given Akira's spear to Bazine, who held the rear boat. Bazine stabbed the river bottom on one side and then the other in tandem to keep from fishtailing. Krank took careful steps so as not to capsize the end boat in his wake. The water was waist deep for him. It would have been uncomfortable had the water not been tepid.

The cavern passage narrowed and widened in various places as they made their way. The cave seemed alive. Crystal glowed like colorful stars, their reflections dancing on the water in lilting patterns. It really was magical. Ashra alone heard the music they sang. She closed her eyes and tilted her face upward. She could actually feel the light patters across her face like an echo. The vibrations were familiar, like a song you've heard before but couldn't quite remember the lyrics. Peace washed over her.

Ashra heard quiet conversation coming from ahead. Shara and Smirah were speaking in hushed tones while Haker quietly held his shell to the lead. Her father sat backward, easily reaching his hand to the shell in front, unabashedly staring at Bazine.

Bazine stood in the middle of the shell, keeping their path steady and carefully avoiding Sheed's steady glare. It was mildly amusing to Ashra and a slight distraction from the burning sensation crawling up her arm. Her arm span was not as long as her father's and she struggled to grip the other shell. Krank fell further behind and Ashra suspected it was a quiet mercy on her behalf. *I do love you, Krank.* The wakes lessened and she was grateful.

Ashra's mind eventually settled back to the unanswered questions of the new members of their group. *We aren't from around here.* She

The Sound of the Stones

played Bazine's words over in her mind. He had glanced at her meaningfully when he said "as to the reasons." *Why?*

They traveled for a couple of hours. The cavern yawned wider, the steep banks becoming a gentle slope. Rucain pulled his boat to the bank, tugging the rest behind.

"Let's rest here for a while," Rucain said. There was a collective sigh of relief.

They pulled the shells to shore. The group stretched and shuffled, making necessary adjustments. Akira knelt by the waterside and brought water to her lips. She smelled the water, tasted it with the tip of her tongue, and took a sip, swishing it in her mouth. She closed her eyes and nodded as she swallowed. She took out her water bag and filled it with river water.

Ashra watched her curiously. She seemed so young, her light hair flowing around her face like a cloud. Her eyes were the color of ice, sitting big in her face, and her lips so full they seemed to dominate her narrow chin. Akira noticed Ashra watching. Ashra smiled. Akira returned her smile but her eyes showed hesitation. In Akira's unguarded moments she looked like a child. In moments of danger, like the ones they just faced, she looked fierce, older.

"Akira, how old are you?" Ashra asked.

Akira's eyes flicked wide and then narrowed. She rose proudly and lifted her chin.

"Thirteen," she said, keeping her ice blue eyes steady.

Ashra blinked and then nodded slowly.

"I only ask because at first I guessed you around that age, but you carry yourself in such a way I second-guessed myself. The way you fought…I thought you might be older than you look."

Akira searched Ashra's eyes for a quiet moment and then a broad smile spread across her lips, revealing her youth.

***

Rucain watched the exchange from a distance as he rummaged through his pack.

"How do our food rations look?" Bazine asked as he walked up behind. He followed Rucain's line of sight.

Ashra and Akira were laughing at something and pointing at various things in the cave. The contrast between the two standing side by side was striking. Akira's hair was bright and free flowing, her eyes light, dancing with amusement. Ashra's hair was dark, escaping her tattered bun in rebellion, her eyes full of fire and secrets.

"We have some dried meat and bread. Enough to sustain us for a day or two if we're careful," Rucain said, pulling the supplies from his bag.

"Good, want me to get some water boiling?" Bazine asked, pulling his eyes from the girls to look at supplies. Rucain grunted assent, but didn't meet his eyes. "Are you well?" Bazine knelt down so that he was eye level with Rucain, but he still wouldn't look up.

Rucain sniffed. "I'm not sure what I expected. But this..." He swept his hand across and looked up, indicating the lot of people and one Giant. He shook his head and looked back down. He stayed quiet for a moment more, then brought his eyes to Bazine. "The way you fought...you..." He stopped abruptly, his eyes asking a question he could not finish.

Bazine rubbed the bridge of his nose and cleared his throat. "Fair enough. Let's wait until we gather to eat so I only have to tell the story once."

A Story Told

The group gathered around the bubbling pot as if drawn by an unseen force. The women made small talk while the men watched quietly, attending to small things in attempt to appear busy. Krank lounged near them, unabashedly staring at the cave wall as the crystals put on their show.

Bazine spooned soup into the only three bowls they had and passed out the last of the flatbread. They each took turns dipping the bread and taking small drinks of soup. It was quiet. It was the kind of quiet that was loaded with unsaid words. Questions brewed in everyone's mind now that the imminent danger was quelled, but no one seemed able to speak their thoughts aloud.

"I come from a land far to the south." Bazine cut the silence like a knife, his gaze cast toward the glowing heat of the crystal fire. All eyes fell to him, anticipation palpable. "The man who helped raise me in the absence of my father tells of a group of twelve families who broke free long ago." Bazine lifted his gaze to meet the eyes of everyone except Krank, who was still staring into the cave. "He told me of a time when things happened in dreams, bad things...unspeakable things." He ran a hand through his hair. "He said that the original families escaped. That they were able to break away because they didn't dream."

Akira and Rucain had heard this story before but they sat patiently waiting for his cue. "My friends here"—Bazine tilted his head toward Rucain and Akira—"come from a land to the west. They come from a different group who broke free from those oppressions."

"Our elders tell of ten families who escaped. We learned to drink tea made from the leaves of frisper. It kept us from dreaming." Rucain shrugged a shoulder. He opened his mouth to continue but was cut off.

"You move like a Bender," Krank said, not taking his eyes from the cave ceiling. Bazine's heartbeat quickened and he swallowed. He nodded slowly. "I was always different growing up. Not so much outwardly. But I dreamed. My mother told me never to tell anyone. That people wouldn't understand. When I turned fifteen I started to notice...other things. I could scale walls, but not like the other boys. I could feel energy coursing through me. Like my body sensed the earth's pulls and pushes."

The Sound of the Stones

It was the first time he had ever voiced aloud what it felt like, and he felt exposed. He looked up, searching for understanding. Their faces were unreadable, except for one. Ashra looked at him with what could only be compassion, as if she knew what it was like to be different. That look gave him the strength to go on.

"My mother was found on the outskirts of our land twenty-one years ago. She was with child and unconscious. She woke when she gave birth to me, but she didn't remember who she was or how she'd gotten there. At least...that's what she told them." He paused and looked down. The air felt heavy and he took several breaths, willing himself to go on.

"Nonsomni is my home," he said, raising his eyes and chin defiantly. "But my mother is from Krad City."

"How is that even possible?" Sheed bellowed. Shara placed a gentle hand on his arm to hush him. Bazine nodded respectfully and continued.

"Her sister fell victim in a dream and became pregnant. One of the Krad helped sneak my mother into the place where her sister was held. She met a guard and"—he made a motion with his hand, not sure how to put the next part—"they became well aquatinted." He dropped his hand and gaze to his lap.

"You have your mother's eyes," Smirah said softly. "Ratha is your mother, isn't she?"

Bazine blinked stupidly. Smirah continued in an attempt to erase the blank stare from his face.

"She is an old friend of mine from childhood. She told me she was in trouble before she disappeared but wouldn't tell me any details. I never knew what happened but..." Her voice trailed off and she looked at Bazine as if seeing him for the first time. "Wait, are you saying your father was a Bender guard? Haker asked incredulously.

"Yes," Bazine answered shortly.

"No." Haker shook his head and ran a hand down his beard. "They don't have children. None of those mongrels have ever had children, and you're telling me your mother bore the child of a Bender and you're him?" Haker asked the question again as if he could elicit a different answer.

"I've only ever seen three humans with eyes the color of his. I'd bet my life he's her son," Smirah said, shooting Haker a reproachful scowl. Haker looked at her for half a moment, grunted, and crossed his arms. Krank rose to his elbow, intrigued.

"That's not all," Bazine said irritably, glaring at Haker. His eyes shifted to Ashra and his expression softened. "In my dreams, I saw you." Bazine held Ashra's stare. The words hung there for a moment.

Ashra shifted uncomfortably. "Me?" she asked, blinking rapidly as if doing so could unlock the sixth sense of omniscient understanding.

"For about a year now." Bazine shrugged. "At first I just ignored them. But the dreams got more intense. You were in trouble. I had to find you." His voice was thick with emotion, his eyes willing Ashra to understand. She looked on mutely. "I told my mother about the dreams. She finally broke down and told me I was dreaming of the place she came from. That's when she told me who I am and how she escaped." Bazine scrubbed a hand down his face. "I told her I had to come find you. It wasn't a choice really. She didn't like the idea but..." He shrugged again as if to say "that's the story, take it or leave it."

"But how did you know I was real? That it wasn't just" — Ashra made an inarticulate gesture with one hand — "I don't know, just a dream?"

"I didn't." His answer was simple. He didn't know, not for sure. He had hoped though.

"Well, what about these two?" Sheed asked abruptly, gesturing to Rucain and Akira.

"I met them on my way to find Ashra. Akira here saved my life when I was almost eaten by a sand worm." Akira grinned, showing teeth. "They convinced me I needed help on my quest." Bazine tipped his chin toward Rucain. "We discovered that we had something in common. Show them." Rucain pulled back his cloak, revealing his armband. At the same time Bazine undid the top of his shirt, pulling it down to reveal his mark. Bazine smiled. "So here we are."

A Song Is Sung

Ashra clasped a hand to her pendant. It pulsed, matching the crystals embedded in the cavern walls. Her face went numb and her head swam. She took shallow breaths, her eyes darting between the armband and Bazine's mark. The pendant matched them. The vibrations grew stronger. It was almost more than she could bear and she braced her hands on the ground as she swayed.

The water behind Akira began to lap at the bank. Small sprays lifted from the water's surface as if dancing to an unheard melody. A breeze swept around Rucain, lifting his white hair in gentle strands. Ashra's heart pounded in her chest so hard that she thought it might burst. The vibrations grew so strong that she could no longer hold herself upright. She slumped to the side, resting her body against her father.

"What's happening?" Ashra managed to whisper.

Water sprays swirled around Akira and her eyes rolled back. Her chin lifted and her body became limp, held aloft by an invisible force. She broke forth in a familiar lilting song. A song that until now had no lyrics.

What once was light turned into dark
Don't worry, little one
The darkness will not always be
Don't worry, little one
When time has come to set you free
Don't worry, little one
The signs I send you in due time
Don't worry, little one
When earth cries out in colored song
Don't worry, little one
She wears the sign around her neck
Don't worry, little one
Trust in me, I'll set you free
Don't worry, little one
Follow her into the light
Don't worry, little one
She'll break the chains, I'll meet you there
Don't worry, little one

The Sound of the Stones

She wears the sign, a torch of life
Don't worry, little one

It was the wordless lullaby all mothers hummed to their children. Akira sang the words and they pierced the air, bleeding into the mind and body of those around her. As the last words rang out Akira's eyes regained focus and her body shuddered. The water fell back to the river and the wind stilled. Akira trembled, eyes wide. She sat on the ground with a heavy thud. Rucain crouched beside her, speaking softly so that only she could hear.

Ashra pushed herself up, rubbing her hands over her face. Her cheeks were wet from tears she didn't even realize she was shedding.

"I don't understand," she managed. "What does this mean?" She looked from face to face but no one had words. They sat motionless. The memory of the song echoed in the silence, leaving more questions than answers in its wake.

Ashra rose but didn't feel her legs. Her face was still numb and her hands felt cold. She put one foot in front of the other and walked off down the bank. Bazine started to follow, but he felt pressure on his shoulder. He looked back to meet Krank's eyes, expecting an angry stare. Krank shook his head gently.

"Just give her time," he said.

Sheed and Shara eyed her warily. Ashra walked a short distance and slumped to the ground, hugging her knees to her chest. She rocked gently back and forth, tears freely flowing. Bazine's heart constricted at the sight. He looked at Krank. He too was watching her, worry evident in his deep-set eyes.

"Can't you do something?" But even as the words left his mouth Bazine felt ridiculous.

Krank let out a heavy sigh and walked in her direction, the ground vibrating softly under his feet.

Comfort Given, a Gift Unleashed

Krank approached as quietly as he could manage. He paused next to Ashra and waited for her to look up. She did, managing a small sad smile. He sat next to her and mimicked her posture. She glanced at him and did a double take. He was hugging his knees to his chest and she giggled despite herself. Krank gave her what she had learned to be a smile though it looked like a menacing grimace.

"It had been a very long time since anyone had smiled at me," he said quietly, his troubled eyes looking out over the water. "The first time you smiled at me, it was like I could breathe." He gave a snuff that Ashra knew to be his laugh. "You're like a light, Ashra." He shook his head. "It's no wonder they were all looking for you."

Ashra touched his arm and sighed. "I'm scared, Krank."

"I won't leave you." His words lingered in the air, his deep timbre resonating through her bones. She felt a small reassurance at his closeness but confusion and doubt still nagged. Where were they supposed to go? What was she supposed to do? Nothing was clear. Ashra drifted to sleep next to the big cranky Giant who had promised never to leave. The ancient song that now had words played over and over in her mind.

***

She woke to the sound of girlish giggles. Krank had slept sitting upright, his hand draped across her to keep her warm. Her lips curved amused and she stood, careful not to disturb him and his great growling snores. She walked toward, Akira who was kneeling at the water's edge. As she got closer she saw the source of Akira's amusement.

Small sprays of water danced from the surface in unnatural spatters beneath her hand. As she pulled her hand up, a tiny spray followed her hand as if attached. When she dropped her hand, the water spray fell, swallowed by the river.

Ashra's foot caught a stone as she approached. Akira jerked her head toward Ashra, her eyes wide. A smile spread across her lips.

"Watch this." She held her hand over the water again, just above the surface. She pulled her hand up ever so slightly. A small spray of water

The Sound of the Stones

lifted to her hand. She moved her hand to the side; the water followed. She shifted back to the other side and it followed again.

"How did you do that?" Ashra asked, her voice sounding ridiculously high-pitched.

"I really can't explain it," Akira answered, her voice pitched high and ridiculous as well. "I've never done this before. I woke up and came over to rinse my face and the water followed my hands when I reached in!" Her voice got louder in her excitement, causing others to snort and stir from slumber.

"That's amazing," Ashra said, trying to keep her voice quiet.

"Do you think it has something to do with last night?" Akira asked, her face drawn in serious contemplation. Ashra pressed her lips in a hard line and shook her head. Last night still felt like a dream. The question felt like a cold slap of reality.

"I'm sure I don't know," she said dryly and rubbed her eyes. Bazine padded up behind them.

"Good morning," he said through a wide stretch. Ashra jumped and inhaled, then coughed when she sucked spit down the wrong way. Akira giggled. Ashra shot her a look. Akira cleared her throat, looking back at the water to play with the spray. Bazine froze mid-stretch, his eye widening. He watched her for a long moment and then looked back to Ashra. Ashra shrugged and snorted.

"Well, that's interesting," he said.

"Isn't it?" Ashra agreed, hugging her arms around herself. She didn't mean to look forlorn. But the way Bazine was looking at her with a clinched jaw, she assumed she must look a mess.

"I'm fine, and no, I don't know what that all meant last night. And I have no idea what this means." She gestured toward Akira, who was still giggling. The waterspouts were getting taller as she practiced. Bazine nodded, opened his mouth as if to speak, then closed it. He cleared his throat and ran his hands through his hair.

"I'm glad you're okay." His expression was a mixture of embarrassment and honest concern. Ashra felt a twinge of guilt for cutting him off from whatever it was he was going to say. Her eyes softened.

"I'm sorry, Bazine. Thank you." She managed a small smile. He didn't smile back but held her eyes. She felt the weight of his stare and began to feel warmth pool in her stomach. It was then that her stomach gave a loud, hungry growl. It was so loud she could swear it echoed off the cavern walls. She blinked. Bazine grinned.

"Come." He held out a hand. "Let's feed the beast," he said through soft laughter. Ashra swatted his hand away but couldn't help but laugh too.

***

Everyone was busy with breakfast and readying themselves for another day of travel. Ashra had smiled for a short time while they all ate but as time neared for them to leave she grew quiet. Bazine wanted desperately to pull her from the dark place her expression so plainly stated. But he was still a stranger to her. He had to remind himself that despite his instant familiarity toward her, she didn't know him. With great effort, he gave her the space to work through the emotions. And with a heavy heart he watched her struggle.

They loaded onto their shell boats and pushed forward much the same as the day before. The terrain was the same winding river and crystal-laced cave. It seemed a living thing, and the air felt heavy. It was full of things that yesterday were unknown. Today things were known, though not understood.

Ashra remained distant as she clung to the shell in front. Bazine kept silent, not sure what to say. Krank trudged behind with ramrod endurance, pushing through the water that came to his chest in the deeper parts.

When they paused for a quick midday meal, the group was chattier than in the morning save Ashra, who kept her distance. Her eyes weren't even focused on the conversations around her. Shara kept a close eye on her, but didn't push her to speak. She sat closely and laid a reassuring hand on her daughter's leg as they sat on the bank.

Again they pushed on only stopping to grab some much needed sleep. They made camp on a wider bank much the same as the day before. They were running low on food and shared a small meal and then fell into fitful sleep. Ashra chose a spot close to her parents and curled up in a tight ball, squeezing her eyes closed against the world. Bazine lay restless, wishing he could lend her peace.

Dreams Reveal

It felt like seconds when her body drifted into mist. She walked along the foggy tunnel unable to do anything else. There were lights ahead, much brighter than the dim lights in the cave. She moved in their direction. Then the light began to touch the mist. She stepped in. There were a cave and a river up ahead, just past the light. It split into two separate directions. The stream to the left went into a smaller passage full of light, while the stream to the right led to darkness.

She pushed forward. The ground seemed to vanish and she found it odd that despite no ground to walk on she stayed upright. Her pulse quickened and she reached out to steady herself but there was no need. She hovered weightlessly. *Now that's new.* It felt strange to hover there. Also, it was slightly inconvenient in that she was stuck, bobbing in the mist. But as soon as she thought about moving forward her body obeyed. *Well, okay then, that's better.* It did not occur to her to wonder where everyone else was, or how she got there. She floated along the corridor toward the light in peace.

Someone began to sing. It was an old song, and the voice was ethereal. She wanted to move closer and that's all it took. She smirked, thinking this was definitely something she could get used to. The closer she got, the brighter the light, and the colder she became. Her mind no longer had control of her movement. She was not so peaceful anymore as she hovered in the light, unable to move. The voice stopped singing.

"Hello, Ashra." The voice resonated through her mind.

"Who's there?" Ashra's voice cracked and her breathing increased. She blinked desperately in the brightness, trying to see. But the light was blinding and she thought it unfortunate, so desperate was she to match the voice to a face.

"Don't be afraid," the voice reassured her. The light dimmed as a figure stepped forward, wrapping herself in a robe of light. She was smaller than her voice. Ashra's pendant lifted from her chest as if drawn toward the figure. She had long dark hair that swirled in an unfelt breeze. Her eyes were dark and curious.

The Sound of the Stones

"You can't stay here long." The woman's eyes turned sad. She shook her head, her hair following the movement as if under water. "I must help you understand something before you go."

"I don't understand," Ashra said, and then realized how ridiculous she sounded. She twisted her face in embarrassment. The woman laughed and her eyes creased into half moons. Ashra smiled despite herself.

Then the woman's eyes turned serious and her hair went still, frozen strands in all directions. "You will come to a place where you must choose a path. It is your choice to make." She paused and searched Ashra's eyes. "One path will lead to complete understanding. All will be revealed, and you will be safe. But you can never return." She emphasized the word *never*. "The other path will lead to sorrow but release will follow." She finished and her hair moved freely again. The woman began to fade.

"You look like my granddaughter," she said as her image dimmed.

All at once Ashra was pulled backward, and she instinctually reached for something to brace herself. Her fingers grazed the side of the wall and came away with a strange sticky residue. The light faded into the mist as she continued to move away.

"Wait!" Ashra yelped.

"They are coming, Ashra. Hurry." The woman's voice was distant and then faded into nothing.

Ashra woke, breathing heavily and covered in sweat. She sat up and brushed tangled hair from her face then jerked her hand away. A strange sticky substance dripped from her fingers.

A Tough Decision

They traveled along smooth water for little more than an hour before a fork in the cavern came into view. Dread settled into the pit of Ashra's stomach. The river divided into two smaller rivers, each leading down its own corridor. A looming decision lay bitter on Ashra's heart. There was a small bank in between the two caverns. She sighed heavily as they pulled up to discuss their course of action.

She paced between the two corridors on the small bank looking, smelling, listening for some sign, some help in the matter. She peered down the caverns, trying to gain some sense of what each held. The path to the left was vibrant with its glowing crystals full of vibrations. The path to the right was quiet and very dark.

She noticed her pendant lay still at the entrance to the vibrating cave. When she stepped to the dark passage her pendant lit and hummed. She rolled her eyes and groaned. She didn't know what that indicated at all. She certainly didn't want to face sorrow, but the release sounded promising. But release from what? And what kind of sorrow? She didn't want to leave her family and the people who risked their lives to help. The path of sorrow and release was the path she would choose. The question was which path led to that?

She closed her eyes against the chatter as the others debated which fork to follow. Bazine was trying to convince Rucain that the river branch to the right would most likely lead south. He supported his claim by pointing out that the flow of the river held stronger current to the right, indicating a greater change in elevation.

"Nonsomni lays south," he reminded.

Sheed agreed with Bazine loudly, while Haker grunted his support for Rucain. Rucain was slow to convince, a scowl prominently displayed on his face. The women tittered back and forth, interjecting opinions. Krank watched the group, an amused expression growing on his face, as the water lapped at his knees.

Ashra hummed what she hoped was a question in her mind. She felt a familiar tingle as her senses aligned with the crystals around her. She tried to connect to her pendant in a way she had not before. She sought its help. She was surprised at the ease with which she evoked a response.

The Sound of the Stones

The vibrations from the pendant formed an answer. It did not answer her in words. Pictures formed in her mind and she closed her eyes and let them flow.

To the left, muddled pictures of light danced and she felt warm and safe. It was simplicity and ease, but there was emptiness there too. A great chasm of life was removed from her heart in that direction. She shivered.

To the right she saw tears of blood running down an old woman's face. Then she saw dead bodies and women weeping over them. At last she saw a long dark tunnel. She swept past the darkness and reached a locked double door of crystal. The doors were so thick that only warped light danced behind. She could not see what lay beyond. In her mind's eye she tried the handle on one door. It wouldn't budge. When she removed her hand, the door began to seep. A thick red substance bled from the edges, but not downward, as gravity would demand. It ran from each edge toward the center of the door as if it had life of its own. Slow, purposeful trails toiled to conceal the doors. Now the doors were crimson, ominous.

In a flash the doors were gone and a wide-open space surrounded her. It wasn't nothingness exactly, more like emptiness filled with endless possibility. There was no light but it also wasn't dark. She was filled with awareness for the first time since the strange old man had confronted her at the mines. Her eyes couldn't see, but her body sensed things beyond comprehension. She was on the cusp of some greater understanding.

"Not yet," a voice said.

She was back on the bank surrounded by the others, any glimmer of understanding ripped from her mind, replaced by frustration.

The gentle argument as to which way the group should take had become more heated. Everyone had their own thoughts on the matter and Sheed was the loudest of them all. Ashra was struck by the tension in the air and stepped forward with her hand raised in a placating gesture. She had been so withdrawn and distant that this made her action more poignant. Everyone stopped bickering and looked.

"We should go right," Ashra said. No one spoke. They simply stared at her awaiting an explanation. She shook her head to the unspoken questions of why. "I..." She stopped mid-sentence and grappled to explain. Her hands worked in tandem with her mouth to form words. There were no words for what she experienced though. "I saw something," she finished lamely.

Krank stood back from the group, still knee deep in the river. He faced the direction from which they had come. He tilted his head up and closed his eyes, breathing deeply. He turned toward the group, his expression grave.

"They are coming," Krank said with a quiet seriousness. "It's time to go."

Rucain looked down at the bank and saw the tracks they left. Ashra and Bazine followed his eyes, realization dawning. Evidence of their travel was all along the banks where they stopped.

"Bring a shell over to me," Bazine shouted to no one in particular as he kicked at the footprints. Rucain followed his train of thought and grabbed one side of the shell and dragged it across the side of the bank closest to the left passage. Hopefully anyone following would assume they had left the bank in that direction. They carefully avoided leaving traces of boarding their boats on the right side and made haste down the right passage. Krank caused a strong wake purposely, splashing the small bank and washing any tracks from the right side of the bank as they disappeared.

Ashra wasn't sure if she had made the right decision. How could she be? She hoped, though, that the path would keep her with them even if it caused trouble. With her heart in her throat, she gripped the boat and drifted into the dark.

A Battle for Misfits

Ashra finally released her breath. She could make out shadowed figures in the dark, lit only by the scarce light they carried. They pushed on. Her arm ached from tethering the boats by hand. Even Krank trudged behind them with labored breath. They were exhausted, but fear pushed them forward. After a while the walls of the cave began to show signs of crystal again. The dim light grew to a level they had become accustomed, and they each took turns to look around and silently count heads.

A bit later a wake tipped Ashra's boat gently to the left. She looked to the water. A large domed shell breached the water followed by an oblong head. The creature huffed out a breath, blowing mist in the air, then dove back into the depths. Ashra blinked and looked at Bazine. He tipped his chin as if to say, "Yes, I saw it too." She silently thanked the creature for the use of its dead relatives.

Ashra allowed her eyes to linger on Bazine for a few moments. His muscles shifted beneath his shirt as he stabbed the river bottom, fighting against the wake. She found this very much enjoyable to watch, then felt guilty for the observation, and then angry at herself for the timing. He must have felt her watching because he looked, his eyes locking with hers. Ashra's face flushed and she looked away, vowing not to do that anymore, look at him. Yes, she could probably just avoid eye contact altogether. That wouldn't be noticeable.

They stopped once to eat, but rest was a luxury they could not afford. So they kept moving. A little while later Ashra felt the hair on her neck stand. The reason why was verified when Krank spoke.

"They grow closer."

The cold fear growing in Ashra's stomach lurched to her throat. She swallowed hard and passed the message up. Haker delivered the message to Rucain. His expression didn't change. He simply nodded and pulled them over to a wide bank that was nestled in a bend to the left.

There was no better option. Benders moved fast. They could not outrun them, even with their two-day head start, and the element of surprise held something. It wasn't much but the guards would almost

The Sound of the Stones

surely expect to catch them with their backs turned. Smirah was familiar enough with Perditus to guess he would not be with the pursuing party. He would likely send others to feel the situation out. They guessed maybe ten perhaps twenty guards would reach them shortly.

Their placement in the bend was clever, really. They were concealed from view, but able to hear anyone approaching. They took stock of their resources: Two spears and their owners who fought well, one knife, which belonged to Bazine who was a weapon in his own right, one small mining pick, which was Haker's, one Giant, one loudmouth father who didn't seem afraid to fight, and three brave women. It wasn't an army to brag about, more like a traveling band of misfits.

Ashra wasn't sure what her gift could lend. She had never thought to use it for violence. Only once had her gift brought death. She shuddered at the memory of the scream that had brought boulders down, crushing the rock eaters. But she wasn't sure how exactly she had done that, or if she could make it happen again. She took a long shaky breath.

Krank smelled them closing in before they rounded the bend. There were eighteen of them in all, seventeen Benders and one Giant. They were as ready as nine misfits could be. Krank lunged forward and made a wave as the Krad neared the bend. The first three Benders rode backward on the wave but jumped from the rafts. Loud shouts echoed from the cave walls as the Benders landed on the bank.

Bazine and Krank stood in front. Benders gathered a short distance away. Rucain and Akira stood to each flank, their hair blowing like white light around them in a sudden breeze. Small sprays of water danced at Akira's feet as if awaiting command. The air grew quiet and heavy. Ashra brushed hair from her face and marveled distractedly at the sensation that she was moving in slow motion. It didn't take long for the Benders to gain their bearings and charge. The slow motion snapped and reality set in at the sound of the Benders' shouts.

Two Benders sprang from the bank. Bazine met them in the air. He nicked the first Bender in the face as they crossed paths but missed the other. That Bender sliced at Bazine's arm with a spear. A trail of blood indicated he met his mark. Bazine jumped to meet them again.

The Giant rushed Krank. A wave surged as their bodies clashed, giving a fleeting shield to the humans. Ashra had seen this dance before.

Krank handled the other Giant with quiet efficiency. He gripped the Giant by the throat and held him fast to the cavern wall. He looked behind and kicked two more Benders in pursuit, all the while holding the struggling Giant by the neck. That Giant looked surprised, legs and arms scrambling for release. The kicked Benders landed with a hard thud against the far wall. Ashra watched in horrified wonder as the life left the other Giant's eyes. Krank released him and he slumped to a watery grave. Krank turned to face another Bender.

Ashra concentrated hard, trying to elicit some power. She hummed ridiculously but nothing happened. Her parents, Haker, and Smirah stood ready but the others were forming a barrier. They waited. Ashra growled in frustration.

Akira held her own with scraping jabs, until the Bender sprang from the ground. Rucain dodged, stabbed, and repeated against another, all the while glancing at his sister. But then his eyes went wide. A Bender had launched, his spear aimed at Akira's head. Rucain threw up his hands and shouted. A gust of wind burst forth so violently it blew everything in its path against the cavern wall.

The wind settled as quickly as it came. Akira was stunned but unharmed. Water dripped from her face as she blinked in disbelief. Ashra thought her expression quite appropriate under the circumstances. Several of the Benders were knocked out from the force of the blast. Akira opened her mouth to scream as another Bender launched his spear. It struck Rucain with a heavy thud, jutting from his thigh. He looked down, his mouth working to speak but no words came. He went to his knees and the water turned pink where he knelt. Akira threw back her head and wailed. Its shrill sound pierced the air. When she lifted her arms a funnel rose from the water, thrashing violently and smashing Rucain's attackers to the wall. They crumpled, unmoving.

Rucain gritted his teeth and stood. The spear in his leg quivered with each step. He lifted his hand against another Bender advancing toward Akira. The wind was stronger this time, and when the Bender hit the wall his skull cracked. Blood dripped from his nose and ears and he fell in a heap to the narrow bank.

Bazine handled two Benders of his own. Krank barely managed four. Scrapes and gashes on his arms showed the brunt of his wounds as he deflected the Benders' aerial assaults.

The Sound of the Stones

Ashra watched the scene numbly, sprays of water and gusts of wind lending an ethereal tone to the battle. But stark reality slapped her when several Benders maneuvered past the wind and water barricade.

Haker crouched, his pickax gripped with a white-knuckled posture. He grunted something that might have been instructions. Sheed stood upright, his bare hands raised, shouting loud taunting bellows barely audible over the wind and clatter. Smirah reached down and found a rock and held it aloft as a makeshift weapon.

"No!" Shara screamed, pushing Ashra behind her roughly. She threw her hands high as if that action might stop time.

It was now or never. Ashra felt a great, welling surge of energy as the Benders approached. Some of the guards bounded above, spears aimed at the men in front. Some flanked on foot to either side, spears pointed toward the women.

"Now, Ashra!" she heard Krank yell.

It started as a low-pitched growl. Ashra bent at the waist, the rush of power so great as to be almost painful. The louder she screamed the more relief came, and she managed to unfold her body to stand.

She didn't remember forming the words, "Hear me!"

She heard it leave her mouth with distant ears as if her mind was separate, watching from outside. The walls shook and the airborne Benders tumbled to the ground. To say they fell wouldn't do the action justice. They didn't simply fall in a gentle arch. They fell as if pulled by force, hitting the ground with a sickening thwack. The crystals in the cave cried ear-piercing pulses, sending the rest of the Benders to their knees, clutching ears.

Akira used the distraction and moved one hand in a circular motion, trapping Benders in a cyclone of water. Rucain continued to call forth wind, smashing Bender after Bender against the wall. Bazine and Krank moved in to finish any Bender not killed by the impact. Smirah and Haker followed suit, wielding a pickax and a rock. Shara and Sheed braced Ashra on either side as her knees buckled. Her body trembled and her head lolled. Then the cave fell silent.

It took several moments for the group to realize the fight was done. Even breathing sounded loud in the silence. Water dripped from the cave ceiling in random pits and pats.

Rucain was the first to move. He limped from the shallow water and collapsed on the bank with an audible thud. The spear in his leg pulsed with every rapid beat of his heart, a stark reminder that they were not unscathed. Akira moved to his side and dropped to her knees, brushing straggled hair from his face. Everyone hobbled closer. Ashra watched from the ground, still unable to move.

Bazine crouched, placing a hand over Rucain's chest, and said, "How do you feel?"

Rucain managed an incredulous look, and it was so out of place that Bazine barked a laugh. Smirah clucked her tongue and shook her head in disapproval, but for the inappropriate laugh or wound, it was not clear.

"Sheed, fetch water. Haker, elevate the leg. Bazine, start a fire. Krank, hold pressure on his thigh while I gather what I need. And someone get Ashra a drink. She looks like she's about to fall out." Smirah's commands were neither forceful nor timid. She spoke with a calm certainty that brought peace as the other set out to address Rucain's wound.

Krank placed a hand on the leg and pressed down gingerly. Rucain clenched his teeth and growled. His eyes shot wide, rolled backward, then his head slumped to one side.

"No!" Akira cried, grabbing his head on either side, then slapped him. She looked around desperately and met Smirah's eyes.

"He's passed out from the pain. He's still alive," she said, as she gathered strips of material from clothing that could be spared. "Leave his head to the side, he may vomit when he wakes." Akira looked at her defiantly. "He could choke on it. Now *that* would kill him." Smirah said this pragmatically and continued to bustle about. Akira scrunched her nose and sniffed. She relented and moved his head to the side but kept her hand there.

The others watched helplessly, having finished their assigned tasks. Smirah boiled strips of cloth, stirring them with a wooden spoon. Then she removed each strip carefully, placing them on a makeshift spit to dry.

"Does anyone have any spirits by chance?" she asked doubtfully, glancing from person to person. Haker cleared his throat and gave an

The Sound of the Stones

embarrassed grin. He rummaged in his pocket and pulled out a water bag. He handed it over with an apologetic shrug. Smirah pressed her lips flat and took the disguised alcohol from his hand. She unstopped the top, sniffed and then hummed.

"This will do nicely." She bobbed her head in approval. Sheed chuckled and Shara shot him a pointed look.

"What?" Sheed feigned ignorance, his mouth curving up slightly.

Smirah knelt down and inspected the wounded leg. "Krank," Smirah said gravely, "pull the spear from the leg." He moved to grab the handle but she stopped him with a firm hand. Krank looked at her with one grizzled brow raised. She raised her own brow back. "Listen, do it clean, and don't pull too quickly, but not too slowly either." She gave these instructions as if there were a perfect measure of "not too quick" or "not too slow" and that the sound of her voice should be sufficient to reveal those measurements. "Don't bend it to the side," she continued, "we mustn't have it break off inside."

Krank ducked his head in agreement, though his expression indicated doubt. The spear made a sucking noise as he pulled it from the leg. Blood began to flow freely. "Grip here." She grabbed Krank's hand and placed it above the wound on the leg. He did so and the bleeding slowed slightly. Smirah ripped the pant leg, exposing the entire gash. She poured a large amount of spirits over the leg and it mixed with the blood, making bright pink streams down his leg. Blood continued to seep as she readied the boiled rags. She tied some of these above the wound, replacing Krank's hand, then packed the injury with small bits of clean rag and applied a pressure dressing. Every fifteen minutes for the next hour, she loosened the rags in small increments. The pressure dressing was bloody but there were still bits that remained dry. Smirah nodded and sat back with a heavy sigh.

"The bleeding has stopped. Now we must keep it from infection. He shouldn't be moved for at least three days."

Bazine shifted uncomfortably. "We can't stay here."

"He can't manage! If he tries to walk he will bleed to death!" Smirah's calm demeanor snapped and her cheeks burned hot.

"If we stay here we all will die," Sheed added with less tact. Shara shot him another glare but didn't speak, quite likely because she agreed with his statement.

"I will stay with him." Akira's voice was soft. "You go on." She was stroking his face with a damp rag.

"No," Krank said. He looked at them, the small, lost girl holding her broken brother in her arms, and his eyes began to glisten. "I will carry him."

Limping On

Rucain woke with a dry mouth and a dull aching throb in his leg. He squinted against the dim light, seemingly bright, and shifted his head. It was a bad idea, he thought, when his head began to pound. He sucked air through his teeth and a wave of nausea hit him. He closed his eyes and concentrated on breathing slow. After a few moments the nausea passed and he heard a soft snore to his right. He opened one eye bravely. Smirah sat with her elbows on her knees. Her face was propped on both hands, ample cheeks pillowed in sleep. He cleared his throat. She snorted and sat up straight, blinking wildly. Rucain lifted himself slowly onto his elbows and then winced, thinking that, too, was a bad decision.

"You should be fine. It's a clean wound. No arteries were clipped." Smirah smiled, her hazel eyes crinkling at the corners. "Here, drink this." She handed him the water bag.

Rucain nodded and took a long drink. He looked over at his sleeping sister and blew out a long breath. "She's fine," Smirah soothed. "You and your sister put on quite a show for us." Smirah's eyes danced with amusement. Rucain grunted and shook his head. "Is that something you have done before?" Smirah asked.

Rucain's eyes snapped to hers, recalling all the details of the day before for the first time. He blinked a couple of times and lay back, folding his arms across his chest. He let his eyes wander to the crystal-laced ceiling of the cave.

"No." He was quiet again for a good long moment and then rubbed a hand down his face. "Never like that." He tried to laugh cynically but it came out as a grunt. He looked back at his sleeping sister. "We have always been"—he paused, deciding how to say it—"different. I have known the wind all my life. Could hear it, knew which way it would move. How strongly it would come. But...I'd never tried to call on it." He looked at Smirah, his expression unreadable. His eyes drifted toward the ceiling. "I suspected Akira was the same." He glanced back at his sister. "It's something we shared but never said out loud." His voice held warmth that he often lacked in conversation.

"It seems to me to be a valuable trait," Smirah added, while lifting his bandage to take a peek. If it hurt Rucain didn't show it.

The Sound of the Stones

"Ashra seemed to pull her own stunt," he added wryly.

Smirah laughed. "That she did. If you include Bazine, the four of you make quite a team," she added.

Rucain grunted a laugh. "Don't forget our Giant."

"Ah, yes, let us not forget Krank, the beast to slay all beasts." That pulled a full-fledged smile from Rucain. He pulled up on his elbows again, then winced and decided against it.

"Careful, you will recover, but you have to take it easy for a while," Smirah cooed. Rucain clenched his jaw and shook his head. "We must move. I need to see if I can bear weight on it." He attempted to sit up again.

"Oh no you don't." Rucain met with Smirah's firm hand against his chest. "We have a plan." Her grin was sly. He narrowed his eyes.

***

With sore muscles, cuts, and many bruises, they loaded the boats to leave. Bazine took the lead and Akira moved to the back with Ashra. Rucain looked pitiful snuggled into the crook of Krank's arm as they brought up the rear. Ashra fought the urge to giggle at the care with which Krank held the wounded man. He looked like a huge, ugly mother holding an overgrown child. Rucain's face, usually stoic, held signs of obvious irritation.

Of course Sheed chided Rucain. "Want a sup of milk and a nice blanket for the ride, Rucain?" He bellowed a laugh that could quite possibly have been heard all the way back in Krad City. Ashra couldn't help it. She laughed too, as did the others, though not all of them as loud as she, nor did they snort like her. Rucain shot Ashra a pointed look.

"Sorry." She mouthed the word as the laughter died down. Rucain grunted and closed his eyes. Akira smiled too, her shoulders shaking from suppressed laughter.

They traveled for the day, taking small breaks. Smirah continued to change Rucain's bandages with clinical efficiency, making it clear he was not to get up and move about. He obeyed her but did so with a stone-faced reluctance.

The others took turns attempting to spear fish in the shallows. Shara ended up snagging the first one. She returned to the bank with a smug look on her face, the spear held aloft with a fish on display. Haker had luck snagging a fish or two, but Shara proved to be the best at it. She waited patiently and struck with swift precision. She was like a lightning strike. Ashra suspected it was a gift honed through the many years of jabbing her husband in the arm for inappropriate and ill-timed remarks. Krank acted as a dam, trapping fish from moving downstream. They had plenty of meat, but the lack of grains and fresh greens would become an issue if they were underground too much longer. Rucain, especially, needed proper nutrition in the wake of his damaged body.

They moved as swiftly as they could for several more days. Rucain began to put weight on his leg for short intervals. The bleeding had long since stopped, and thanks to Smirah's good work, no infection was present.

Akira and Ashra shared long talks and a comfortable quietness with one another. Ashra noticed that Haker seemed fond of Smirah's warm but bold personality. Bazine remained somewhat distant, as if giving Ashra time to accept the newness of the situation. He was still kind and friendly but she did not catch him glancing as often. She thought she would find relief in the lack of attention. Instead, she felt anxious.

Coming Home

There were no crazy events over the next week of travel through the winding underground river. Aside from a few slaps on the head from Shara, given to Sheed for saying things loudly at inappropriate times, the trip was calm. They stopped when they could go no longer. They speared fish for food. They shared company by the fire. They slept when they could. No wild winds blew. Akira left the water at peace. Ashra continued to hear the vibrations all around her but did not seek its reaction. There were no troubling dreams. No answers were found. They all simply fell into a rhythm that a traveling band does.

Krank continued to keep his sniffer tuned. He did not smell anything that would lend to worry. It was in the back of everyone's mind. More Benders would come. *And when they did...* It was inevitable, but for now they seemed safe and no one talked about it.

It was the fifteenth day after the Bender attack that the cave started to show fewer signs of glowing crystal. They became more sparsely located, until at last there were no more of the iridescent crystals. The glowing crystals were replaced by a more common species that they all were accustomed to seeing. They used their own crystals to light the way.

Then a light other than their crystals came from downriver. As they proceeded forward, so too did the light grow. It became clear that they were nearing an outside entrance, or exit as it were. Butterflies formed in Ashra's stomach. She was about to enter a world she thought she would never know. She would be a free woman. Her mind raced. What would it be like? How would they live? Would they remain together or go their separate ways?

***

Bazine tensed when he realized where they were. The slow-burning anxiousness he was harboring sparked to a much larger fire in his chest. He recognized the cavern walls as the ones he explored as a child. This was the river that flowed in the large cave of Nonsomni. It was the river that fed into the fresh spring pool of his own land. He was home.

His stomach soured as he waded through swarming thoughts. What would his people think of the band of people he brought back? What

The Sound of the Stones

about Krank? How would they react? He would have to reveal who he truly was to them. He pulled the boat to the side, not ready to face them.

"Why are we pulling over? We aren't far from daylight," Sheed complained.

Rucain was well enough to travel by shell now and sat with Bazine up front. Bazine held out a shaking hand to him as he exited the shell. Rucain looked from the shaking hand to his eyes. Bazine pressed his lips in a line and shook his head.

"We're close to my home." Bazine looked down at the ground and wiped his hands on his pants. He looked over at Ashra and she looked at Krank. He stood in knee-deep water, his arms crossed over his chest. His shirt had long since disintegrated, leaving him in tattered pants with a hulking bare chest. He looked menacing even to familiar eyes.

"Why don't you go ahead while we wait for you to..." Ashra made an inarticulate gesture.

"Announce our arrival," Krank finished for her with an embarrassed grimace. Ashra's lips turned up at the corners. Bazine nodded and blew out a long breath.

"I will be back shortly." Bazine hopped into a shell and sailed toward home.

***

Several children were playing at the mouth of the cave. They shouted his name and one boy left in a hurry. Bazine greeted them warmly though his stomach was in knots. They laughed and shouted questions over one another.

"Slow down, one question at a time," Bazine said through amused laughter.

"Where did you go?" "What did you see?" two boys peppered him.

"Well..." Bazine rubbed his chin, looking serious. "I traveled north to a city you have never seen." The boys started shouting again but quieted when Bazine held up a hand. "I saw things that no one knew were there." He held up one finger. "I will tell you all about it, but first I need to speak with Abrack and Ratha."

The boys gave grunts of disappointment at their lack of immediate gratification. Bazine patted them on the head and continued his walk toward home. He heard them all excitedly making plans for a long journey as he walked away. He shook his head. *Nonsomni will never be the same.*

Bazine meandered up the familiar path and plucked fruit from a tree. He brought the sweet-smelling berry to his watering mouth but paused. A twinge of guilt bit him for leaving his friends behind, and instead he tucked the treats into his sack for later. He emerged from the tree line to see his mother rushing down the stairs of the cliff. Her hair blew behind her like a flag of hope and when she caught sight of him she cried out a garbled mess of happy exclamations. Rushing over dirt and rocks like a dasher, she threw herself into his arms, sending him backward. She buried her face in his chest and sobbed. He had to laugh to keep from crying. They spent a long moment in a quiet embrace. Then she pulled back, wiping tears from her face, and checked him over.

"Are you well? What happened? Did you get there? What did you find?" She laughed and shook her head. "I'm so glad you're home." She let out a shaky sigh as though she had held her breath for the last two months.

Abrack peered out from his home and smiled. He disappeared back inside and returned after a moment with some fishing tackle in his hands. He tottered over the path toward them.

"Hellooo, my boy!" Abrack called his familiar greeting.

Bazine's heart swelled and he draped a loving arm around his mother's shoulder as he watched the old man approach.

"You're back just in time! I broke my favorite lure." He beamed. Bazine laughed and grabbed him in a rough hug. Abrack patted him wildly on the back. "Ah, it's good to see you, my boy." He pulled back and searched Bazine's face with serious eyes. "You found what you were looking for." It wasn't a question.

Bazine tensed. He darted looks between his mother and Abrack and ran his hands through his hair. Ratha cocked her head to the side in question.

"Well, I do need to show you something. Can you both come with me?"

Ratha looked at Abrack and he at her.

The Sound of the Stones

"Let's go," Ratha agreed, and they followed him back down the path.

When they came to the mouth of the cave Bazine stopped and turned to Abrack.

"Abrack, the pictures people form in heir minds..." He paused and looked to Ratha. She tipped her head in approval. "I dream, have for about a year now. That's why I had to leave." Bazine watched him. Abrack's face showed no sign of surprise and he nodded an indication to continue. "I brought some people back with me," he said, and then held his breath, watching for their reaction. They stared at him. "They...they are back up the stream a ways." He gestured over his left shoulder with his thumb and blinked.

"Okay, so why did you leave them upstream?" Ratha's face clouded with confusion. Abrack looked a bit frozen.

"Well, you see, one of them is not a human," he said, dropping his voice at the end so it came out muffled.

"Not human?" Ratha squalled.

"One of them is a Giant," Bazine said and cleared his throat. Abrack rasped a laugh, slapping his bony knee. Ratha dropped her jaw and stared. "It's not what you think, Mother." Bazine made a mollifying gesture, as she looked ready to burst into flames.

"Not what I think! I grew up near those nasty beasts! Now you've brought one home like some feral animal! I can't believe you would lead one home!" Her arms flailed wildly and her face turned bright red.

"Now, Ratha, hear him out." It was Abrack's turn to make a mollifying gesture. "Look at the poor boy. It looks like you beat him with a limp fish!" Bazine took his cue and hunched over, making his best sad eyes. "And what do you mean you grew up around those beasts? Do you remember more than you've let on?" Abrack rebutted.

She crossed her arms and huffed. She glared her best motherly disappointed look, ignoring Abrack's pointed question.

"Mother, please, he helped me when I came into Krad City. The Giant actually freed the girl I went in search of. He has saved our lives in many ways."

Ratha's expression softened from piercing to simple irritation. It was a step in the right direction. Abrack cracked a smile.

246

"I never thought I would live to see any more people come into Nonsomni. What is this Giant you speak of?" Abrack rubbed his hands together like an eager child waiting for a treat. His eyes twinkled and he hooted a happy noise. Bazine blew out a long breath and shook his head.

"You really have to see him to understand. My words will not do him justice. Come." He started toward the cave, and with one last glance between them they followed.

Introductions and Reunions

Bazine led them down the narrow bank toward the place where he had left the others. Ratha trailed behind in apprehension for the Giant beast she was about to encounter.

Ashra and the others were huddled along the edge of the bank. Krank sat with his legs lying in the water, as the bank was too narrow to hold all of him. They were a weary, tattered mess. They all rose to their feet at Bazine's approach.

"Ratha!" Smirah cried from behind the others. She pushed forward and ran toward her long-lost friend. Ratha stood mutely for a moment, searching her face. "It's me, Smirah." Ratha covered her mouth and stifled something like a laugh or a cry.

"Little Ratha," Smirah whispered as she embraced her friend from years gone by. Ratha held her at arm's length after a nice embrace and smiled warmly. "The years have been good to you, my friend," Smirah said.

"How is your family?" Ratha asked.

Smirah shook her head and pursed her lips tightly.

"I'm so sorry, Smirah."

Smirah's mouth curved up slightly through brimming tears. "It happened years ago," Smirah said softly, momentarily taken to a dark place.

Ratha was silent for a moment, a look of dread washed over her face. "What of my parents?"

Smirah shook her head. "Losing both daughters was too much. They died not long after you left."

Ratha choked on a sob and sniffed. She bowed her head and wiped tears from her eyes.

"It's good to see you, old friend," she managed with a shaky voice. She eyed the group behind Smirah. They were all respectfully watching the reunion. Ratha dropped her voice low. "Tell me of this Giant. Is he really safe to have around?"

Smirah glanced back at Krank. He was nervously shifting from foot to foot, looking pitifully at the ground.

The Sound of the Stones

"Yes, I would have never believed it had I not been there when he broke us from the holding cell in the palace. He has been a loyal friend to us through this whole ordeal," Smirah said resolutely.

Ratha's mouth curved up to one side tentatively and she tipped her head at Krank. He smiled back and the awkward grimace wobbled. Ashra patted him on the arm and he sighed.

"Bazine, how about a proper introduction," Abrack prompted. His chin rose, dignified. His body language was easy, as if he had met hundreds of new people in his life.

Bazine gestured to each person and gave a brief synopsis. He made his way down the line and reached Ashra. "This is Ashra, the girl of my dre...er...*from* my dreams," he amended, and his face flushed hot. Abrack made a noise in the back of his throat.

Ashra waved. "It's nice to meet you," she said breezily.

Bazine glanced at Ratha and her lips curled into a smirk. He caught Rucain's eye. He was grinning at Bazine like a cat. Bazine shot him a look but that only made Rucain bark laughter. Akira slapped him on the arm. Sheed crossed his arms and brooded. Shara snorted. Haker grunted and mumbled something under his breath.

"You must be hungry." Abrack broke the awkwardness, and both Bazine and Ashra sighed in unison, causing the group to fall into a fit of laughter. Krank watched as if he were too dignified to participate, but his tattered pants and bare chest painted such a disparity with his expression that Ashra laughed harder. Krank did smile when both Shara and Ashra fell into a fit of snorts.

Abrack suggested it would be best to hold a tribal ceremony in which he would introduce the newcomers. They would wait just out of the Nonsomni walking grounds until the formal meeting took place. Abrack found the same group of boys hanging around, waiting for Bazine. He sent them to spread the word for all to meet him at the mouth of the cave as soon as they could. Word had already started to spread as some had witnessed Bazine reunite with Abrack and Ratha. People were already gathering before the boys went to tell the others.

Abrack peppered the small group with questions. He needed to explain enough that they were not frightened of the outsiders. Where did they come from? What is a Giant? Where is Krad City? Where did

250

Rucain and Akira come from? The fact the Rucain wore the Nonsomni symbol was something of a novelty to Abrack. He hummed in interest and scratched his bearded chin.

"It looks like most of us are gathered," one of the boys panted. He stopped, almost running into Abrack, and blinked up at Krank. His eyes grew big and his mouth fell wide. Krank waved. The boy made a strangled noise. He waved a hand and promptly turned on his heels and ran.

Abrack sighed and shook his head, eyeing the group of newcomers. "I would have liked more time, but they will be restless for answers." He took a sharp breath through his nose and nodded. "We will make the best of it. Will we not?" A warm, self-assured smile spread across his face and his eyes twinkled. He winked at Ashra. "Follow me," he said, turning in the direction of his people.

It went as well as could be expected. The Nonsomni were attentive. They listened to the outsiders as they spoke of their journey. Only a few openly gawked at Krank. Krank even spoke on his own behalf, careful to keep his tone gentle. None of them shared the part about their gifts. That part was left for another time. The Nonsomni were gracious and accepting save for a few older cranky folk.

Places were provided for the newcomers. Ashra and her parents shared a home. Rucain and Akira shared a home with Smirah. She became something of a surrogate mother to the two. Haker had his own place and Krank made camp on the outskirts of Nonsomni.

Settling In

Over the next few days Abrack's questions were answered in regards to Ratha's origin and how Bazine came to be. The pieces of the puzzle slowly fell into place. Bazine confided his talents as a Bender to Abrack and his mother.

Abrack rubbed his hand down his beard and eyed Bazine. "Yes, I see now. I suspected burdens, my boy. But the secrets you both carried..." He shook his head and looked at Ratha.

Ratha placed a hand on Abrack's shoulder. "I'm sorry I didn't tell you. I was afraid." She searched his face for a long moment. He held her eyes, no indication of how he felt. Then a leisurely smile spread across his face and he waved a hand in dismissal.

"Ratha, I only feel bad you had to bear it alone. I understand. Some things are not ready to be said until they are." He shrugged.

Ratha laughed. "No wiser words were ever spoken."

Abrack feigned utter seriousness and touched a finger to the side of his nose. "Indeed."

Later that evening, as they gathered in Abrack's home to share a meal, Bazine described Ashra's, Rucain's, and Akira's gifts.

"Show me." Abrack was in no way shy about his request for a demonstration. In fact, he looked like a child waiting for someone to entertain him. They obliged, but were unable to reach the same degree of success they had under the duress of a fight. Their gifts came out calm and subtle. It didn't matter though; Abrack was no less excited. He whooped with delight, eliciting laughs from the leery crew. His sense of wide-eyed wonder and air of acceptance made settling in a much easier transition.

***

Ashra remained distant from Bazine. She did start making eye contact with him again, but they were fleeting looks that broke as soon as he noticed her. His heart ached for her attention. Perhaps his purpose was done. Maybe he had already completed the task he was meant to. Ashra may not be meant for him, though his heart felt otherwise. He would wait. He wouldn't push.

The Sound of the Stones

It was his third full day back. Bazine sat with Abrack at the water's edge. He felt a moment of peace in familiarity of the routine. They dangled fishing sticks in the water and Abrack smoked his bone pipe, blowing shapes in the air.

"The Krad will send others through the underground river." Bazine's voice was grave. Abrack nodded and took another pull from his pipe. "What should we do?" Bazine asked almost rhetorically. He had been asking himself that question since they came. The initial joy of being home had worn off, leaving a looming dread in its wake.

Abrack looked sideways at Bazine and gave him a measuring look.

"Seems to me you have been doing all right so far." His mouth curved knowingly.

"I have done nothing without the help of others. There isn't one thing I can take credit for on this journey. I can't even get the girl I went for to look at me longer than an instant."

Abrack chuckled. Bazine looked at him, irritated.

"Ah, my boy, you have grown so much in such a short time." He took a pull from his pipe and then pointing it at him. "We do not accomplish the big things on our own. We pull from one another." He winked. "That is when you know what living is about." Abrack took another pull from his pipe, looked back at the water, and sighed contentedly. "As for your young lady, it seems to me a lot has been placed on her shoulders. Just give her time." He looked at Bazine. "But make sure she knows you have eyes for her." He smiled as if enjoying a memory.

***

Later that evening Bazine and Rucain gathered the group. It was time to address the issue of defense. They decided that a watch of two would be posted deep in the cave and relieved in shifts. Men and women were armed with what hunting gear was available, while others set out to make more. Women and children got crash courses on tactical basics. Akira led the women and children. Rucain led the able-bodied men.

The next day, after the men had finished training, Bazine wandered off. He found a hill with a view of the women's training ground and sat alone, letting his mind wander and his eyes follow Ashra. She was struggling with a move and Akira slapped her elbow, eliciting a startled yelp. Akira, not used to such a reaction, yelped back. They both fell into fits of laughter and had to start over. Bazine smiled then looked to the left. His smile dropped. Bisha was there too.

He had avoided her to this point. She hadn't really made eye contact nor tried to talk to him. He felt the situation would eventually need to be broached and it lay quietly in his mind like a snake poised to strike. Bisha was better with a spear, more graceful, serious. When she moved, it was with purpose, as though she was born to do this very thing and only now been given the chance. Maybe Bazine was not the only one who had changed.

Bisha stopped as if sensing something. He was caught. She saw him. Her eyes went from his to Ashra, then back to him again. So many unspoken words lived in that look. He shifted uncomfortably. Ashra didn't notice and he was grateful.

"Who is the one there full of fire?" Rucain asked, nodding his head toward Bisha.

Bazine jumped.

"What? Where?" He looked back at his friend and blinked. Rucain kept his eyes downhill. Bazine ran a hand down his face. He followed Rucain's line of sight. Bisha's hair flowed behind her like yellow flames with each angry move, her gray eyes piercing like daggers in his direction. Bazine cleared his throat.

"Bisha," Bazine said, avoiding her sharp stare.

Rucain watched her quietly for a while.

"She has feelings for you."

Bazine winced. "She did. But as you know I was pulled in another direction."

Rucain nodded.

"Would it offend you if I spoke with her?" Rucain said this never taking his eyes from the girl. Bazine studied him for a moment before shaking his head.

"No. She is her own person," Bazine answered.

Rucain grunted acknowledgment and sat beside him until the class was over.

The Sound of the Stones

When the women and children disbanded. Ashra glanced up and saw them. She smiled and waved. Bazine waved back and then felt silly. Rucain shot him a sideways look.

"Not a word," Bazine said under his breath. Rucain gave him a rare, wide grin.

Ashra climbed the small hill. "Hey," she greeted them warmly and sat. She smelled like the grass after a heavy rain. Her cheeks were flushed, and her hair in straggles. Bazine thought she couldn't look sweeter if she tried, then laughed at himself for thinking it.

"What?" She cocked her head, searching his face for the answer. He shook his head and looked away.

"Nothing. I was just thinking about your class. It was fun to watch." It wasn't a lie in that it was fun to watch. But he was thinking other things as well. Rucain coughed and then sniffed.

Bazine looked at him harshly and gave him a solid thwack on the back. "You okay, buddy?"

Rucain grunted and smirked. Ashra's cheeks turned an even brighter pink and she turned her face back out over the hillside.

They watched in silence as some of the children in the distance played near Krank. He laughed at their antics and beamed. One little boy approached him tentatively and Krank reached out to him. The boy tottered forward and Krank rewarded him by lifting him high above his head for a better view. The boy squealed with delight and the other children clamored for a turn. Ashra laughed and looked at Bazine. Their eyes locked and her smile fell. They didn't see Bisha still standing at the base of the hill. She was watching. She was angry.

Rucain cleared his throat and stood. Without a word he walked down the hill. Ashra and Bazine watched as he approached Bisha. She was still staring at Bazine. Rucain bent to her and said something. She looked up at him as if seeing him for the first time. She adjusted her posture to stand taller but still only reached his chin. Her face changed at once from stormy to pleasant. She tucked a piece of hair behind her ear and rewarded him with a slight curve of her lips. Rucain held out his hand to her and bowed. She took his hand and he placed a gentle kiss there. They walked slowly away toward the cliff. Rucain leaned in and said something else. She threw her head back and laughed.

256

"I wonder what he said to her," Ashra said and then pulled her knees up, hugging them.

Bazine looked over and studied the gentle lines of her face and the way her hair escaped her bun as if willing itself free. She looked younger now, innocent and small. He tried to imagine what she felt. What it must be like to have people show up out of nowhere and claim she is something she knows nothing about. And it struck him. "I'm sorry, Ashra. I didn't think about how my finding you would affect you."

Ashra looked at him with tired eyes. Her hair flared around her face, a small spray of freckles lending to her youth. His heart swelled. She was here, so close he could reach out and touch her. He wanted to brush a stray hair from her cheek but instead clenched his fists and looked away.

"I know." She shook her head and sighed. "If Krank hadn't found us and broken us from that cell, my parents and I would probably be dead." She turned her eyes back to him. "But if you hadn't come, those Bender guards may have killed us all right there before we left Krad City." Ashra shrugged and leaned forward, resting her chin on the top of her knees. "Do you wonder how it all began…what it was like before the Krad?"

Bazine nodded and looked off in the distance. "Yes, it seems like someone should know…something." He gestured with one hand helplessly.

"Oh!" Ashra lifted her head, her eyes coming alive. "I had a dream…at least I think it was a dream, back in the cave when we had to choose which way to travel." Ashra paused and eyed him for a moment as if taking his measure. Bazine struggled to find an expression that might lend to a sense of trust. He settled for a polite nod. It seemed to be the right answer as she continued.

"I met someone in a lighted place. She told me I had two choices." She held both hands out as if weighing something. "One choice was an easy path but I would leave everyone behind." She pulled one hand down to indicate the weight. "The other was a harder choice with death and heartache, but release would follow." She pressed her lips in a hard line and bobbed her hands back and forth, showing the difficulty in judging which held more weight.

The Sound of the Stones

Bazine tilted his head, considering. "So, you chose the hard path then," he said quietly.

Ashra looked at him, eyes worried. "I did, but what will it bring us? What do we do from here?" She dropped her hands to the ground and blinked. Bazine placed his hand on the ground near hers. He wanted to touch her hand for reassurance but was afraid that might push her away. So he settled for words.

"I believe we will be shown the way," he said, and was surprised to find he actually believed it.

Ashra searched his eyes for a good long moment before speaking. "I think I am the only one who is unsure of this whole situation. I was busy trying to save myself and family while the whole human race is waiting to be saved." She shook her head and looked out at the landscape as if it held answers.

"I think we've come a long way. Don't be so hard on yourself. The answers will come in time."

Ashra looked at him again. She placed her hand over his tenderly. Ashra's pendant began to hum and even Bazine could hear it this time. He jumped. Ashra gasped and took her hand from his. The pendant went silent.

"What was that?" Bazine's eyes were as wide as the moon.

"You heard it?" Ashra asked, with mirrored wide eyes.

"Yes?" he answered, but it sounded like a question.

Ashra placed her hand back over his. The pendant hummed again, but she didn't let go this time. She closed her eyes and let the song wash over her. Bazine watched her and listened to the song as well. They sat for a long while just listening.

"That's amazing," Bazine said, breaking the trance that held her.

"I have an idea," Ashra said, still holding his hand. He cocked his head to the side in question. Ashra's eyes danced. "Come on, let's find Rucain and Akira."

A Surprise Gift

It felt good to talk with Bazine. Ashra hadn't been avoiding him, but she hadn't made an effort to see him either. She was glad she made herself walk up that hill and smiled like an idiot as they walked to find the others. They found Akira with a group of girls and Rucain still hand in hand with Bisha. Ashra didn't know Bisha well, but she didn't seem to be friendly, in that every time she looked at her the expression she wore was not a pleasant one. It was awkward.

They gathered together in Rucain and Akira's home. Bisha came too, upon Rucain's request. Ashra inwardly rolled her eyes and tried to avoid looking at her. But Bisha kept glancing back and forth between Ashra and Bazine. She may as well just say it. This tension was killing her mood.

"I'm sorry, have I done something to offend you?" Ashra finally asked after several uncomfortable moments.

Bisha sniffed. "I just don't see what Bazine sees in you."

Her statement slapped Ashra in the face. Ashra's mouth hung open and she stared at Bisha in disbelief.

"What?" was the only word Ashra could think of, and she was mad at herself for not having something more articulate to say. The room fell silent as everyone watched.

"Bisha…" Bazine started to say more but was rudely interrupted.

"Shut your mouth!" Bisha gestured between Bazine and Ashra and her voice came out in a shrill, heated tone. "Don't tell me there isn't something between you two. Everyone sees it!" As her arms flailed back and forth, sparks poured from her hands. Bisha didn't notice but everyone's eyes were fixed to the light show dripping from her hands like liquid fire.

"What is wrong with you people?" Bisha cried, as their expressions changed to surprised confusion. She stopped and followed the direction of their stare. She screeched. Her body began to tremble and she clasped her hands together in an attempt to stop them from leaking fire. It seemed an appropriate reaction under circumstances, Ashra thought. Rucain stepped forward and placed his hand on her shoulder. She looked at him with horror-filled eyes.

"Calm down, Bisha," he said firmly. She blinked at him and stopped squealing. She took a few slow breaths and the sparks stopped. She

The Sound of the Stones

stood for a long moment, staring at her hands still clasped, then looked up.

"I don't know what's happening," she finally managed, tears brimming in her eyes. Rucain kept his hand on her shoulder and murmured to her under his breath.

"It looks as if you have a gift," Akira offered in a small voice, looking uncertain of her place in the situation. "It all started when we found Ashra."

Ashra was not at all sure she appreciated that Akira had named her as the perpetrator. Bisha shot her a withering glare. Nope, didn't appreciate it at all.

Akira ducked out of the home for a moment and left Ashra to stand there awkwardly. Akira bustled back in, holding a bowl of water, just in the nick of time. This was a good thing in that Ashra was tempted to say or do something that would quite likely enhance the awkwardness, sing, dance, anything to change the subject.

"Watch," Akira said, looking every bit as young as she was. She placed her hands over the water and called it up in silent concentration. The water lifted from the bowl in one solid sphere. Everyone watched as she slowly directed the water sphere back and forth between her hands. Then she raised it higher and pushed it into the middle of the room. Bisha made a strangled noise in the back of her throat. Rucain lifted his free hand and pushed the orb back toward his sister. Akira lost her concentration and the sphere broke shape. Water splashed into Akira's face. She squeaked and blinked, water dripping from her eyelashes. She shot Rucain an incredulous look. Rucain's eyes flashed amused and then settled back into a blank stare. Bisha looked back and forth between the two of them her hair swinging wildly.

"What does she do?" Bisha gestured dismissively toward Ashra.

"I hear crystal vibrations. The earth speaks to me."

Bisha snorted dismissively and looked at Bazine in a way that made Ashra want to claw her eyes out.

"Look, I don't know what's going on here, but I want nothing to do with you people." Bisha's anger flared and sparks poured from the tips of her fingers again. She looked down and ran from the home, hands thrust forward. She was shrieking ridiculously and Ashra found that she very much enjoyed Bisha's frustration, much more than she probably should have. Rucain followed her. Ashra, Bazine, and Akira stood silently for a moment.

"Well, so much for my plan," Ashra said with a sigh.

"I'll be back," Bazine said, walking swiftly out the door, leaving Ashra with a strange twinge of anger.

***

Rucain attempted to comfort Bisha as she knelt, sobbing, on the outside ledge of the home. Bazine approached quietly and cleared his throat. Rucain shot him a sharp look.

"Give us a few minutes?" Bazine asked. Rucain's eyes flashed anger and then returned to ice. He breathed deeply through his nose and tipped his chin.

"Bisha, I will be just inside." She sniffed. He got up hesitantly, leaving his hand to rest on Bisha for a moment longer. Then he walked inside, remaining close to the door.

Bazine knelt down beside her. "Bisha, I'm sorry. I never meant to hurt you."

She blinked through tears. "Why couldn't you look at me the way you look at her?" Her voice choked.

Bazine sighed and sat on the ground beside her. He gathered her hands in his, giving her a measured look. "I just couldn't give you what you deserve. You are such a bright, sweet, beautiful young woman. You deserve someone who will give you every bit of himself. Not just parts." He pulled his lips up at one side but concern still riddled his eyes. She pressed her mouth in a hard line. "Bisha, I think my life will always be full of complications. I do have feelings for Ashra but I have no idea how she feels about me. You don't deserve the kind of pain I would put you through while I try to figure out my life."

Bisha lifted her hand from his, wiping tears of pain and frustration from her face. She sat back against the wall and sighed. She was silent for a few moments. Her face settled into peace as she nodded. "I know." She barked a humorless laugh. "I've always known, really. I just thought that maybe you would change your mind." She gave an apologetic grin that made Bazine laugh. She smiled a more genuine smile at his amusement. "So, tell me about Rucain." Her eyes danced and Bazine grunted.

"Well, now that will take a while. It all started with a sand worm." He settled back to tell the tale.

Rucain leaned against the wall and crossed his arms. Warmth spread through his chest and his mouth curved to one side as he listened to Bazine tell their tale.

Seething

Perditus sat hunched in a chair staring at his hands. He recounted his heated conversation with Fleuric and ran a hand through his hair. Revealing Ashra's escape had brought a fury of mostly one-sided admonishment from Fleuric. He said things to Perditus that made him wonder if he had ever been in his father's good graces at all. He clenched his teeth, his jaw muscles jumping as he ground them in anger.

He would not, could not, meet with his father again until she was found. He blew out a long steady breath and leaned back heavily in his chair. It creaked under his weight as he shifted. He pressed his fingers to the bridge of his nose and shook his head. The humans were becoming restless. The Glasne had been on a rampage, and more women turned up pregnant and in a coma every day. The birth sanctuary was full, and the human helpers were run ragged under the influx.

Humans in general were resisting sleep to the detriment of their jobs. And though the Krad were stronger, the humans still outnumbered them two to one. The possibility of an uprising loomed thickly in the air. He would be forced to slaughter them all if that happened.

Perditus scrubbed his hands over his face and stood to pace the floor. His boots echoed heavily with each step. It wasn't the slaughter of all humans that bothered him, but the thought of the Krad having to step into the jobs they left behind, that made his stomach sour. Where was the team he sent after Ashra?

Several Benders had reported a Giant and eight humans fleeing. He knew about Smirah, Ashra, Sheed, and Shara. Haker had come up missing, as well as Krank.

"That son of a wench," he mumbled. But there were three humans no one could account for. He stopped for a moment and shook his head. "No." He discounted the rumors of one who might have been a Bender and chalked it up to embarrassment for letting them escape. He walked to the window and stared blankly into his city. He was pondering his next move when a Bender entered the room.

"Sir, they still have not returned. What will you have me do?" Mesheleck asked hesitantly. Perditus kept his back to the head guard,

The Sound of the Stones

his shoulders tense. Mesheleck shifted uncomfortably and cleared his throat.

"Gather the best of our Benders. I want one hundred waiting by the mines to leave in the morning. I will be going this time. You will stay here in my stead." His voice was gruff and he turned to face Mesheleck, his eyes fierce. Mesheleck was forming words with his mouth, but Perditus stopped him with one swift move of his hand. Mesheleck closed his mouth, nodded curtly in tandem with a bow, and exited.

Perditus looked at the empty doorframe for a few long moments and then turned back to the window. His eyes swept to the mine. How had he not known about the underground river? Perditus growled and slammed fists into the sill. They made a loud thud and the pain from the impact served as a temporary relief from his flare of rage. He would find them, kill them all, save Ashra. He thought about the things he would do to her and a sneer graced his lips. Then a twinge of something foreign pierced his chest as he pictured Ashra's horror-filled eyes. His sneer faded.

"Curse her," he whispered. He ran a hand through his hair and sighed. "Curse you, Ashra." He turned toward his quarters and began to pack.

Visions Given

Ashra put her hands on the table, palms up, and looked around the table. Bazine placed his hand in hers and then reached to take hold of Akira's. Ashra's pendant lit. Akira grabbed Rucain's hand and Bisha completed the circle. They could all hear it now. The pulsing vibrations from her pendant bled into their minds like slow-growing frost. Ashra closed her eyes and the others followed. Fragmented pictures formed, unclearly at first, but then came into view in startling color.

Ashra saw the woman from the cave. Bright lights swirled and the woman's mouth moved as if to say something.

The lights in the room flickered and a breeze blew through. But they didn't notice.

Rucain saw a white-haired woman. She danced like trees blowing in the wind, but stopped to look at him. She motioned behind her. He moved past her and hovered over familiar surroundings. It was his homeland. People gathered, watching an approaching storm. Dark, ominous clouds toiled above. Lightning flashed and the winds blew strong.

The lights in the room flickered faster.

Then the white-haired woman soared through the sky, carried by the wind. Lightning made a fury of patterns behind her.

Akira saw a woman immersed in water, long white hair moving around her in slow motion. She moved her hands up, gathering the water above. Then at once, she stood dry on top of a mountain, the water suspended over her head. The water moved in rolling circles held by an invisible energy. She looked down into a valley where a great mass of angry travelers marched. With a wave of her hands, the rolling water moved. It crashed upon the menacing group like a wave. Then she stood by a river and met Akira's eyes. She paused for a moment and pointed to the water. She dipped one finger, and with the flick of her wrist, changed the direction of the water's flow.

Bisha saw a woman with golden hair. She stood brazenly in a burning forest, untouched by the lapping flames. Her hair flowed free, dancing like fire. She raised her hands to the sky and called out. A great flaming bird circled ahead. Lightning struck the trees and they fell at her

The Sound of the Stones

feet. Still she stood unharmed. She looked back at Bisha and motioned toward her. Was she showing her something? No, she was offering.

Bazine saw Ashra sitting in the middle of four women. Two had white hair, one dark brown, and one with golden hair that moved like flames. They surrounded her. She looked startled. He moved forward into the circle and reached for Ashra's hand. She noticed him then and her eyes softened. He pulled her up and they stood together, watching the women move in graceful circles.

"Release comes through dreams," they chanted in unison.

The dark-haired woman was shrouded in light, mouthing a word over and over. They strained to hear her above the wind. They looked past the woman and saw the people of Krad City. They cried in the streets and tore at their clothing and hair.

"Free," they cried. "Free".

Ashra was the first to let go. She dropped her head to the table, her shoulders shaking with silent sobs. Bazine hesitated for half a heartbeat but then gathered her into his lap, cradling her head against his chest. Ashra continued to cry as the others watched. Akira stood swiftly and bolted for the door.

"Where are you going?" Rucain shouted.

"I know what to do," she said over her shoulder and left. Rucain and Bisha exchange a brief look then followed, leaving Bazine and Ashra alone in the room.

"Ashra," Bazine said softly.

She pulled back to look at him. "They are suffering." Her eyes held every ounce of pain those people felt.

"They want to be free," Bazine said quietly, and traced the line of her jaw. Ashra blinked and then sniffed, scrubbing tears from her cheeks.

She licked her lips and her eyes got wide. "We have to do something."

Bazine nodded. "We will." He brushed wet strands of hair from her cheek. Then his eyes met hers and she was struck by his compassion. All of the hurt, all of her pain, was reflected there in eyes like oceans, eyes like infinite violet stars. His eyes so familiar bore resemblance to ones she had known before, one who had caused so much pain. But these eyes were safe. These eyes knew her.

"Please," she whispered and pressed her lips to his. Bazine froze, reluctant, but she did not pull away. She brought her hands to his face gently. She kissed the side of his mouth, his nose, his chin, then brought her lips back to his. It was not lust but something deeper.

"Please," she said against his mouth. A sigh left his lips, as he buried his hands in her hair. They were lost to one another for a moment, time frozen, nothing wrong.

Abrack cleared his throat where he stood in the doorway. Ashra jumped, stumbling backward onto the floor with a heavy thud. She was flushed, eyes wide, and her hair stood in every direction. Bazine stood and helped Ashra from the floor with a crooked smile fixed on his face. She didn't think her face could grow hotter but it did. She felt like a ripe tomato. He settled her into a chair and sat next to her still holding her hand. *Still grinning!*

"Abrack." Bazine made it a question by raising one brow. Abrack had a broad smile on his face and his hair stood wildly as if frozen in an erratic wind. *Is everyone going to smile inappropriately except me?*

"I thought I might give you two some warning. Your mother, and Ashra's parents, are just behind me." The footsteps came behind Abrack. They heard him before they saw him.

"What happened? All the lights were flickering and the wind picked up. Then it just stopped. We saw the others running toward the cave," Sheed shouted as he came into view. He studied the two sitting alone in the room and his expression turned dark. He crossed his arms and pelted Bazine with a stare.

Nope, not everyone is going to smile. Bazine's smile dropped and he ran a hand through his hair. Then he cleared his throat to fill the silence. With messy hair and flushed cheeks Ashra sat there, giving her best impression of an innocent blink.

"Well?" Sheed demanded. Shara rolled her eyes and pulled him by the arm to sit at the table.

Abrack leaned casually against the doorway with a self-satisfied look on his face. Bazine shot him a hard look. Abrack laughed. Ratha followed in behind, casting a glance between the two. Her eyes went wind and then she frowned. She looked at Bazine with pursed lips. He grinned sheepishly and shrugged. Ashra snorted.

Ashra and Bazine took turns finishing each other's sentences as they explained their visions and answered questions. No, they didn't know what Akira and the others were doing. Yes, this was the first time this kind of thing had happened to them all. Yes, they kissed. They were grown adults, and yes, that's all they were doing. Sheed brooded at them across the table. Ashra stared at him defiantly. Bazine blew out a long breath and Shara laughed.

Abrack clapped his hands together, breaking the tension. "Let's go see what the others are doing." His mouth tugged up at the sides. They followed him out the door in silence.

A Turning Point

Akira stood near the water's edge. Rucain and Bisha stood silently behind her, staring at the water flow. Abrack and the others followed their stare. The water was no longer flowing forward. It flowed against nature, back toward Krad City. Akira turned, beaming. Her silvery hair stirred in a breeze, eyes dancing with amusement. She looked unearthly and wise beyond her years. She cocked her head to one side and giggled. She was young again.

"It will slow them down." Akira's voice was singsong.

Abrack chuckled. "Yes, that might give us some time." His eyes crinkled warmly as he assessed the odd girl.

"What does all this mean?" Sheed bellowed and then blinked unapologetically. His question was met with blank gaping stares.

"It means that the time has come." Krank's voice came from behind.

Startled eyes turned to him expectantly. He let out a long breath and ran a hand over his head, ruffling straggled hairs. He looked at Ashra and shrugged. "There was a time when all humans had gifts." He gestured to Ashra and the others. He grunted in half amusement and shook his head. "When this all began, humans did not understand why some women would not wake up, why they died while giving birth." He sat on a boulder and rested his arms on his knees. He looked up slowly. "The Krad were born, and cast out of human tribes when some became violent." His deep black eyes looked hollow. "It was messy. But not all Krad turned. Not at first. There were some who were loyal to humans...our families."

His voice dropped low when he said the word *families*. "But when the truth was revealed,"—he dropped his eyes to the ground—"I can still remember the look on my grandmother's face when she learned what I was, why her daughter died." His voice was thick. Ashra stepped forward and placed a gentle hand on Krank's. He looked up and tried to smile but it wavered and fell. Then his expression turned grave as he searched her eyes.

"It's not safe to stay here. They will come, and keep coming. They will take Ashra and kill everyone else." He was looking at each of them now. "They will use her until they figure out how to set the Glasne free."

The Sound of the Stones

He shook his head solemnly. "I don't have any other answers. I don't know how you are to do the things you must. But I do know that staying here is like waiting to be slaughtered."

The hair on Ashra's neck stood on end. The air felt thick with tense energy.

"But how? How do we convince the people to leave when they know nothing of these things?" Abrack looked desperate. His normally jovial face was set in deep lines of concern and he looked every bit of the years he had lived.

"We can go to my lands." Rucain spoke boldly. "We were sent to look for her." He gestured to Ashra.

Akira bobbed her head. "Our people have been waiting for this since the first families founded our land." She stepped closer to her brother. Rucain looked down at her with rare affection.

"We were chosen to find Ashra when the colored crystal began to glow. The crystal woke when Akira was born. My people have trained for this." Rucain placed a hand on Bazine's shoulder then swept his gaze around the group. "They will be expecting us."

Abrack was quiet for a moment, then spoke darkly. "I think there's more to the story." He looked at Krank. "You know how it began, don't you?"

Krank nodded. "The gifts were not all as strong as yours." He gestured toward the four and shrugged. "But the they were present. Some used them more, some less. Some refused to use them at all." Krank looked at Ashra. "Before my grandmother found out"—he made an hesitant gesture, his face drawn in painful memory—"what I was, she would tell me the story of creation."

Ashra moved closer to Bazine and he placed a reassuring arm around her. Krank cleared his throat, swiping a hand under his nose. He looked at Ashra and lowered his voice. "There is a prophecy at the end."

Ashra nodded mutely and swallowed.

"Go on," Abrack urged.

"It's been a very long time, but I remember every word." He looked past them, his eyes fixed in a far-off place, somewhere long, long ago. "It happened deep in the eleventh dimension. A place so large you could never reach its end. It's a place that holds all smaller places, like liquid crystals full of energy. And even those smaller places are so immense that the mind fails to understand their size."

Krank paused and looked around him. "That is where He lives." His voice was hushed as he met their eyes. Then his eyes fixed back into a distant stare.

The ground beneath Ashra's feet seemed to pull harder and her face went numb. *Where He lives.* The phrase echoed over in her mind.

"In the eleventh dimension between the smaller places, He spoke. His voice vibrated in seven-part harmony and the crystals moved. They clashed, one against the other, and burst. That's when it happened. Out of that chaotic dance, an explosion of pieces and parts scattered. Clusters formed. He held them together with effortless breath and made shapes." Krank held his hands out as if holding something delicate. Ashra shivered.

"He created the stars and planets all with His voice. They unfurled from a central place." He made a sweeping motion with both hands. His eyes followed as if watching it unfold. "At first they moved quickly, in a hurry to reach their appointed place." His hands slowed, then stopped. "Eventually they slowed to a lazy crawl and he ordered them to stop." He dropped one hand and held the other out as if cupping something small in one palm.

"He chose a place perfect for His plan. He spoke man into existence with love in His heart and smiled down on him." Krank dropped his hand gently to his knee. He blinked, his eyes sweeping over the watching faces. "It was more beautiful then. This place is a shadow of what it was before." He pressed his lips together and shook his head.

"What happened? Why did it change?" Akira's hushed tone drew Krank's dark eyes. The briefest curve crossed his lips.

"He called the first man Epatras. He woke the first day, freshly made and fully formed. His skin was light, and his hair black as coal. His eyes were dark but held flecks of amber, a reflection of the Creator's wisdom." Krank looked at Ashra.

"Epatras was the only human. And though he spent his days in wondrous beauty, his heart held longing. He wished for another to share it with." Krank looked down at his hands sullenly as if he understood that longing.

The Sound of the Stones

"The Creator saw his loneliness and created the first Mother. He called her Timera. She had skin rich and warm, hair bright like the sun. Her eyes reflected colors of violet, blue, and green, a reflection of His love and patience. When Epatras looked into her eyes, he saw forever there. She was his home, his ending and his beginning. Their love was the first between man and woman. Pure. The love by which all others would be measured."

Krank stopped and rubbed his neck. Ashra looked at Bazine, feeling sentimental. He must have sensed her looking and turned. Bazine's eyes lingered but he reluctantly turned away when Sheed spoke, his voice loud, shattering the reverence of the moment.

"What happened? How did the Krad come to be?" He spread his arms wide with impatience.

"This is where the story takes a turn." Krank gave Sheed a sharp look. Sheed returned it without hesitation.

"There were others. The Glasne. They were strange and wonderful creatures created to keep company with the Creator. The first Glasne, Fleuric, was inspired by the harmonies that the Creator sang. He wanted to be like Him, to create his own universe. But he only had a six-part harmony. It wasn't enough. The crystal orbs that formed life did not obey him. He convinced other Glasne to sing with him, hoping to find the right mixture of vibrations. But no matter how they tried they could not create. Fleuric confronted the Creator. He was patient at first and told Fleuric that only those who were one with him, those pure of heart, could learn.

"Fleuric's frustration grew and he became bitter. He tried to turn the Glasne away from the Creator, and succeeded in turning nine others. They followed Fleuric into the first universe. His intention was to lay claim and steal it from the Creator. But when he crossed over, he broke the seal of protection around the universe. Once the seal was broken, time was unleashed. Time changed everything. It brought decay and destruction. Weather became violent. Life became difficult. Humans were forced to fight for survival.

"The Creator became angry. He created the second universe and banished Fleuric and his followers there. The second universe was but a shadow of the first. It lacked warmth and beauty. He bound them there until the time was right. But Fleuric found a way in through dreams."

Ashra moved closer to Bazine. He tightened his grip on her hand. She had been there, face to face with Fleuric. She had felt the draw of his power, and heard the desperation in his voice when she escaped.

"But why? If the Creator is so powerful, why do we continue to be subjected to the Glasne? Why doesn't He just get rid of them?" Ashra felt a mingled sense of fear and irritation. Her voice was pinched and she tightened her grip on Bazine's hand, causing him to flinch. "Sorry," she said, loosening her grip.

Krank nodded grimly. "There is more. I am not wise enough to know the answers to all of your questions. I have lived a very long time." He frowned. "I can only tell you the story as it was told to me." Ashra nodded and swallowed.

Krank leaned forward and lowered his voice. "The Creator had a purpose and a plan for all. Although Fleuric broke the seal of protection over the first universe all was not lost. He promised to set his people free from the destruction. He blessed Epatras and Timera with four daughters, each gifted in a different way.

"Aquia was gifted with the ability to hear the water. With this gift she could hear where the fresh water dwelled, and sense the changing of the tides. Terrea could hear the earth. The rocks would sing her the story of creation, and events yet to come. Bresia could hear the wind. She knew when the seasons would change, and when a storm was coming. Fumia could hear fire. She could sense the elements and know which ones would bring a spark. She could feel the lightning before it hit and know where it would strike.

"Each daughter was blessed with a mate and the earth filled with sons and daughters. The gifts to hear the elements were passed on as the earth grew in population. But then the Krad were born. As time passed they forced the humans to forget. For hundreds of years the human gifts lay dormant. But the Creator is faithful. He promised one day someone would be born, and she would remember how to listen."

He stopped for a moment, looking at Ashra. "That time has come."

The air held tension as each person processed the story and its impact. How had they never heard this story before? How did an entire race forget something so important?

The Sound of the Stones

Shara's voice broke the silence. "My grandmother used to tell me a story about a bird just learning to fly. It became trapped in the cleft of a rock. The space was tight and it could not spread its wings. The wind blew and called to the bird, but it was afraid to jump. Rain fell and tried to wash the bird free, but it clung to the rock for fear of falling. Sparks poured down from the rock face, but the bird pushed itself further into the cleft to avoid getting burned. Finally the rocks shook, the wind blew, the sparks poured down as a storm raged, forcing the bird from the cleft. It jumped because it had no other choice. When it passed through the raging storm, the land transformed into a colorful world of peace."

"I remember you telling our little bean that story," Sheed said, with a wistful glance at his daughter.

Bisha's eyes went wide. "There is a story very similar to that here in Nonsomni. But instead of a bird in a rock, it's a tree climber stuck on a high limb."

Krank tipped his head. "The gifts were given to set you free. It's time to use them."

Ratha got a thoughtful look and tapped a finger on her lips. "I have an idea."

The Hidden Prophecy

The Nonsomni people dreamed that night and it unsettled them. A crowd gathered at the mouth of the cave awaiting Abrack to address them. Anxiousness was the common attitude as they spoke to one another, comparing the pictures that had played in their minds. There was a recurring theme, people suffering in a strange land. The dreams varied in detail but the one prevalent similarity was people begging for freedom.

Abrack stepped onto the rocky outcrop, his hand held high. A hush fell over the crowd. Full ceremonial garb further enhanced the seriousness of what was about to come.

"Good people of Nonsomni, I have a story to tell. It is an old story. One we have told our children since long ago."

Bazine bounded to a high point on rocks above Abrack. Chatter broke loose as they witnessed his Bender skills.

Abrack waved a hand flat and the crowd silenced. "A very young tree climber climbed to the top of a tree." Abrack pointed to Bazine. Some of the children giggled. Abrack raised his brows and they went quiet. "The tree climber was scared. He had climbed too high and would not come down for fear of falling."

Rucain stepped onto the lower rock next to Abrack. "The wind picked up, trying to blow the tree climber down." Rucain lifted his hands and sent a strong gust of wind toward Bazine. The crowd gasped and murmured. Bazine clung to the rock dramatically.

Abrack raised his voice. "But the tree climber did not move."

Akira stepped up next to Rucain. "The rains came down, urging the tree climber to be free." Akira cupped her hands, lifting a ball of water from the lake. She positioned it above Bazine. As she wiggled her fingers, tiny drops fell from the sphere until the water was gone. Bazine clung to the rock as he was dowsed with water.

The crowd whispered fiercely under their breath as Bisha stepped onto the rock. "Sparks poured from the limbs, urging the tree climber down." Bisha lifted her hands. She shifted back and forth and huffed when nothing happened. The crowd fell silent. Rucain leaned in and whispered something. Her cheeks flushed pink and she raised her hands again. A small orb of fire flickered in the center of her hands.

The Sound of the Stones

Rucain nudged the glowing ball forward in a mass of sparks with a flick of his wrist. It landed just below Bazine. Water sizzled and the sparks died. Bazine jumped, pushing himself flat to the back of the ledge. Bisha blinked, Rucain smirked. The children of the crowd giggled, most likely due to the indignant expression Bazine wore. People murmured and pointed with wild gestures.

Bazine edged back in place and grabbed hold of the rock. Abrack held his hands high once more. "The tree climber still refused to come down!"

Ashra stepped onto the rock and joined hands with the others. Her pendant lit, the stones sliding into a pattern. Abrack lowered his voice and the crowd leaned in. "Then the earth began to tremble."

Ashra closed her eyes and let go of the others. She knelt down on the rock and tilted her head, listening. She whispered. The ground began to shake, sending tremors up the rock cropping. It was a small tremor, not so much as to split the rock, but enough that the crowd felt it under their feet.

"The earth shook, and the winds came!"

Akira lifted more water. Rucain blew gusts of air, sending sheets of water down. Bisha shot bursts of sparks.

"The fire burned, the wind and water swirled even as the ground shook. The tree climber jumped."

Bazine flipped dramatically and landed in the crowd. All went still. The ground ceased trembling, the water and the fire stopped. It was silent.

"The tree climber landed safely but he was not where he was before. The land was new, full of hope and peace. It was a new beginning. He was home." Abrack dropped his hands. With a tip of his chin, Bazine revealed the mark on his chest, Rucain showed his arm band, and Ashra lifted her pendant. The crowd shifted silently.

"Good people of Nonsomni, this story holds a truth. A truth we didn't understand until now. This symbol is a message. We have a greater purpose here than we know. These people have been sent here to show us something. Something wonderful."

He paused and scanned the crowd. "But we are in danger. There are others who will come and try to take what we have. They are coming even as I speak." He waited for the crowd to understand. "But there is a way. We must follow Rucain to his land. His people too escaped long ago. They have been preparing for this. They wait."

He looked around at the myriad expressions. Not everyone would believe, that much was clear. "For those who will follow, we will leave in three days. This is not a command but an urgent plea. Come with us. Save your lives. Discover the truth."

The crowd stirred, as if broken from a trance. Loud shouts of disagreement rose. Children cried in confusion. Then a voice rang out. The crowd did not hear her at first, so Akira repeated the first verse again. As the song washed over the crowd a hush fell in recognition of the familiar tune.

What once was light turned into dark
Don't worry, little one
The darkness will not always be
Don't worry, little one
When time has come to set you free
Don't worry, little one
The signs I send you in due time
Don't worry, little one
When earth cries out in colored song
Don't worry, little one
She wears the sign around her neck
Don't worry, little one
Trust in me, I'll set you free
Don't worry, little one
Follow her into the light
Don't worry, little one
She'll break the chains, I'll meet you there
Don't worry, little one
She wears the sign, a torch of life
Don't worry little one

The wind picked up and the water lapped heavily at the shore. Sparks rained from Bisha's hands and the earth trembled. Ashra closed her eyes and the pendant glistened, sending vibrations through the crowd. It whispered to their hearts. Not everyone openly received the call. Some pushed it away, swallowing the well of emotion and steeling themselves against it. Those who refused to hear stood frightened.

They Left

"Are you ready?" Bazine asked.

Ashra turned, throwing her pack over one shoulder. There was so much more to that question than three simple words. It was the look in his eyes, the way he tilted his head. He smiled and looked back to the top of the cliff.

"As I'll ever be," Ashra answered. But her mind reeled and her heart beat in anticipation of the unknown.

Not everyone was convinced to go. The people who stayed behind were dots on the cliff, watching them leave. The dots blended into the cliff the farther they went, as if no one was there. Ashra looked back over her shoulder until the cliff faded from view. At first she wanted to turn back as her heart cried out. *They will die!* But no. You can not make someone believe. They will, or they will not.

"We can only trust and move on," Abrack told her. But it did not take the sadness away. She thought of the people in Krad City. Could they help them? Would they listen?

"One step at a time," her mother said. Yes, this was the next step.

"It's hot," Sheed grumbled. Shara doused him with water and kept walking. Ashra smiled. In danger and facing things they knew nothing about, they would love one another. She would cling to that. Love. Hope. A new beginning.

***

Those that stayed behind had long since left the cliff peak. But Branish and his small sister stayed, blinking into the desert. He was old enough and had almost told his grandfather that he was leaving with them. He looked down at the reason he stayed. She would not have been allowed to go with him.

"Will we see them again?" Her eyes were wide as she blinked back tears.

"I don't know." He turned his eyes back to the desert. "I hope so."

An old man watched from the distance. His white hair blew gently in the breeze. He grinned.

"You will see them again," the old man whispered.

Listen

Frankie woke, her face pressed to the book. She sat up, peeling her cheek from the page. The story flooded back in her mind. It felt real. A gentle knock on the door startled her.

"Frances, it's time to get ready for school," Mr. Abenstein called.

Frankie blinked. "Be right down," she said automatically, though she felt more out of place now than she had ever felt before. Her surroundings were a cardboard cutout, and she, a character on a stage.

Then her arm began to tingle. She pulled up her sleeve and swallowed hard. The wine-colored mark had grown darker. She pulled the sleeve back down and drew a blanket around her shoulders as a shield against weirdness. Then she realized the window was open. As a breeze blew through her room she heard something like a voice. The pages on the book rustled. One word carried on the wind.

"Listen."

CPSIA information can be obtained at www.ICGtesting.com
Printed in the USA
BVOW06s0139020216

435118BV00009B/72/P